PAL JO

a novel

by

Clifford Cawley

first edition

All characters and events in this novel are imaginary; if the names of any actual persons appear, it is only by coincidence.

University Editions
4937 Humphrey Road
Huntington, West Virginia 25704

Copyright 1985 by Clifford Cawley
Library of Congress Catalog Card No: 85-51767 ISBN: 0-916383-03-2

Cover by Bonnie F. Thomas

PART ONE
IN RE THE PRENTICE ELECTRIC
Boston, September 10-13

CHAPTER		PAGE
I	Jo Brings Disturbing News	1
II	Christopher Beanfield Sees a Ghost	6
III	Sampson Rowbottom's Dilemma	12
IV	How Tarzan Learned to Swim	17
V	Prudence Prentice's Electric	23
VI	Young Caller with Flowers	29
VII	Mrs. Stambulov	35
VIII	Barney the Cop	41
IX	Lucy	47
X	In the Noo-Wud	53
XI	Jo Makes the Best of a Bad Situation	59
XII	The Cigar-Store Indian	65

PART TWO
THE MATTER OF THE CARRONADE
Nantucket, September 18-21

XIII	Pal Fizzo's Problem	71
XIV	The Bachelor's Friend	77
XV	The Carbide Kid	83
XVI	The House Warming	89
XVII	Mayhew Stubbs' Diary	94
XVIII	Rowbottom Reveals Unexpected Depths	100
XIX	Homer Hart Inspects the Secret Room	106
XX	Fizzo and the Warlord of Mars	112
XXI	Disaster	119
XXII	Jo Accuses John Kettleworth	125
XXIII	Beriah Stubbs Still Refuses	132
XXIV	Gully Must Burgle for Winnie to Marry	138

PART THREE
CONCERNING ONE PR. ITEMS
Kittery, October 11-13

XXV	Sampson Rowbottom's Torch	144
XXVI	Bunnington Wood Falls Again	150
XXVII	Salesman Gulliver Gates	157
XXVIII	A Princess of Mars	163
XXIX	Bunny Buys a Present	170
XXX	All Blurry-Like and Perfume	176
XXXI	Gully Betrays His Own	182
XXXII	Pete McGlue's Revenge	188
XXXIII	Officer Pinzio	195
XXXIV	In the Dean's Office	201
XXXV	Victory and Defeat	207
XXXVI	Shuffle Off to Buffalo	213

CHAPTER ONE
JO BRINGS DISTURBING NEWS

"...nine whites," said Jo.

"And finally, twenty-five reds."

"Right." She turned the flashlight around and began to flash again. I held my breath, listening for the hoped-for reaction. "...twenty-five," she ended.

The bulky mechanism clicked.

"You did it!" I cried.

I opened the door and we entered my attic lab, where Jo made the rounds of my inventions-in-progress, ending at the working model of the Gates Automatic Bed: my most promising bid to date for quick fame, fortune and a life of well earned leisure. She then turned.

"Darling," she said, "bad news."

I eyed her apprehensively.

It was, for the record, three o'clock of a Sunday afternoon, September the tenth, to be exact—and I had been hard at work on the balky prototype of the Gates Photo-Electronic Combination Door Lock when cousin Jo, some seven years my junior and a pal from birth, came bounding up the attic stair of the Back Bay house I share, if share is the word, with my Aunt Orpha.

"What?" I asked.

"Marj is despondent—a tiff with Randy."

I eyed her with concern. Senior-stately Mrs. Florence Miller, Aunt Orpha's widowed younger sister, lived in Cambridge with a) son Norman, a red-headed hellion of twelve, and b) junior-stately daughter Marjorie, twenty-three. The latter was engaged, due largely (and so far thanklessly) to my efforts, to Randolph Bohr, a Hackamore pal and now a well-paid electronics engineer for an R & D firm out on Route 128. Marj, although no cloak-and-dagger type like Jo, was a good bet for the long haul, and it was in the manner of one always ready to rush a finger to the dike that I requested details.

"Christopher Beanfield is the trouble," said Jo.

"Chris?" I said, puzzled. He, another Hackamore pal, was now a heat engineering expert with a Boston firm. Some months ago, I had arranged a date for him with a junior league type named Ellen Hill. They promptly had become engaged, and I had heard nothing from him since.

"It seems," Jo went on, "that Christopher wants to enter a partnership, but there's some hitch. If he can't enter it, then he and Randy are taking off for Brazil—up the Amazon, and all that."

I shook my head. The idea was not new. Early in our senior year, the pair had started shoving at me Harry Franck's old *Vagabonding Down the Andes* and Hudson's *Green Mansions*. The fever had gripped me briefly and passed. But with them it had lasted longer, and now for some reason was flaring up again.

"So Aunt Flo thinks Marj needs a change," Jo continued. "She has decided to take Marj to California for a few months."

A chill shot through me. "You mean," I asked slowly and distinctly, "that she has decided to take Marj *and Norman* to California for a few months?"

"No. Norman can't miss the start of school. She'll leave him with Aunt Orpha."

"No!"

I clutched my head. You know those carnivals where the brawny fellow whangs the big mallet down on the platform and the weight shoots up and rings the bell? My head felt like that mallet. Norman—established under our own roof! Free, while I served out my time at the office, to pick and pry his way into my lab! For a *few months*!

"See Chris first thing tomorrow," Jo said hurriedly, as the voices below grew louder, indicating that her mother and Aunt Orpha were nearing the front door. "Get the facts, and Tuesday we'll come up with something."

She was catching the bus for Kittery, for scholarship and registration preliminaries for her sophomore year, and would return to Boston Tuesday, arriving at the St. James Avenue terminal at four—where, I now confirmed, I would meet her, drive her down to Woods Hole and see her off on the ferry back to Nantucket, where she was finishing up a summer's apprenticeship with the Music Circus.

"Oh, Darling!" she cried, springing at me. A most uncousinly hug and kiss ensued. Then Aunt Effie called and she started down the stair.

The empty feeling she left behind persisted until bedtime—when, sitting on same and eyeing the adjacent row of books, I at length pulled one out. In my hand it fell open and the words sprang out: *"Die, cursed thern!"* Then the empty feeling was gone. For she was Dator Xodar, the black pirate of Barsoom; I, in the disguise of a hated thern, was climbing to the rail of her air vessel; and she, with a grim smile, was aiming her radium pistol at my head and hissing, *"Die, cursed thern!"*

I was in Quincy's first grade, going on seven and living with my Aunt Orpha and late Uncle Orville, when—to Uncle Eustace and Aunt Euphemia across the street—Jo arrived. Small, brick-red and yowling, she at first sight was a shock and disappointment. But later, when I was allowed to hold her and she promptly latched onto my thumb, I was touched. When I served as baby sitter, she only stared at me. "—never cries when he's around," Aunt Effie often noted.

When Eustace Parkington Gates, an Edgar Rice Burroughs fan to the hilt, passed on to his reward, it befell me to supply the paternal element of young Jo's upbringing. Eustace had left behind in his den a well stocked shelf of the adventures of John Carter and of Tarzan; and there, on many a rainy afternoon, appropriately sprawled on the tiger rug, I read these gripping accounts to the infant Georgette, and later she to me. For Jo, there was no Peter Rabbit: we started right in on Tarzan, and to this I attribute her precocious reading ability and early evidenced high I.Q. Inevitably we were moved to act the stories out—sometimes only we two, and sometimes, until their interest flagged, with a supporting cast of other imaginative spirits of the neighborhood. That to myself always went the role of Captain John Carter of Virginia, later Martian prince of the house of Tardos Mors, Jeddak of Helium, as well as that of Tarzan of the Apes—who, unknown to himself, was Lord Greystoke—went without saying. As did to Jo the roles of Tarzan's Lady Jane and of Carter's black-haired, ever beautiful Dejah Thoris, Princess of Helium.

We were close pals by the time she could walk. We spent a chummy, carefree youth in Quincy, she the small tagalong tomboy, I the hero in her adoring eyes. When we moved to Back Bay, I saw less of Jo; but thereafter, on the occasions of Christmas and birthday, she one by one had given me the volumes, after having added the inscriptions which made necessary their shelving in the privacy of my bedroom. I turned back to the flyleaf, where, in her distinctive violet ink and vertical hand she had written:

To The Only One I Ever Will Love.

Jo was hardly eight when she pointed out in confidence how, while Orpha and Flo and my late father John Gates were brother and sisters, Orpha's late husband Orville Albright's sister Euphemia—Jo's mother—had married a Eustace Gates—her father—who happened to have the same name as, but was no relation to, my father. Thus, she concluded, while we were cousins, we were not blood relatives, "so if you ever wanted to marry me—why, you could."

3

This had surprised and disturbed me.

"But if I did," I asked, "would we still be pals?"

"Of course," she said, and there the matter had stood.

When Hackamore U., out in Hackamore Heights, in due course turned me out into the workaday world. I at once became keenly aware of the implications of a free enterprise society; of what wealth meant and what the lack of it meant; and of the all-important difference between employer and employee. To Jo I had revealed my determination never to marry while forced to serve another: "I'm not a radical, Jo! I'm all for capitalism and capitalists. I just want to *be* one!" And the only way I could see to be one fast was through my inventions.

The crack of Monday's dawn found the old VW, laden with Aunt Orpha, luggage and self, entering Callahan Tunnel. As we neared the East Boston end, she, with a rustling sound, busied herself at her handbag—inside of which was a smaller one, and so on—eventually producing two tolls which she punctiliously handed over, the second being for my return. The Old Party, a real estate broker of considerable clout, in her customary taciturn way had revealed only that she had business in Philadelphia. I previously had gathered, however (Aunt Flo to Marj to Jo to self), that she had been retained by Prudence Prentice—ancient and wealthy aunt of Teddy Prentice, Aunt Flo's suitor—to dispose of some of Prudence's Philadelphia properties. Now, as we entered Logan Airport, she added that she would return Thursday or Friday. At the curb I extracted her bags, hailed a porter, wished her well and watched her deceptively frail appearing figure, old laced and ramrod straight, cut a thin swath through the crowd to the doors.

During a tie-up in the Westbound tunnel, I reflected upon my pressing new problem. And pressing it was, for in the eyes of Aunt Orpha, young Norman Miller could do no wrong. Once, in the Miller living room, I happened to glance out the side window and was startled to see that the adjacent VW apparently had sunk down through the driveway. I rushed out. A female child of ten, the only gang-member left behind, pointed down the street and screeched: "*The cats made a scooby rod!*" And peering in the direction indicated, I made out the rapidly receding forms of Norm and colleagues astride what would have been an ordinary homemade racer with little red wheels—except that these now served as hubs for my VW's wheels. "How clever!" Aunt Orpha said to Aunt Flo afterwards, meanwhile patting his head. "Norman will become another Henry Ford." And to my plea that in my absence he be enjoined from entering my attic laboratory, she had returned a frosty stare and exclaimed:

"But Norman likes to *play* there!"

Clearly, Christopher Beanfield must be caused to achieve his partnership at once; thus quashing the alternative of his and Randy Bohr's trip to Brazil; thereby curing Marjorie Miller of the vapours; thus negating the need for her change of air—and so keeping young Norm to his own side of the Charles.

Searching for some clue as to the nature of the problem, I recalled how, at the zenith of their delirium, Chris had taken to singing *Rolling Down to Rio*. You probably remember it: all that guff about never having sailed the Amazon, never having reached Brazil; the bit about the steamers white and gold—namely, the *Don* and the *Magdalena*—going there when they will; the acrobatic rendition of the word "roll" over a total distance of four bars; the business of the armadillo dillowing in his armour; and then a second four-bar go at the "roll"—by which time any red-blooded American has had it. In the face of which, Chris once had sung this riot-inciting ditty twice through in a beer hall, was dared by a paying customer to try it again, and did. During the next subsequent "roll" the riot started. School champion boxer Randy had gotten fragile Chris out, thus sealing their friendship.

My first move, as Jo and I had agreed, would be to contact Chris and elicit the facts. Accordingly, an hour late for work due to the tie-up, I entered the lobby of the Witherspoon Building and was heading for the phone booths—when to my astonishment I saw him standing at the cigar counter, as tall, spindly and diffident as ever.

"Chris!" I cried.

CHAPTER TWO
CHRISTOPHER BEANFIELD SEES A GHOST

Why it is, I do not know, but upon chance-meeting an old pal, it is remarkable, in my case at least, how often a more-surprised-than-pleased expression flits across the face of the latter. Sure enough, one now flitted across his. Then he forced a smile and held out his hand.

"Gully, old man," he said.

"What a coincidence!" I exclaimed. "I was humming *Rolling Down to Rio* (I hadn't been, but I threw it in) and thinking of you—and here you are! My sources report," I shot in fast, "that for you it's either a partnership or Brazil."

He appeared torn by conflicting emotions. Then he shrugged, relaxed and stated the facts. He had a chance to enter a desirable Boston partnership. The ante was ten thousand dollars, of which he had only five. If he could not borrow the rest by Wednesday, he was out.

"You mean *this* Wednesday?" I asked in dismay.

"Yes. And if I'm out, then Randy and I take off for Brazil."

"But," I protested, "you're both engaged to be married!"

He shrugged. "If we don't go now, we never will. On the other hand, I want the partnertship. So we agreed to let that decide it."

I eyed him thoughtfully. I had the picture. I even entertained a sneaking admiration for their daring to propose, at this late date, to kick over the traces—but it just wouldn't do.

"So what brings you here," I asked.

"Ellen. It was her idea. My last chance."

"How do you mean?"

"She's up there now, in his office." He glanced at his wristwatch. "Her uncle. I've never met him, but she wants me to try him. Sampson Rowbottom—ever hear of him?"

My jaw dropped. Ellen Hill at no time during our acquaintance had revealed having this uncle-to-end-all-uncles.

"Why," I stammered, "he's my boss. A great fellow," I added firmly, accentuating the positive. "You'll like him."

"The question," said Chris, "is will he like *me*—five thousand dollars worth." And squaring his shoulders, he headed for the elevators.

I had to know the outcome. Purchasing and munching at a bag of peanuts, I sourly compared to my own the circumstances of a Hackamore pal who, by his own admission, had accumulated *five thousand dollars*. By now, I had held and had lost, due to various misfortunes, a number of lowest rung engineering positions. And those with certain other companies were self-denied because of my secret ambition—their hiring agreements contained the patent assignment clause I never would sign. Indeed, my present job with Bell, Rowbottom and Witherspoon was the last local possibility in my field. In the face of which, I recently had effected a change in my relations with Aunt Orpha which was both glorious and dangerous.

Her present business had always kept us comfortably, and had made possible our move from a Quincy flat to our present more metropolitan quarters. But all the while, and notwithstanding my advancing years, she staunchly had maintained the dimmest of views toward modern democratic government. This attitude finally led me to propose that I bear half our household expense in return for half a voice in its top-level decisions. And when she, with ill-concealed delight, proceeded to itemize the staggering tab, I had found myself, though left with barest pocket money, at long last elevated to separate-but-equal status. That was the glorious part. The dangerous part was that to lose my present job would precipitate a domestic disaster too horrible to contemplate—a return to conditions of the Old South.

Hardly five minutes had elapsed when the elevator doors opened and a chalk-faced Christopher Beanfield burst out. He loped across the lobby and lunged through the street doors. Mystified, I gave chase. Half a block away, I caught up with him. He eyed me without recognition. I grabbed his arm and slowed him to a walk.

"It's me, Chris! Your old pal! What happened?"

He gave me a dazed look. Then, in the manner of one who has just seen a ghost, he stared ahead. "I never knew his name was Rowbottom," he said.

"You never knew *whose* name was Rowbottom?"

"Rowbottom."

"Oh," I said, still mystified.

Two long beers in a bar at length drew from Chris what proved to be a fearful secret of his undergraduate past. A desirable, heat-engineer-dominated fraternity had offered him membership but, because of its notoriously rough initiation, Chris had held off. The brothers then offered him an alternate test. The president of a brother house "across the river" had been flunked out by a professor of sanitary engineering. It had been a matter of a fraction of a point, but the professor would not reconsider. Revenge was called for.

"This professor gave demonstration lectures, and always called for a volunteer assistant. The brothers needed a fake student. So I—" Chris shrugged. "I finally agreed. This particular demonstration had to do with a complicated chemical treatment of sewage."

"Sewage!" I gasped. "Not old—?"

"The house chemistry majors had it all figured out. They gave me everything I needed and told me exactly what to do. When he turned to the board, I added the ingredients." Chris paused, his eyes lighting with pride over a job well done. "When he turned the switch, it was Fourth of July in the glue factory. Fire and stench—! During the excitement, I walked out. I ran all the way across the bridge."

"You pulled it off!" I said, eyeing him with new respect; he had revealed unexpected depths.

"Yes. But I never did know his name until just now. When I went up, there he sat—Professor Rowbottom. He recognized me at once. It was lucky," Chris ended soberly, "that Ellen was there."

"How about the five thousand?"

"I didn't stop to ask."

"Don't give up," I said, as we parted. I laid my hand on his shoulder. "It's only Monday. And remember, it's always darkest just before the dawn. I'll think of something. And when I do, I'll call you."

Walking back to Beacon Street, I thought of my parting speech. To buck up Chris, the speech had been necessary. But it also had been phony. I had assured him that I would think of something. But all I could think of was that, with the background which Chris had just revealed, the chances for last-hope Rowbottom lending him five grand were zero. And that, therefore, the chances for a Norm visit were excellent. Hoping that my lateness had gone unnoticed, I made my way to my drafting board. But it had not. On that board lay a memo slip which read as follows:

FROM: *S. D. R.*
TO: *G. Gates.*
SUBJECT: *Report my office.*

One way these professorial I-Led-Two-Lives busters get started is at the beer barrel after the society session. There, a struggling young assistant professor is accosted by a short-handed architect or engineer named Bell or Witherspoon who inquires *sotto voce*, if the y. a. prof would consider taking on an item of moonlighting. The y. a. p. can't resist the green, sneaks most of the job on university time, and comes back for more. Meanwhile he writes learned papers, assembles them into a book or two, his name becomes known in the profession, he rises to associate professor, and at length he holds out for a partnership.

Such a buster was Sampson Denhardt Rowbottom, B. S., M. S., author of *The Sewer* and *Some Aspects of Sewage*, professor of sanitary engineering at the institution across the river, and one of those who, as they say, keeps one foot on each side of the Charles. Once a day he strode up and down our drafting room aisles, honor society keys dangling, superciliously eyeing our efforts, and, in my case, usually with the air of a professor about to issue a failing notice. At his door, I took a deep breath, lightly rapped, and, to the anticipated shattering roar, entered.

"Yes, sir?"

Professor-partner Rowbottom, a hulking bachelor of forty-five, sat staring at a picture frame on his desk. Now, he rubbed a hairy paw across his bull-ape features, lowered his shaggy black brows and glowered at me, and I did not doubt for an instant that a bawling out was in the works. To my surprise, however, he began to strain toward a smile.

"Mr. Gates!" he said in a softer tone. "How are you?"

I blinked in surprise. Had he just finished phoning a client and forgotten to turn it off? Or was this the sarcastic buildup, to be followed by the thus more devastating knockdown?

"All right," I said, eyeing him apprehensively.

"Sit down, please."

As I did so, he swung away, bent down over a file drawer and slowly pawed through its contents. Was he setting me up for the kill? Or was he still doing a slings & arrows over the fake student who had boobytrapped his lecture and now had turned up engaged to his niece? It would be prudent, should the subject come up, not to mention that Chris and I were pals. Loudly he cleared his throat.

"Do you, ah—" he asked over his shoulder, and with what to my ear was a forced casualness, "—do you still belong to that gymnasium of yours?"

He must have been looking at my employment application, on which I had listed the old Ajax Gym under *Memberships*, and "Squash" under *Sports*.

"The Ajax Gym? Yes, Sir, I still belong."

At quarter speed, he resumed his leafing.

"Go there much?"

"Why, when I can. A quick game of—" I hesitated over the word, recalling the office story of how he once achieved a unique revenge at squash. "—of squash, or a swim. I try to keep in trim."

"There *is* a pool?" he asked, pouncing upon the word.

"Why—" I stopped, astonished, as he shut the drawer and slowly turned. For in his manner was a diffidence which was entirely out of character. "Yes, there is a pool."

He gripped the desk edge and reddened.

"Mr. Gates, I—" He stopped and gulped in air. "Mr. Gates—" he tried again, then stopped for more air. "Cigarette?" he asked, producing a pack.

I took one, he held out his lighter, and soon smoke mushroomed over the desk. I waited. He made a desperate gesture.

"Mr. Gates, what I have to say must go no farther."

I nodded gravely.

"Mr. Gates, I find this—" He stopped and scowled fiercely, "—an embarrassing admission." He eyed me appealingly. "Mr. Gates, the fact is, I can't swim."

With a quick movement, I recaptured my cigarette, which, due to the sudden dropping of my jaw, had become unmoored.

"I see," I said. "And you'd like to learn."

"It's not that I'd *like* to learn. I *have* to learn."

Somewhat at sea, I considered. Had we been fellow passengers in mid-Atlantic on a sinking raft, his remark would have come as no surprise, but here it did. In particular, one thing puzzled me. According to the revenge-on-the-squash-court tale, Rowbottom belonged to an athletic club in Cambridge. It was as swank as mine was not, with a beautiful pool, high and low diving boards—and, almost certainly, capable swimming instructors. Why did he not engage one there? But this was no time for such questions. He wanted help and had come to me. I smiled encouragingly.

"Mr. Rowbottom, I, myself, had trouble learning. But after I was shown a few preliminary tricks, the rest was easy. First, in the bathtub, you hold your breath and put your face in the water. Then—"

He shifted impatiently.

"Mr. Gates—"

"Then you duck your whole head under and open your eyes—it

smarts a little, but you get used to it. Then you try to pick up a penny from the bottom—or a dime will do. Then you are ready for the actual pool. There, you repeat the same things. You find—"

"Mr. Gates—"

"You find," I hurried on toward the happy ending, "that you can't stay down even if you want to. Before you know it, you are doing the jellyfish float." I flung out my arms and thrust our my legs to illustrate. "—and then dog-paddling. And as the days go by—"

Determinedly he signalled a halt.

"Mr. Gates, I feel that a stranger who is a professional instructor would be best, and under conditions of the utmost privacy possible. Furthermore, as to the days going by—it won't do. I should like to become a proficient swimmer today."

I eyed him in surprise.

"Proficient?" I asked. "In one day?"

"Then let us say passable."

"Today?"

"Yes, today. You do not think it possible?"

"I don't know. It's like riding a bicycle. At first you can't. Then you can. All of a sudden it happens."

He digested this, then nodded.

"I suppose so. Well, I can ride a bicycle."

"Can you? Good! Then you can learn to swim," I affirmed.

CHAPTER THREE
SAMPSON ROWBOTTOM'S DILEMMA

Such a conclusion doubtless would have drawn frowns in the better logical circles. But on the face of my companion it produced a hopeful smile.

"I am glad to hear you say that. You see, I was wondering if you might be able to arrange a lesson for me, and under the conditions I have outlined."

"At the Ajax?"

"Yes."

I considered. Ajax Vieille, former wrestler and weight lifter and still the spitting image of Tarzan, was a first rate instructor in the gym and in the pool as well. As to imparting the art of swimming, his method—uniformly successful as to the youngsters I had witnessed him with—was quite the reverse of the one I had just described. Without any preliminaries, and with a circular "water wing" about their midriff, Ajax started them in at once on the elements of the crawl. This being explained to a Rowbottom who literally hung upon my words, he nodded eagerly.

"He sounds like the right man."

"Then the only problem is privacy. When you say by today, do you include by tonight?"

"Yes, certainly."

Again I considered. Of late, Monsieur Vieille had found it profitable to set off the main part of his morning for ladies' classes, aiming at the lucrative field of the figure conscious matron, bringing in formidable lady masseuses and barring men entirely. Toward noon, however, with a disconcerting reek of menthol, alcohol and perfume, the place reverted to the males, and there was constant activity all the way to ten P. M., when he officially closed. Afterwards, however, he often remained by appointment to administer one of his renowned "twenty minute specials" to some harried minister or physician who needed to sleep especially soundly and thus awaken especially fit for an arduous morning's go at scalpel or pulpit. At ten o'clock tonight, then, M. Vieille might take on my employer, and with privacy assured.

"Yes, yes!" he cried, when I had explained. Nodding hard, he sprang to his feet. "Fine! That's it."

"I could see him this noon."

"Better still, hop along right now." He was beaming. As I arose to go, I was sure that, but for the intervening desk, he would have slapped me on the back. "And phone me from there. I'd like to know."

Happily I exited. Bands were playing; the sun was shining. In my relations with old Rowbottom, a new day was dawning.

Half an hour later, I dialed B,R & W and asked for Rowbottom. "He'll do it," I informed. "Tonight at ten, if agreeable to you."

"Certainly!...Fine." He paused. "I don't suppose, er—" He then began a hemming and hawing in which I detected a definite uneasiness. "I wonder...would you be able to meet me there?"

My heart leaped. "Glad to," I said.

"Fine. I would appreciate it."

"Not at all. I could be waiting outside at ten."

"All right, fine. Outside, you say?"

"Outside, yes."

"Outside at ten?"

"At ten, yes."

"...Outside?"

"Outside, yes," I confirmed.

"At ten?"

"Yes."

"All right, fine."

I hung up feeling I had been clutched at by a drowning man. Teaching him would be no snap. But Ajax, like Tarzan, could do anything—and assuming a successful evening, then what? To a Rowbottom won over by his new skill, I should be able to bring up *in re* Chris Beanfield: how he regretted the follies of his youth, now faced with a bright future, was a desirable mate for niece Ellen—and, to get the thing clicking, needed a loan of five grand. Right now, then, the shoving into old Chris of some words of hope and cheer would be wise, so that he would not go ahead with any irrevocable plans for Brazil. I dialed his office, where, upon hearing my voice, he did not sound overjoyed.

"Chris! The dawn is breaking. I'm doing Rowbottom a great service. Afterwards, he'll be receptive when I put in some solid words for an old pal."

"Look, Gully! Stay out of this."

"Just as you wish," I replied, and with no intention of doing so, signed off.

I was in the attic making final adjustments on the Gates Automatic Bed when, at seven-thirty, Rowbottom phoned, his tone that of one about to chicken out. The gist of his disjointed statements: a) he was at home alone; because b) his sister had taken off for Florida; and so, c) rather than meeting him in front of the Ajax Gym, as to the location of which he was uncertain (never have I heard a flimsier item c), would I consider coming by for him? In fact, why not come right now? I replied that I would start at once. Whereupon he babbled out detailed directions for my getting there, ending with the fervent plea that, should I go astray anywhere along the way, I head for the nearest telephone and call him for further directions.

Skirting the northerly edge of Roxbury and approaching South Boston, I turned down a side street into an old and deteriorating neighborhood. His particular block, however, proved to be an oasis of large single houses, the plain exterior of the Rowbottom residence concealing, as I saw a minute later, a richly furnished interior. Hardly had I rung when a distraught Rowbottom wrenched the door open, pumped my hand and urged me to sit. He sat down, immediately sprang up again, and headed for a cabinet, announcing that we might as well have a whiskey and soda.

"Mr. Rowbottom," I said, steeling myself for my babysitting stint, "I would strongly advise against it."

He stopped, harrumped and came back. "...Suppose you're right." He sat down and began to fidget. Suddenly, as if having had the greatest idea of all time, he arose and made for an end table. "A cigarette!" he cried.

I raised my hand. "Mr. Rowbottom," I said firmly, "at this particular time, I would advise against that also."

He stopped, frustrated. Upstairs, the phone rang. He bolted up the stair. A moment later, he stomped down again. "Wrong number!" he fumed. "At a time like this!"

"A pipe, perhaps," I suggested.

"Yes!" Futilely he ransacked a drawer. Then, with a happy cry, he bounded up the stair again. "In my bedroom," he flung back. He descended with pipe and pouch and fumbled at the makings. My advice had been sound; he now had plenty to do.

"You will find Ajax Vieille an expert instructor," I remarked. "There is really nothing to worry about. It's too bad, though, that you can't start out in sea water. More buoyant, you know."

"But I have to swim in *fresh* water!"

"You *have* to?"

"Have to—yes." He slumped back. "I might as well explain," he muttered, "if you can keep it confidential." And upon my prompt assurance that I could, he unburdened himself of his dreadful secret. "Last Saturday, when I went to New Hampshire..."

It was a moving tale. A small New Hampshire town had acquired a new electronics plant and with it growing pains, and so was concerned over pollution of its lake, a revenue-producing tourist attraction. To its town committee, salesman Rowbottom had described B, R & W's highly successful installation in a Rhode Island town with a similar problem.

"The big question in their minds was as to the purity of the liquid flowing from the final effluent tank. To convince them, I stated that the Rhode Island effluent was so pure that I would not hesitate to swim in it. Then the chairman, a hard-headed fellow, said that if I would favor them with a demonstration this Wednesday, they would be convinced." He gave a wry laugh. "Only then did I recall that I could not swim."

I sat back. Not often does the lad out at the drafting board get the inside look at the executive mind in action. But there it was, and the stakes were high. Either he got in that tank and swam, or he lost a client and the firm's reputation.

"You can do it," I said firmly, eyeing my wristwatch. "And we'd better be on our way."

"Who's the clumsy oaf?"

"Sampson Rowbottom."

"New member?"

"No. My boss."

"Oh, sorry."

"No need," said I.

Ajax's final patient, barefoot Dr. Amos Clarke, now clad in the sheet from his massage table and looking like a small Halloween ghost, stood beside me at the office window looking down upon the little drama at the pool's far end. There, Monsieur Vieille, head and shoulders out of the water, voiced encouragements in his—though we could not hear it—rich baritone to his new pupil, who, hands on Ajax's shoulders, desperately thrashed his legs and desperately tried to keep *his* head and shoulders out of the water. M. Vieille, a patient man, gently shook his head.

"All wrong," said my companion, shaking his. He whipped his sheet into more toga-like form. "I mean, the man obviously has a phobia."

15

"A phobia?"

"Hydrophobia—scairt of the water," said Dr. Clarke, chuckling over his own joke.

I forced a weak laugh. This, to me, was no time for jokes, for things did not look too promising. A snicker now escaped Dr. Clarke—one in which I, not sharing his detachment, did not join. Rowbottom was climbing the ladder, wearing around his middle the inflated "doughnut" of the Vieille method. M. Vieille himself followed rather thoughtfully. Some indistinct business took place in the background; then Rowbottom reappeared wearing *two* doughnuts.

"Oh, no!" quaked Dr. Clarke.

In taut silence I watched the pair re-enter the water. It was M. Vieille's practice to sweet talk the leg-thrashing pupil into releasing his hold of Vieille's shoulders and instead to begin flailing his arms against the water. Meanwhile Vieille's hand would support the pupil's chest, lightly at first, and finally not at all. At which time, to his pleased surprise, the pupil would—*voila!*— find himself swimming.

But not this time.

Hands on Ajax's shoulders, Rowbottom desperately thrashed his feet. He then raised one hand, flailed out wildly and, from the waist up, disappeared from sight. His kicking legs rose out of the water. Then his arms reappeared, grappling with Ajax. For the first time in my life, I saw Ajax stagger, then recover his balance. Then I saw him double a fist. I closed my eyes. When I opened them, Ajax, erect, was mounting the ladder like Tarzan, with Rowbottom slung over his shoulder like a freshly killed buffalo.

"Gully—"

I turned. I had not been aware that Dr. Clarke had left my side, but he must have, for he stood behind me sheetless and holding out his key case.

"Better trot out to my car and fetch my bag," he said.

I grabbed the keys and shot off.

CHAPTER FOUR
HOW TARZAN LEARNED TO SWIM

Tuesday morning, passing Rowbottom's door, I heard his familiar roar. So he was all right. At my board I pondered the Chris-problem. So far, he never actually had asked for the loan. Suppose, then, that with me at his side, he simply outlined the pressure of the undergraduate situation which had led to the classroom debacle, apologized, and...Inconspicuously I made for the back stair, pattered down and headed for Christopher's office. There, to my knock, the sharp young chap who shared his room opened the door. Chris was on the phone. As he hung up, I braced myself, but need not have, for he swung around with a cordial greeting.

"You sound happy," I said, surprised.

"Yes. That was Ellen. She just saw her uncle again. She said that when she mentioned I played squash, his eyes brightened. This noon he wants me to have a game and then lunch with him."

A chill shot through me. Involuntarily my hand sought the back of my head. "Chris," I said, sadly shaking the latter, "you'd better come outside."

Puzzled, he arose. At the stair, I told him the story. A young firm-member, after causing B, R & W to lose a valuable award, had been vastly relieved by Rowbottom's cordial invitation to squash. Their game, however, had been adjourned in mid score after Rowbottom's accurate and bulletlike return "accidentally" hit the back of his opponent's head and flattened him.

"Revenge!" gasped a crestfallen Chris. As had mine, his hand sought the back of his head. "He only wanted to—"

"I'm afraid so," I said absently, for in my ears was a dictum of Jo's to the effect that situations fraught with peril can also be fraught with opportunity. Then it hit me: this was one of them! I grabbed his arm. "Chris!" I cried. "I've got it!"

Skeptically, to my insistence that the plan called for a walk in the fresh air, he followed me down the stair and outside, where I asked him if he knew the story of Tarzan.

"Tarzan—! What has Tarzan got to do with it?"

I sketched out how the Greystokes were marooned, Lady Alice died, Lord Greystoke was killed, and brave she-ape Kala foster mothered the tiny man-child. And how, as he leaned over the bank of the lake, old Sabor the lioness sprang—and Tarzan, ten, although he had been taught by the apes to fear the water, instinctively jumped in and felt the chill waters close above his head.

"Chill waters! Did you get me out here to tell me a bedtime story?"

I held up my hand. "Chris, do you know what Rowbottom wants most of all?"

"Revenge on me."

"No, he wants to learn to swim."

"Swim? He can't swim? How do you know?"

"Last night, an expert instructor failed to teach him. But you are—right after your game. He'll be so grateful that he'll write out your check at lunch."

Chris shook his head. "I can't believe he wants to learn to swim that bad."

"You will, when I tell you why."

As I proceeded to do so, his eyes widened. At one point he cackled: "And he agreed to swim in a sewerage tank?"

"That water is about as good as any other. He simply proposed to dramatize it. So after you teach him, you'll walk out of that club arm in arm."

"H'm," said Chris, trying, apparently without success, to picture that improbable exit. "But if an expert couldn't, what makes you think I can?"

Triumphantly I tapped him on the chest. "Chris, how did Tarzan learn?"

"Oh...that. But I don't see—"

"Then listen," I said, and outlined my plan. Owl-eyed, he listened. At one point, with a wild look he broke away from me and took off down the street. At an adverse traffic light I collared him. "Chris!" I said, breathing hard. "It's your only chance!" Ahead, I saw the same bar we had visited the day before. Locking my arm in his, I gently but firmly steered him toward it.

Fifteen minutes later, side by side at the counter, I was worn to a frazzle but Chris was whipping into shape. "Once more," I encouraged. "First the squash game. You keep your head down and go through with it. You carry it off, the good sportsman, no matter what."

"Head down. Good sportsman, no matter what."

"Right. Then, you want to swim."

"Why?"

I flung out my arms. "You just *want* to, Chris—the pool being right there, and all. You say you've never been in it."

"But I *have* been in it."

"You have? Then don't tell him so. Just say you want to try it—anything."

"Want to swim. Got to swim."

"That's it. Good. Then he confesses he can't swim."

"Why?"

"Because he'll have to."

Chris squinted doubtfully, then shrugged. "Well, all right," he said.

I raised my arms in a show of astonishment. "You are astonished. You tell him how you once feared the water more than anybody. Then a friend cured you instantly by the secret Hindoo method."

"The secret *what* method?"

"The secret Hindoo method."

"Not the Tarzan method?"

"No. Actually, it is, but—"

"Then why not the Tarzan method?"

"Because he may have read the book. So we play it safe—we give it a different name."

"I see. Good thinking, there. I would never—"

"All right. A friend cured you instantly by the—?"

"—secret Hindoo method."

"Good. Then you get him to walk out to the end of the diving board and stare down."

"The three-foot or the ten-foot?"

I considered. "The ten-foot," I said firmly.

"The *ten*-foot?"

"Chris, this is no time for half measures."

"No, I suppose not."

"All right, then. With an awful scream, you push him off. He feels the chill waters close above his head, his instinct for self-preservation conquers his fear of the water, and he begins to dog-paddle because he *has* to."

Chris squirmed miserably, as if not fully convinced. "And that worked for Tarzan?" he asked.

"Yes, it worked for Tarzan. And," I said firmly, "it will work for Rowbottom."

Chris squirmed again. "That's the way it was in the book?"

"Yes."

"Do you have it handy?"

"The book? It's at home. Why?"

"I never heard a lioness scream."

"A lion will do just as well. Roar. Like this."

I gave out a roar, and, in the manner of one pushing a Rowbottom off a ten-foot diving board, pushed at the counter with both hands. In imitation, Chris pushed doubtfully and squeaked like a mouse. "Good," I lied, trying to accentuate the positive. "But throw more weight into it. And open the mouth more. Snarl."

He tried again: the counter creaked and a fair-sized roar came out. The third time was better still. By now, however, the bartender and several bystanders were eyeing us with concern. I got off my stool.

"You'll do fine," I said.

Outside, I said I would phone him afterwards to learn how he had fared, and we parted, he rather cataleptic and glassy eyed.

Well pleased by my efforts, I strode briskly toward the Witherspoon Building. It had been an idea such as Jo, given the circumstance of a revenge-bent Rowbottom inviting an unsuspecting Chris to his club, would have conceived. Then I slowed: I did not want to run into Rowbottom before hearing from Chris. I strolled aimlessly, regretting that Jo could not have helped rehearse him, for long ago we had acted out that very scene, I in the role of the young Tarzan, she as Sabor. But anybody, the mechanics being explained, should be able to do Sabor. And as for Rowbottom in the role of Tarzan—well, it was simply the matter of getting him out to the end of the board and the element of surprise. The idea was soundly based. But would Chris muff his lines? My doubts were erased by a happy thought: he, no champion to the naked eye, successfully had pulled off Rowbottom's classroom debacle. There was good stuff in Chris. Older, now, and with a lot more at stake, he could not fail.

At length, on edge to know the outcome, I phoned his office. The young chap answered. I asked if Chris was back.

"He came back, but—you the fellow was here?"

"Yes."

"He went home. Not feeling good. Had a chill."

"Do you?" I asked, having one of my own, "know how he made out in Cambridge?"

"Way I got it, he pushed some joker off the diving board. Joker went down like a rock. Then they pumped him out and he took after Chris. Chris ran for a taxi in his swim trunks—sent me back for his clothes. Real crazy, the whole thing, if you ask me."

I hung up with my opinion of Rowbottom at a new low. He had not even exhibited that most primitive of instincts: to struggle and thrash about when unexpectedly deposited in the water. No Tarzan summed up old Rowbottom.

Walking back toward the Witherspoon Building, I thought fast. Chris was a spent force: it was up to me. In the lobby, I thought of Jo. "There are times," she once had said, "when the simple truth is the best answer." Suppose, then, that I simply went to Rowbottom and explained about Sabor and Tarzan? How the whole thing had been an earnest attempt, based upon sound principles, to teach him to swim—and how Chris had had his best interests at heart. Then, in the elevator, I recalled Jo's addendum."—but," she emphatically had added, "*not often.*" By the time I arrived at his door, I was doubting that this was one of those times. Still, there just wasn't any other idea around. I rapped. A roar wet with watery overtones bade me enter.

Sampson Rowbottom sat at his desk in what had become a characteristic pose. Just so, last night, had I left him sitting on the edge of his bed, head far over to the side, palm pounding it with a measured beat. I swallowed, overcome by the enormity of the statement I was about to make. He straightened up and glared.

"Well—?" he demanded.

I opened my mouth. Nothing came out.

"Mr. Gates—" He gave his head an angry shake. In my mind's ear I heard the splashing waters within. "You knocked. You entered. Doubtless you had something to say. Say it!"

"Well, no," I stammered, certain by now that this was not the best of all possible times for any simple recital of the facts. I grabbed for the doorknob.

"Mr. Gates—"

I turned; he eyed me strangely.

"I was about to call you in. Sit down."

I did so, sensing behind the lowered brows some raging debate. It is prudent, at such times, to try to put yourself in the other fellow's shoes. I tried: in those shoes was a man who, having failed to carry out a well-planned revenge, then found himself tricked by his intended victim into being pushed off a ten-foot diving board. Such a man would not now be in the best of moods. And to sum it up, my recent idea of setting forth the simple facts was strictly for the birds.

Meanwhile, he turned his head from side to side, apparently weighing alternatives. At one point he started to turn toward his files for another of those refreshing sessions of pawing through a drawer. Then, appearing to think better of it, he turned back. With a final slow nod, he regarded me.

"Mr. Gates. As a junior member of the Society, you may have met our secretary, Mr. Theodore Prentice."

"Oh, yes," I said.

He paused. "Do I take it from your tone that you are acquainted?"

I hesitated. Teddy Prentice, middleaged widower and town engineer for Meldonville, was, as already noted, courting Aunt Flo—a match approved by family council and self. But in adversary proceedings one does not reveal all one knows. On the other hand, this was no time to cross old R.

"He and my Aunt Florence have an understanding," I said.

Rowbottom exhibited surprise. "I was aware of his feelings for a Mrs. Miller," he conceded. "I did not, however, realize that she was your aunt. Well! You would know, then, that Mr. Prentice, quite against his will, now drives an ancient electric automobile?"

"Oh, yes," I said again.

CHAPTER FIVE
PRUDENCE PRENTICE'S ELECTRIC

Prudence Prentice, seventy-five and worth half a million, lived with nephew Teddy, her only remaining relative, in Meldonville—where, some months ago, bowling along at ten miles an hour in her electric, she had failed to note the presence of a well-meaning traffic officer in her path. Well, I don't know how closely you follow Burroughs, but you may recall how John Carter, surprised by a score of green Martian warriors, was able, due to that planet's lesser gravity, to save his life by leaping thirty feet into the air. At any rate, after such a John-Carter-like leap, this officer had flagged down the next car, given chase, arrested Prudence for reckless driving and filed personal action for assault as well. Through Teddy's efforts the action had been dropped; in traffic court she had drawn a suspended sentence and a stiff reprimand. Afterwards, incensed, she had announced that she would drive no more in Massachusetts; that she was turning over the durable and economical electric to Teddy; and that, there thus being no need for two cars, he was to sell his own. Heir-apparent Teddy, not daring to offend, meekly had done so.

"You are aware," asked Rowbottom, "that this has placed Mr. Prentice in an onerous position?"

"Onerous is right!" I seconded, for from all reports, Teddy was taking a real razzing and was being kidded to death—"Git a hoss!" and the like. Aunt Flo had opined that he could not take it much longer. On the other hand, if he balked, down would go his chances to inherit half a million dollars.

Rowbottom leaned forward. "Mr. Gates, a solution to my friend Mr. Prentice's problem occurred to me. I offered to help and he gratefully acepted. In carrying out the plan, I had intended to enlist the help of my niece's fiance. But this noon—" He leaned over for a session of head pounding."—I discovered the boy to be mentally unbalanced."

My jaw dropped. How wrongly I had interpreted Rowbottom's eyes brightening! With Ellen Hill's mention of squash, it simply had occurred to him where and how to put the proposal, whatever it was, to Chris. He now slowly shook his head, as if reliving the noon's stirring events. Then he eyed the ceiling.

"I have decided to ask your help in this matter."

"Help?" I asked. "How?"

"You will steal the electric."

As I eyed him, speechless, he outlined the plan. The Society's monthly social was to be held tonight at the popular Pickersgill Grotto in South Boston. Teddy would drive Prudence to Cambridge, pick up Aunt Flo, and proceed to "Pigles', " as it is locally known. There would be no problem of a parking stub, for frugal Prudence always refused to park in a pay lot. Teddy simply would park at the curb as near to Pigles' as he could. After the affair, Rowbottom would "happen" to run into the trio, sociably would walk along with them to where they would find their electric missing, then helpfully drive them to the police station to report the theft, and as helpfully drive them home. The event started at seven-thirty and ended at nine-thirty. Before the alarm went out, I thus would have two hours plus to locate and drive—Teddy had given him a duplicate controller key—the electric to our Tilborough Street garage.

Very neat, I thought, as he eyed me for my answer—and with, should the scheme go sour, only Gulliver Inchmore Gates to be marched off to the clink. Also, I was sure there was more to this than he was telling.

"Mr. Rowbottom," I said coldly, "yesterday you wanted to learn to swim. Today it's stealing cars. What—?"

"As it happens," he said with a wry laugh, "there is a close connection." And he proceeded to reveal it.

Remember the hardheaded committee chairman? A representative of a rival Philadelphia firm afterwards had visited him. Told of Rowbottom's forthcoming swim, he had countered that, if the chairman instead would accompany him to one of *his* company's installations which used the patented Prentice Process—he personally would *drink* the final product. Whereupon the impressed chairman had advised Rowbottom that the swim was off. Prudence's late father, I knew, had invented the process. She long had licensed it to the Philadelphia firm. Aware of this, Rowbottom had sounded out Teddy—to be told that the license presently was up for renewal and that Prudence, dissatisfied with her share of the take, had instructed him to look around for a likely new licensee.

"And B, R & W would like that license?" I asked.

"Of course! And so I offered to arrange about the electric if he, as a favor, would recommend our firm to his aunt. Being familiar with our high reputation, he at once agreed."

And that was the story. Having lost, due to his rival's even more dramatic offer, the need to learn to swim, but determined not to lose a prospective client, Rowbottom now was preparing—good executive that he was—to pull the rug out from under the Philadelphian.

"So what do you say?" he asked hopefully.

I considered. It had not occurred to him to ask me if I even could *drive* an electric, and I did not enlighten him. Actually, at rallies with my Uncle Roscoe Miller (Flo's older brother-in-law) up in Indian Mound, I had acquired a considerable knowledge of same. Also, at Teddy's invitation, I once had driven the electric in question—a Halrick & Sears with the unusual feature of an inboard charger—around the block.

"You would be demonstrating your loyalty to the firm," noted Rowbottom in a kindly tone. "—resulting in your immediate advancement from junior engineering aide to senior engineering aide, with, of course, the accompanying increase in salary."

"Oh?" I said, not too enthusiastically, and considered some more. If I decided to go through with it, I would need help, preferably Jo—to, for one thing, tail me from South Boston to Tilborough Street. I glanced at my watch: three-ten. When I went for her at four, I would ask Jo—never one to miss an adventure—to stay over. But what about Aunt Orpha? When, on her return, she inquired as to why I had left the VW standing out in the driveway instead of putting it in the garage, and I informed her that the garage in question was presently occupied by her client Prudence Prentice's stolen electric, she would have conniption fits until I got it through her head how this furthered her own sister's romance. But again—and on the bright side—with success, Rowbottom should be receptive to my last-minute pitch for Chris.

"On the other hand," he now added, "considering the firm's loss should you refuse, you could expect two weeks notice."

My head shot up. To be fired at this time, as already explained, would precipitate that domestic disaster too horrible to contemplate. The decision made, I arose and held out my hand.

"Do you have the key?" I asked.

I stopped in the lobby to dial Christopher's home. He answered with a sneeze, followed by, when I identified myself, a roar of anger worthy of Sabor.

"Good news!" I said in a rush. "Rowbottom and I are pals again, so don't give up hope."

"Gully! I'll thank you to keep your fat—"

"I'm doing him a great service, Chris! By tomorrow morning, he'll be eating out of my hand, and I'll put in the winning pitch for you. Chin up, old man! You'll be hearing—" I then rang off, for he,

25

saying something I did not catch, had hung up.

At a few minutes after four, I pulled to the curb at the St. James terminal and a waiting Jo bounced in beside me. Hardly had I completed the plot's first paragraph when, as predicted, she declared her confederacy. We at once took off for South Boston, where from Pigles' we scouted a back-street route home, carefully making revisions due to one-way streets. During our second pass, a helmeted pair in a police car, who had eyed us only casually the first time, this time turned for a second look—a disturbing action which caused us reluctantly to agree upon a change of plan. For suppose someone reported seeing an electric followed by a Volkswagen, and Prudence Prentice heard this from the police. "Gulliver Gates drives a Volks," she would say thoughtfully, and at length would arrive at only one conclusion. So Jo would not follow me in the VW, after all, but in it would go on by herself. I dropped her in Quincy and returned home to make final preparations for the heist.

In Quincy, again, I pulled up at Aunt Effie's and beeped. The front door promptly opened and Jo dashed out. I reached over and opened her door.

"Hello, Gully, Dar—*Yikes!*"

She froze.

"It's all right," I said reassuringly.

Giving me a wide-eyed stare, she got in.

My appearance, I knew, was striking. Indeed, it was the result of no little thought and preparation. For I would be operating in an area of festive nightclubbers, and so had best be one of them. I therefore was formally dressed, the whole thing topped off by my special-occasions fedora—the real thing, dark, wide brimmed and crease crowned. But it was not this which had given my young cousin pause, for she had seen me thus before. No, it was two additional touches—touches inspired by the chance that I might be seen in the vicinity of Pigles' by someone I knew—that had succeeded in shaking this steel-nerved child. These two touches, in brief, were my red wig and red moustache.

"Gully! Where in the world did you get them?"

"Cast your mind back a few years. Have you forgotten the kit that came with my private investigator's course?"

"Oh, yes. But do you really think—"

Crisply, as we took off, I explained my reasoning.

"Another thing," I said, pointing behind.

She looked around.

"What's in it?"

The package on the back seat represented the solution to a problem the very existence of which, to one of less background, starting out to steal an electric automobile from in front of a brightly lighted nightclub—might not have occurred until too late. The problem was how, under the bright lights, without arousing the suspicions of bystanders, are you going to transfer your locksmithing tools, brought along just in case, together with your extension cords, assortment of plugs, etc., etc., from the Volks to the electric?

The answer, as I now explained, was the gift-wrapped, beribboned box on the back seat. I made a show of lifting it.

"A well-dressed man, out for the evening, obviously bearing a gift for his beloved—you see?"

"Yes. But Gully, let me tell you this, fast."

"It won't wait?"

"No. It might change your mind."

"Let's have it."

"Well, while Teddy and Prudence were in Aunt Flo's living room, they saw a white flash, outside. So Teddy—" Jo sighed, and a premonitory chill ran up my spine. "Do you remember Norm's racer with the little red wheels? The one he—"

"Yes!" I said.

"You can imagine how nervous Teddy must have been, anyway. So he rushed out, and—"

"And—?"

"Well, it seems that Norman had been experimenting with an old electric motor on his racer. He knew that Teddy's electric had batteries, so he connected wires from the electric to his motor, but apparently he had the wiring wrong. Anyway, the wires were white hot. Teddy grabbed a stick and knocked them loose."

I groaned. Twelve-year-olds, it has long been my conviction, should be drowned at birth, and here was the final proof.

"So afterwards, the question was, would the electric still run or not? To find out, Teddy got in alone and drove it around the block. And apparently it still was running all right."

"But Jo, how do you know all this?"

"After Aunt Prudence and Aunt Flo got in the car, he told them he had suddenly remembered an important call he must make, and went back in. He tried you first, but no answer. Then he called me."

"Norman Miller—!" I fumed.

"He wanted to get the facts to you at once, because he realized you might have trouble with the car."

"*Might* have trouble—!"

"Gully, why didn't the electric blow a fuse?"

It was a good question, but one to which I long ago had learned the answer. At a rally up in Indian Mound, I had accidentally shorted the batteries of a buggy-type electric belonging to old Nicholas Parr, Uncle Roscoe's deadly rival. Happy Uncle Roscoe, afterwards congratulating me in private, had explained how the electric auto was the one electrical machine that could not have a circuit breaker or fuse in its main power line. Because on a steep hill or in a mudhole, just when the most power was needed, such a safety device would blow. Instead, they simply made the motors rugged. Which explained, incidentally, why Prudence Prentice's electric was still around.

"Because they don't have them," I said shortly. Then I saw the answer. "Look, Jo. We'll drive past Pigles'. If the electric isn't there, it means they didn't make it, and the evening is over. If it *is* there, the chances are good that there's enough juice left to drive it back to Tilborough Street."

CHAPTER SIX
YOUNG CALLER WITH FLOWERS

Hardly having run through her careful check-list of "what if's," we turned onto a busy avenue in South Boston. Several traffic lights later, we made out the garish front of Pigles' ahead. My attention being demanded by the heavy traffic, I left for Jo the scanning of the curbside for a parked electric. Suddenly she gasped. Turning my head, I saw why: on our right, the stately form of the Halrick & Sears showed directly in front of a brightly lighted florist's shop. In the entrance, a small, aproned man with the air of the shop's proprietor was pointing to the electric and talking, presumably about it, to another man.

"Keep going!" said Jo. "Turn your head away."

My heart pounding, I did so.

"Of all the fat heads!" I exploded, when we were safely past. "Why in the world would Teddy park in a spot like that?"

"He probably stopped to buy corsages, and then Prudence probably said that it looked like a good safe place, being so well-lighted."

Two blocks later, I turned down a side street and stopped.

"And the chances are good," said Jo, "that the proprietor has a good memory of a middleaged man and woman and a little old lady getting out of that car. But I don't think he noticed you." She sat back. "Any ideas?"

I sat back, too, snookered. Of all the unpromising setups for a car snatch, this was the prize. And then I sat up again, for the old brain was still hitting on all four. Quickly I outlined my plan.

"Yes, said Jo, after thinking it over. "In your getup, I think you can pull it off."

Standing where Jo could still make me out from the parked VW, I flagged down a taxi, placed the "gift" box on its rear seat and got in.

"Where to, Buddy?" the cabbie asked.

"I'm looking for an electric."

He turned his florid face.

"An electric? Electric *what*?"

"An electric automobile."

His brow puckered derisively.

"Look, Buddy. It is a well known fact that they do not make electric automobiles any more." He paused for an emphasizing shake of his head, then added: "Not for some time, now, do they not make electric automobiles any more."

"They don't make my aunt any more, either," I retorted, getting into the spirit of the thing.

The man extended his arm along the top of the seat and impatiently tapped his fingers.

"Look, Buddy—you been having a few?"

"Sure," I said with a gay laugh. "But nevertheless, I am, believe me, looking for my aunt's electric automobile. A Halrick & Sears brougham, to be specific. She was going to leave it somewhere here on the avenue. Just drive along, if you will. You can't miss it."

He turned forward and tentatively grasped the steering wheel. Then, in the rearview mirror, he stole a glance at me. Finally he shrugged and started off.

"Halrick and Sears," I recited. "Electrics that will run for sixty years."

Mirrorwise, he eyed me with concern. "Look, Buddy," he said in a friendly manner, "I could take you home. How about that?"

"And how about *that*?" I countered, triumphantly pointing ahead to the elegant plate glass cabin that towered above the adjacent parked cars.

Spying it, his jaw dropped. He pulled up beside it.

"How about that!" he said.

He shook his head and laughed; I joined in loudly. His meter still showed the minimum fare. I slapped an extra five into his hand, then gathered up my gift box.

"Thanks for the ride," I said, laughing.

"And I thought you were crocked!"

"How about that?" I said, and with a final hearty laugh, I slammed the door hard.

Box in hand, I stood there laughing and nodding while he called a final thanks and pulled away. Then, turning and blandly but keenly taking in the storefront and interior, I mounted the curb and matter-of-factly strode to the electric's door. All this laughter, as I had intended, had caught the ear and eye of the proprietor inside. I was keenly aware that he was watching, as, on the sidewalk, I ostentatiously opened the door and deposited the gift box on one of the forward, backward-facing tete-a-tete seats—the interior furnishings of such fancy old electrics, I perhaps should explain, being laid out more on the lines of the old fashioned parlor than of the modern automobile. Then I turned. The proprietor had come out, and stood in the doorway.

"Quite a rig you have there," he observed—a disarming opening behind which, I was sure, there lurked dark suspicions.

As one with pressing matters on his mind, I strode toward him. "Quite a rig, yes," I replied. "But not mine, I am happy to state."

"No?"

"Definitely not. My aunt's. As for myself, I would not take it as a gift, believe me. And now—" I had passed him, but he continued to stand and eye the electric, as if turning something over in his mind. Well, too much of that would not do. I turned and gave him a businesslike clap on the shoulder. "—and now a dozen roses, if you have them and can trot them out pronto."

He turned and blinked. "Roses?"

"Roses, man! Red, red roses!" I said with an expansive wave of my arms. "For a dear old lady."

He came to attention and strode in.

"Red, red roses. Yes, sir! Long stem or short stem?"

"Long stem, of course!"

"Of course," he said, his tone apologetic.

"In a beautiful long box with a beautiful red bow."

"Beautiful long box," he repeated, his arms beginning to jerk in the flustered manner I was after. "Beautiful red bow."

"Precisely."

He started for his wrapping counter, then about faced and wrenched open his refrigerated case. "These, sir?"

I eyed them critically. "Your best?"

"My very best. Yes sir."

"Fine, then!" I said, with a happy nod. "Beautiful."

"Beautiful," he repeated, darting away.

Deftly he began to go about his task, and I, feeling the episode in the bag, stood eyeing the gleaming electric outside and humming *I Could Have Danced All Night*, until, obsequiously, he came up behind me.

"Here you are, sir," he said, holding out the box.

I turned, eyed it critically, then granted him an appreciative smile. "Magnificent!" I exclaimed.

He beamed. "Thank you, sir! Would there be anything else?"

"Anything else?" I snapped my fingers. "Yes. Two of the little ones."

"Little ones, sir?"

I pointed. "Little red roses. For the vases, of course."

"Ah! For the vases, of course!"

And in the manner of one accustomed to supplying flowers for the vases of electric broughams every evening of his life, he again dove into his case. "These, sir?"

I eyed them critically. "Well—" I said, and then, playing it up a bit, shook my head.

"Or perhaps these?"

I studied the new offering, then nodded. "Just right."

"Ah!"

I paid him in a careless manner. He picked up the long, beribboned box and I, with the two roses in my hands, strode out to the car and opened the door. Carefully I placed the roses in the vases, then studied and readjusted them. "Makes all the difference," I remarked.

"All the difference! Yes, sir!" he said, nodding hard.

I got in behind the tiller and took out my key case. Carefully he set the long box inside—his excuse to peer with great curiosity about the interior.

"Is it much of a trick to drive?" he asked.

"No trick at all. And what is more, you don't have to worry your head about breaking any speed laws."

"I suppose not," he said, with a knowing smile, and withdrew, carefully closing the door.

I unlocked the controller and snapped on the headlights. As I looked behind, I saw that he was watching with approval. I raised my hand in salute, and he waved back energetically. When a lull came in the traffic, I turned the cylinder forward and came over hard on the tiller. Silently the car responded. I pulled out into the inner lane. As I glided along the avenue at ten miles an hour, the car's only sound was the faint whine from its high pressure Firestones.

In the middle of a grubby dark block, I stopped at the curb. Jo, in the Volks, pulled up beside me.

"Everything O. K.?" she called across.

"Fine. Mission accomplished. Ouch!" I ended, peeling off the moustache. I then removed my wig, placed the two items in the fedora and handed it across to her.

"How did it go?"

"Not a hitch. The attentive young nephew. I gave it a big play. I don't suppose you caught any of my act? "

"No, Darling. I kept my eye on the top of the electric. When it moved, I moved. How about the batteries?"

"They feel O. K. So go on. Park in front and open the garage doors, so I can sail right in."

"Gully, where is your short wave?"

"Up in my bedroom."

"Well, I thought I'd take it downstairs and listen to the police calls."

I gulped. "Good idea. Go ahead."

She took off, and I suddenly felt very alone. I glanced at my watch and started off. Eight thirty-five. Still fifty-five minutes before Teddy, Prudence and Flo, accompanied by Rowbottom, would discover the electric to be missing.

My back-street-and-alley route led through a tough neighborhood. Now, in the dark, it appeared tougher than ever. I had gone perhaps a mile when I sensed the power slacking off. I twisted the cylinder hard. Nothing happened. I broke into a cold sweat. The car poked along for a dark block. Then, though I held the cylinder hard forward, it slowed to the barest walk. Out of "gas"! I thought of Jo, waiting. Was all our effort to be for naught? With a sudden resolve, I looked hard at the old frame houses I was passing. Lights showed in most of them, but there were no passersby. Ahead, on the right, I saw a house with a dim porch light but with no lights showing in the windows. As if divining my intent, the car crept up to this house and died.

I snapped off the headlights, pushed the ribbon from my supply box, took out the longest extension cord, and thrust some plugs into my pocket. As I got out, I was inspired to take the long box of roses along. At the rear of the car, I connected the extension to the coupling. Stringing the extension across the sidewalk, I stepped up onto the porch. With my handkerchief I unscrewed the hot porch bulb, screwed in a plug, and into this inserted the extension plug prongs. All this I did casually and matter-of-factly, in case anybody was watching. I then put my finger on the doorbell button's molding and made out to push. I did not, of course, actually push. Meanwhile, I eyed with interest the name on the nameplate: *A. STAMBULOV.* I then stood back, to all appearances a smartly dressed young caller bearing a box of flowers and waiting for the object of his affections to answer the bell.

A little later, I repeated the fake button-press. I glanced at my watch. Eight forty-five. Swiftly I calculated. From what I had gathered of storage batteries and rectifiers, the charging rate was highest at the start: for the few miles I still must cover, a half hour's charging should do it. All I had to do was maintain my role of young-caller-with-flowers for half an hour. The front door now opened a crack and my heart shot into my mouth.

CHAPTER SEVEN
MRS. STAMBULOV

"...yes?"

A stout little woman of middle years peered out. Her head was round and she had no neck at all. A retired circus performer, I thought wildly, or perhaps a retired gypsy. Her eyes, small at first, gradually widened. I swallowed hard and reached for my hat to doff it, but to my surprise it was not there. Then, recalling that I had given it to Jo, I forced a happy chuckle.

"My hat," I said apologetically, repeating the movement and indicating my hatless head. "I was going to take it off, but now I remember that I gave it to a friend. Well, well! Mrs. Stambulov?"

"...yes?" she said again, in a small, round voice that seemed to emerge from a bottle.

"You *are* Mrs. Stambulov?"

She gave a cautious nod, and her eyes, by now quite circular, dropped from their observation of my no doubt puzzling performance to regard my long white box. She appeared, in fact, about as baffled as I felt. For until that door opened and sent my heart skyward, I had grown accustomed to the empty porch and to my role of young caller with flowers, and had long since concluded that I had nothing to fear from inside. I yearned for the presence of Jo, who in an emergency such as this could be counted upon to come up with something fast. And so thinking, there flashed into my mind our alias routine. I chuckled apologetically.

"I'm afraid that I have never had the pleasure of meeting you," I said in a courtly manner. "—up to now, that is. Snodgrass is the name—Samuel Snodgrass."

"Oh?" Her words seemed to make their escape from the bottle only after a struggle. "Well, I'm happy to make your acquaintance, Mr., ah—"

"Snodgrass," I said again, seizing and pumping the limp hand she gingerly extended. But her glassy eyed stare persisted, and it struck me that, much as she had startled me, she had only placed second. "Sammy to friends," I added cordially. "Most everybody calls me Sammy. It's quite all right."

She laughed nervously.

"Well, all right, Mister, er—, Sammy."

"Yes, that's it," I said, nodding happily.

"At first I thought you wanted to see Al," she said, eyeing the box again.

"Al? Well—I—"

I hesitated. Whoever "Al" was, I most definitely did not want to see him. Nor did I want to see Mrs. Stambulov, for that matter. All I wanted was to charge my batteries.

"—but I suppose you've come to see Lucy?"

"Lucy?" I stammered.

She gave a doubtful nod.

"Yes, Lucy!" I said, nodding hard. For suddenly it had flashed upon me that since Lucy—presumably a daughter—had not answered the door, she undoubtedly was out for the evening. The young-caller-with-flowers act might scrape through, at that.

""Well—" she said, still in her doubtful manner.

"Not in, I take it?"

She shook her head, then inclined it to the right as if to indicate a well known direction. "No. She's around the corner boozing."

"Oh, is she, really?" I said with a gulp. Tentatively I had been piecing together a conception of some sweet young thing. I would have to start over from scratch.

"Yes. But if you'd care to come in and wait—?"

I thought fast. All I had to do was stall for half an hour, hoping that Lucy, whoever she might be, would meanwhile remain around her corner, at which time I would make my excuses and leave. I could still pull it off. I nodded happily. "Why, yes, of course, if you don't mind."

"Not at all," she said doubtfully. She opened the door farther, and, becoming aware that for some reason her porch light no longer was on, reached along the inside wall to flick a switch, then peered out to note the expected result. She now first spotted my extension cord, and, her eyes following its outward course, made out the darkly gleaming brougham at the curb. I had not supposed that her eyes could grow wider, but they now did.

I flung out my hand in an apologetic gesture and gave another chuckle. "I hoped you wouldn't mind my taking the liberty, Mrs. Stambulov. You see, I'm always having to 'gas up' a bit. Recharge, I mean. And believe me, it's no end of trouble. My friends are always kidding me about it."

She swallowed. "Why no," she said, with more than a slight tremolo. "Not at all."

"A nuisance, just the same."

"Quite all right," she managed, and stood well back for me to enter.

But after I had done so, she did not at once close the door. Instead, in the doorway, she for some time stood looking out in silent thought. I made use of this interval to check the switch which she had been flicking, and was relieved to note that it again was in the "on" position. At last she closed the door.

"Won't you sit down?" she said, still with the tremolo.

"Thank you," said I, doing so.

Nervously she turned to the front window's roller shade, which was already fully drawn down, and gave it an extra tug.

"Al likes to keep it dark up here," she apologized.

"Oh, yes," I said. "I suppose he does." Though why he did, on top of whom he might be, was a second mystery to me.

She nodded primly. "He doesn't want any trouble."

"Oh, no," I tried gamely. "Of course not."

She sat down and eyed the box which I had propped between my knees.

"A little something for Lucy," I volunteered.

"Oh? Well, she'll like that—I guess."

She ended this on her customary note of doubt, but, sensing that I might be getting into deep waters, I did not inquire as to why. But on other matters, meanwhile, the Gates brain was working overtime. Quickly I checked and double-checked my present plan. I was inside the house and my batteries were charging. What more could I ask? My immediate task, then, was to prattle my way through the required half hour. And racking my brain for a suitable subject, it occurred to me that it stood at the curb.

"You may be surprised," I remarked, "to see that I am driving an electric."

She gave a laugh that hinted at hysteria not far behind.

"Well, yes. But everyone to his own taste, I always say."

"Yes," I agreed, laughing heartily.

She sat back nervously. "I guess they don't make many of them any more," she hazarded.

"No, indeed. That is, if you leave out golf carts, fork lifts and the like. Don't forget those," I pled.

"Oh, no," she agreed, with a glassy eyed nod.

"I mean, you can't write off the electric like the Dodo."

"The what was that?"

"Dodo. Extinct bird."

"Oh, yes," she said, rather baffled.

I gave an apologetic chuckle. "I'm sure the car must have been rather a surprise to you."

She swallowed hard. "Well—"

"I mean, I'm sure Lucy couldn't have mentioned it to you."

"No. In fact, she never even—"

"Because," I hurried on, "she has never seen it, herself. I acquired it only very recently." And I could have added that it would take a lot of looking to find anyone who had acquired an electric automobile any more recently than I had.

"Oh, I see."

"But I haven't been going out of my way to show it around, you understand, because frankly, some people think I'm a nut to drive it at all." Here, I was following the sound principle of calling oneself names openly before the other side starts doing it privately, thus taking the edge off. And that this principle was sound was now confirmed by Mrs. Stambulov, who sat silently struggling for an answer, but with nothing coming out. "The truth, however," I went on soberly, "is that I have certain practical reasons for owning this car."

"I suppose you must have," she said hopefully.

"Yes. You see, I am conducting certain experiments."

"I see," she said, with a gulp.

"And the fact is, Mrs. Stambulov," I stated roundly, "I believe the electric automobile will be the car of the future—what with atomic energy coming along, and all that."

"Atomic energy. Oh, yes," she said brightly.

I smiled knowingly and raised a finger. "The problem, of course, has always been the uneconomical ratio of power to weight. But in the very near future, given a light, compact source of electrical energy—" And with a significant pause, I raised my arm in a gesture characteristic of my Uncle Roscoe, whom I had been quoting.

She nodded brightly, "Who knows?" she said.

"Yes, exactly! And when you consider the enormous complexity of the modern gasoline engine—" I paused—another of those significant ones.

"Complex. Oh, yes."

"And smog. Do you know what causes it?" I raised an accusing finger. "Automobiles. They're what causes smog. They use hydrocarbon fuels, and the combustion products go up in the air and stay there and react and accumulate as smog. And do you know what they propose?"

"No."

"Filters on the exhaust."

"Filters? On the—"

"Yes! That's what they propose. And it's ridiculous. Suppose it cuts the air pollution output in half. Pretty soon you are going to have twice as many cars, and the total output is going to be just the same as it was before."

Mrs. Stambulov, apparently after a losing battle with the mathematics involved, shook her head.

"And do you know what the answer is?" Dramatically I pointed toward the front door, causing her to take a rather puzzled look in that direction. "It's right out there at the curb! The answer is to do away with all those internal combustion engines and substitute electric automobiles!"

"Oh," said Mrs. Stambulov, overwhelmed.

I nodded hard. "That's the answer. A more modern design, of course. And—" I broke off for a disparaging chuckle. "—more efficient batteries, by all means. And a public system of charging outlets. It wouldn't do, of course, to have everybody stopping by to plug into your porch light, as I took the liberty of doing, just now."

"Quite all right," she breathed.

"And look at the reduction in noise! You wouldn't have the roar of gasoline engines all day long, starting and stopping and accelerating. When I drove up, I dare say you didn't hear me at all."

Mrs. Stambulov gave way to a hysterical laugh. "No. As a matter of fact, I didn't. I was quite surprised when I opened the door, and—"

She gave a helpless wave.

"I'm sorry if I startled you."

"Oh, not at all. Quite all right."

"But you must look upon me as a pioneer. In the future, as I see it, when you drive up to a metered parking spot, that meter will have a plug receptacle, and you will simply plug in and charge up while you're in the store, shopping. It would be the simplest thing in the world. The nickel you put in the slot would pay for your power. Wouldn't that be simple?"

"Simple. Oh, yes," she murmured.

I arose, carried away by my vision. "For that matter, there is the possibility of power from the sun. They've had some success with that, you know."

"I suppose so, yes."

"There would be some sort of a pick-up affair on the roof of the car. You simply would let the car stand out in the sun, and—" I stopped, for over the small mantelpiece, a large portrait had caught my eye.

Mrs. Stambulov, turning in the direction of my gaze, smiled and nodded. "I see that you have noticed Lucy's new picture."

I swallowed hard. "Is it, really?"

"Yes," she said proudly

I forced my rubbery legs to move. At length, I stood before the portrait, meanwhile feeling my hair rising straight up. It was a colored enlargement of a shapely, well muscled girl in a spangled bathing suit. Around her flat midriff was a wide belt of elaborate design; it bore an enormous silver ornament in front, on which I distinguished an eagle with wings outspread. She wore small, high laced wrestlers' shoes. And at the bottom was the title, *"MAGNITA"*, a name which faintly stirred my memory.

"Magnita!" I exclaimed.

"Yes. That was taken after she won the world's championship in Cincinnati."

A cold trickle of perspiration ran down my back. "Oh, was it?" I said brightly.

"Yes. That was the night Boris met her," said Mrs. Stambulov, with a faint note of censure.

"I see," I said cautiously.

I had scarcely begun to puzzle over the significance of her statement and of its tone when there came a heavy stomping of feet, apparently ascending a basement stair at the rear. A door opened.

"Hey, Ma—"

I turned. A rangy man of forbidding and gangsterlike mien, who could have heroed *Have Gun Will Travel* and no questions asked, had stopped and was staring at me. I turned, as I say. But I did not jump. And neither did I gulp. As a matter of fact, the look which I returned was rather a jaded one, liberally sprinkled over with *ennui*. For I had about had my share of developments for the evening. I was through with jumping very high over any new surprise. "Just toss it in with the others," summed up my present attitude toward any new surprise.

CHAPTER EIGHT
BARNEY THE COP

"This is my son Al," said Mrs. Stambulov, rising to the occasion. "Al, this is Mr., ah—"

"Snodgrass. Samuel Snodgrass." I extended my hand and he crunched it. "Sammy—ouch!—to friends."

"—Came to see Lucy."

"Oh?" This bit of news appeared to surprise Al. He eyed the long box which I cradled in my arm. He looked at me, then at his mother, visibly nonplused. With a scraping sound, he rubbed his chin.

"We were just talking about Sammy's car," said Mrs. Stambulov, nodding hard toward Al and furtively—though not so furtively that I was not aware of it—rolling her eyes in a meaningful manner.

"As it happens," I announced, "I am interested in the possibilities of electricity as the prime motive power for the automobile, replacing the present internal combustion engine."

Al Stambulov gave me a blank stare. "Oh," he said. And abruptly raising his hand to call time out, he turned away. "Hey, Ma. What happened to Lucy? I asked her to cart over a case of beer."

"She went." Mrs. Stambulov shrugged. "Hasn't come back."

"Oh..." Al said knowingly. He turned to me. "Well, then, why don't you join us while you're waiting, Mr., ah—"

"Snodgrass," I supplied, meanwhile wondering just what it was that he was inviting me to join."—Sammy."

"Sammy it is—hey, Ma. You'd better go get her."

My jaw dropped. Of all the things I did not want—! "Oh, no!" I protested. "Don't bother. I'm sure—"

"It's all right, Sammy," he interrupted. "Besides, we need the stuff. Now, what do you say?"

I gulped. "Glad to," I said.

"Good." He clapped me approvingly on the shoulder and ushered me toward the rear. "They'll rob you if they can."

"Oh, I don't know," I said. I didn't know exactly why I said it, but it somehow seemed appropriate. I glanced at my wristwatch. Come what might, the fact was that meantime my batteries were steadily charging. Fifteen minutes to go. Whatever he meant, I would go along with it for fifteen minutes, then make my break.

In the kitchen, Al opened a door and indicated the stair to the cellar. "After you," he said.

"Thank you," I said, and bravely started down.

"Ace bets," said Gunnar, a hard-eyed Swede.

My tablemates and myself each had two cards down and two showing. And my ace was still high, as Gunnar in his impatient manner had just indicated. I thought fast. I had three to a straight, true, but Gunnar had chosen to deal deuces wild. And according to Randy Bohr, a straight in seven-card stud with deuces wild was nothing. Indeed, Randy had once counseled that, as to this particular game, he himself ordinarily would not stay at all unless he held the makings of kings full. Still, it would cost me nothing to check.

"Check," I said.

"Ten," said Dommie, the fierce featured Italian on my right, gently pushing in a dime. His fierce appearance was due to his singular—and by singular I mean not plural—eyebrow, which extended, luxuriant, black and unbroken, from above and beyond one eye to above and beyond the other. From his build, I was sure he was a wrestler. Indeed, if memory served me, he had played the role of the "villain" in a preliminary match I had once witnessed down in North Attleboro, making out to deal illegal gouges to the "hero," and, in plain sight of the crowd—who, for some reason I never will understand, seemed to eat it up—producing a concealed brass-knuckle affair from his trunks and hammering the hero with it. At my side, however, he appeared the mildest of men, and I thought it best not to bring up the subject.

"Twenty," said Gunnar, raising the house limit.

Dommie silently folded, and so did I.

"You play tight," he observed mildly.

I shrugged. "At least when I don't have them."

Dommie nodded approvingly.

"You can't bluff these tigers," he said with a laugh.

I smiled knowingly, then stared down at my stake of silver and roughly counted it by eye. Thanks to old Randy's lessons and to one small win, I so far was only into my third dollar. Meanwhile, Dommie's glance dropped curiously to the box which I held awkwardly between my knees.

"You a friend of Lucy's?"

"Why, yes," I said, cautiously and unencouragingly.

Desperately on guard lest I give myself away, I yearned for what I now realized had been the comparative safety of upstairs, expounding the future of the electric automobile to Mrs. Stambulov. But most of all, I yearned to be in my particular electric, speeding away—if speeding was the word—from Al Stambulov's establishment before lady wrestler Lucy weighed in. Meanwhile, the play of those remaining went on.

"—and up *again!*" roared Gunnar, pushing more silver into the pot. This appeared to give the others food for thought, and during the lull he shot a hard glance at me. "Kind of rushing it, ain't you?" he demanded.

I blinked. All the way, in this Lucy business, I had been the unknown actor suddenly thrust onstage into an unknown scene of an unknown play. I wished somebody would hand me a script. "Well," I tried, "I wouldn't exactly say that."

"Don't mind Gunnar," said Dommie, raising his thick arm to give me a gentle pat on the shoulder. He turned to the others and nodded knowingly. "They'll all be after her, now. You'll see."

"Kings full!" roared Gunnar, triumphantly flipping over his down cards and raking in the pot.

Off the hook again, I tried to fathom the situation which, apparently common knowledge to all present except myself, lay behind Dommie's statement. The only result was to reaffirm that I wanted out, and fast. I surveyed the smoke-blue cellar. It held five round tables, and at each sat six or seven players. Kibitzers stood behind them. Others were gathered at the small bar behind which Al Stambulov held forth. Men entered and left through a doorway at the back; it apparently was served by a well-worn path to the alley. The play was all seven-card stud, with the dealer's option of calling deuces wild or low hole card wild. A lettered notice on the wall, "NO BASEBALL," referred not to the national sport but to a wisely outlawed further version. The reason for the stud games, rather than draw, I by now appreciated, was that they went faster. Also, they were more exciting to watch. I glanced at my watch. I had been here fifteen minutes; the batteries should be charged. I would make my excuses to Al and take off.

"Deuces wild," announced the sad Italian on Gunnar's right.

Our antes—a quarter—were scarcely in when a hatchet-faced youth appeared for the house cut. As he did so, to my dismay I saw Al Stambulov disappearing up the stair.

I tapped the boy on the back. "Where is Al going?"

"To get Lucy."

A wild exasperation shot through me. Everybody was rushing off to get Lucy! "But," I protested, "a little while ago, Mrs. Stambulov went!"

He gave me a condescending look. "Well, you see, sometimes you got'ta go after *her*, too."

"I see," I said with a gulp.

The dealer dealt two down and one up; three deuces showed around the table at once. Dommie promptly folded. I, deuceless but with an ace down stayed (Randy's rule) to see the fourth card.

"What's all this with Lucy?" asked the dealer.

"I heard she had a fight with Boris," said Gunnar. "Up a dime."

Upstairs, Mrs. Stambulov also had mentioned the name Boris. All ears, I tried to keep my mind on the game. When it came around to me, I reluctantly met the raise, although I have long thought Randy open to argument on this point.

The sad Italian dealt another card around. "Ten," he said, as he now was high. He tossed in a dime. "How long have they been married?"

With nerveless fingers I reached for my up cards and turned them down. "Out," I said faintly.

Gunnar raised his eyes in calculation. "Three months, I would say."

"But what happened? Didn't she say?"

"Boris insulted her—that's what she told Al."

"In*sult*ed her?" Dommie laughed. "This Boris must be one brave man!"

Gunnar shrugged and held out his free hand. "Al says he's only about that high. But two days ago, he insulted her. So she slugged him and came home.That's what Al said." He reached for a dime. "Up ten."

Dommie turned to me. "Is that the way you got it?"

"I'm afraid I haven't been in touch," I said weakly.

Out of the hand, I sat back to take horrified new inventory of the situation. The girl for whom I had played—and still was playing— young man with flowers had turned out to be not only a lady wrestler but a married lady wrestler as well, though currently on the outs with her spouse. I now realized why Mrs. Stambulov, then Al, had looked askance at my box of roses. As Swede Gunnar so bluntly had accused, I indeed was "kind of rushing it."

Five minutes later, frantic to be on my way, I made a show of looking at my watch. It was nine-thirty. My mind made up, I shuffled and laid the deck in front of Dommie for his cut.

"Nothing wild," I said. "My last hand."

I dealt three around. My up card was a five. Gunnar, with the first ace, tossed in a dime. I snapped my down cards for a quick look. Both fives! This, according to old Randy, was it: lay low, stay in regardless, and hope—with the best chances in the world—to pair for a full house. The deuces dealer raised. All stayed. After the sixth card, Gunnar had four low hearts showing, Dommie three high clubs. And the pot was big. They either had their flushes or high hopes. I hadn't hit. I dealt the final down card, then snapped mine for a look. A queen, to pair my up queen! I had my full house! Gunnar, still high on the board, looked thoughtfully at my cards.

"Well?" said Deuces.

"Check," said Gunnar.

"Ten," said Deuces, pushing a dime toward the pot. Then he raised his head and squinted toward the ceiling, meanwhile drawing back his unreleased dime. A sudden hush fell upon the room. All around, heads were raising. Slowly but inexorably, the faint but ever mounting siren's scream grew until it was unbearably loud. Directly overhead, it abruptly cut off and whined down to silence. Hearing grunts and shuffling feet, I looked around. The rear door was open and the immediate area looked like the St. James terminal the Sunday after Thanksgiving. I saw the boy race behind the stair; then the lights went off. There sounded the quick scooping up of silver and Gunnar's voice: "Divvy at Dave's, O. K.?" A couple of "O. K.'s" came from the doorway, then utter silence.

I sat there in the dark, refreshed by the cool air rolling in from the open doorway. On one point, at least, I was decided: I was not running off down any strange South Boston alley. I felt along the tabletop. Gone was the pot which would have put me well ahead, as were all the stakes, mine included. I felt for my glass and raised it. And as I did so, another siren sounded. Surprisingly, my hand remained steady, and as the howl cut off overhead, again, I calmly finished the glass. Two police cars! A real raid. By now, I should have been entitled to one good hysterical laugh, but I did not make it. For some reason, I just did not care.

"And then there are other times," Jo once had said, when we were discussing tactics in general, "when you might just as well stay in your seat."

Well, this was one of them. Still, if things got rough, there was no need to be shot at in the dark. I gathered up my box of long-stems and groped toward the wall, planning to follow it around to the switch. I had just collided with a table when there came a click from above and the lights flashed on. I turned and blinked. From the top of the stair a ruddy-faced young policeman peered down. I laid the box on the table and raised my hands.

"Snodgrass," I said. "—Samuel."

He eyed me in a puzzled manner. "What's in the box?"

"Roses. Long-stems."

"Oh...Well, glad to know you. Barney, here."

"My pleasure," I said, also puzzled.

"Where's Mrs. Stambulov?" he asked.

I let out an uncontrollable guffaw; at long last, I knew something that somebody else did not! "She went to get Lucy," I informed.

"Thanks." And so saying, he abruptly turned and took off.

CHAPTER NINE
LUCY

Alone in the cellar again, I pondered the situation. It was an odd sort of raid, to say the least. Or were two car loads of cops already chasing the others down the alley? I strode to the doorway and looked out, but saw no movement and heard no sound. Or could it be that the alarm already had gone out for the stolen electric, and these were the police after my car? I hardly thought so: to recapture a parked electric did not warrant two carfuls of cops. I turned and headed for Al's bar, deciding to help myself to another beer—where I found that, thanks to unreliable Lucy, there was none left. Well, I would simply go upstairs and find out what this was all about. If it did not concern myself, I would get into the Halrick & Sears and be on my way.

I headed for the stair. Above, the lights were on, but, to my surprise, no one was around. Whatever was up must be outside, and I found myself in no hurry to go out. In the front room, I looked at Lucy's portrait. She was a handsome girl, probably in her early twenties, and not at all the gorilla type you might suppose. However, married to her or not, I would not have ventured, as her Boris reportedly had, to insult her. I now realized why her professional name, Magnita, was familiar: I had seen it on a North Attleboro bill of coming events. Standing there, I became aware of a low hum of conversation outside. Cautiously I opened the front door a crack, and quite as Mrs. Stambulov had done not long before, peered out.

A police sedan, then a police ambulance, were parked closely behind my electric, which reared up ahead like a startled partridge. The center of interest, however, was my friend Al Stambulov, who sat on the sidewalk, experimentally turning his head. A white-jacketed figure was bending over him in a professional manner, and the small group surrounding them included Barney the Cop, who in a notebook was laboriously recording the event for posterity.

I now became aware of a blue flame, intermittent and close at hand. It was clear that no one was interested in me, and so, stepping out on the porch, I discovered that the flashes emanated from the juncture of my plug and the porch socket. With a shock, my eyes followed the course of the extension cord to the electric at the curb. Originally, I had laid this cord in a straight line. Now, it was stretched into a broad "V," its apex where Al Stambulov sat.

47

I gave the cord a yank: the plug came out quite hot. With dismay, I wondered if the batteries had been shorting back through the plug. Trying to make my approach as inconspicuous as possible, I gathered up the cord until I reached the edge of the group, where several people were standing on it. Tapping a spectator on the shoulder, I politely invited him to step off. As he did so, Barney made me out. He stared at the cord, then at me.

"Sorry about the cord," I said.

He said nothing.

Tapping another shoulder, I took in another turn. Beyond, I noted the approach of Mrs. Stambulov, arm in arm with an imposing girl of medium height, who on her opposite shoulder carried a large carton.

"What's up, Barney?" the girl called, in a mellow and engaging voice.

"Al tripped!" a helpful chorus informed. "—fell and conked his head!"

"Oh, *Al!*" cried Mrs. Stambulov, rushing to him in mother fashion.

"I'm all right, Ma," he growled.

"It was that wire," the chorus advised.

The girl, who could only be Lucy, lowered the carton to the grass and came up to Barney. "What wire?" she asked.

In answer, Barney silently inclined a thumb in my direction. Lucy at once turned and strode up to me, and at last I stood face to face with the generally supposed object of my affections.

She eyed the cord, then the white box, then myself.

"You're Sammy!" she cried. She flung out her hand. "Ma said you'd been waiting."

"Well, I was. I just dropped by."

"I'm sorry I wasn't in. How've you been?"

"Fine, just fine. Ouch!" I ended, due to the grip which seemed to run in the family.

She turned excitedly to Barney, who had been looking on rather critically. "Barney, I want you to meet Sammy."

"We have met," said he, in a distant manner.

I held out the box. "Here's a little something for you, Lucy."

"Oh, Sammy!" She made a grab for it. "Thank you so much." Eagerly but futilely she fumbled at the ribbon. Then, with a fairly ladylike oath, and quite as Alexander had dealt with his knot, she with one yank ripped open the end and peered within."Roses! Oh, *Sammy!* My favorite! Thank you!"

"Not at all." Quickly I looked at my watch. Nine twenty-five. Any minute, now, the flash would come on Barney's car radio and I would be standing there for the easiest pinch of that copper's career. By now, my batteries either were charged, or, due to the short, dead. I took a long breath. "Lucy, it's a little crowded, here. How would you like to go for a spin?"

She eyed me happily. "Why, Sammy! I'd *love* to."

And seizing my arm in a vise-like grip, she accompanied me to the car. Quickly I stowed the cord under the back flap, while Barney thoughtfully looked on. Beside him, Mrs. Stambulov, in a confidential tone, but not so confidential that I did not hear it, remarked: "Lucy sure picks some queer ones."

"Yeah," snorted Barney.

I swung in behind the tiller, snapped on the lights and gave the controller a twist. To my immense relief, the car responded strongly.

"We're off!" cried Lucy.

"Tallyho!" said I.

Silently we glided away.

My fair companion sat back in silence, curiously eyeing her strange surroundings. She extended a shapely leg, then retracted it, doubtless surprised by the car's roominess. By now, a tingling aroma of alcohol and perfume, reminiscent of the Ajax Gym, pervaded the car. With the controller hard over, we bowled along at ten miles an hour.

"Sammy, at first I thought I might have had one too many, but isn't this a funny car?"

"I suppose most people would think so. It's an electric, quite old, but quite good."

"I guess that's what Ma was trying to tell me. Is it yours?"

I hesitated. True, making my getaway from Barney by inviting Lucy for a spin had been pure genius of the short order, tactical kind. But it was not the overall strategic answer. I had to get this electric home and out of sight in a hurry. But meantime, what of Lucy?

"Well, no," I said. "I borrowed it."

"Oh. But another thing." She laughed apologetically. "—if you will forgive me. I can't even remember where I met you."

"I will hazard a guess," I replied gallantly, "that a lot of men you have met remembered you long after you had forgotten them."

She cocked her head, for this one took some unravelling, then smiled. "Thank you, Sammy, for that nice compliment. But was it North Attleboro?"

"I was there."

"Oh, of course."

"I'm sorry about the cord," I said quickly, for it would be well not to dwell on the subject of our first meeting.

"Think nothing of it. When Al couldn't find anything else, he tripped over his own feet. That's why he never made it as a fighter." Curiously she eyed the vases. "I never saw a car with roses before."

I plucked the one on my side and held it out. "For your hair. Put it in."

"You're a romantic one," she said, laughing. She thrust the stem into her hair and turned to me. "Do you like it?"

"Just the touch."

She lay back and appeared to be having sober second thoughts.

"Look, Sammy, you knew I was married?"

"I heard."

"I guess you heard about the scrap, too?"

"Yes. But not the details."

She sighed. "Well, Boris insulted me. Never mind the rest. He's still in Cincinnati, and I haven't heard from him."

"I see," I said, struck by an idea. Here was a problem in my special field! "Listen, Lucy, I don't mean to butt in, but if I knew the details I might spot some angle you had missed."

She sighed and shook her head. "Thanks, Sammy, for wanting to help, but it would be just too embarrassing. I don't want anybody to know. I couldn't tell Al, or even my mother. Thanks, anyway." She lapsed into a spell of brooding, then roused. "Sammy, where are we going?"

I had been working on the answer to this one. By now, I had it ready. "I promised to take this car to a friend's house. We could borrow his—it's faster—and look in on a couple of night spots."

"I'd love it. You know—" She giggled. "—this one isn't exactly a hot rod!"

"No," I started, and then I stopped, for with a chill, I recognized the old symptoms. The car was losing power.

Quickly I analyzed the situation. We were on the northerly edge of Roxbury—only a couple of blocks, in fact, from Rowbottom's house. I made my decision. This car was the last thing he would want to see, tonight, but he was going to, just the same. If he wanted to ingratiate himself with Teddy, he could hide the electric in his own garage and like it, and lend me his car to go on with Lucy. And having made this decision, the car made another. A block from the turn, it stopped dead. I sat back and sighed. So near and yet so far! Snookered again summed it up.

Lucy looked expectantly at the adjacent house.

"Is this it?" she asked.

"No."

"Then why the stop?"

I sighed. "I'm afraid the batteries have gone dead."

"Then why are the lights still on?"

I stared at her, amazed. I recalled how, when I stopped at the Stambulov residence with my batteries dead, I had *switched off the headlights!* Now, just as then, they were blazing away as brightly as ever. They likely were hooked to a separate storage battery!

"You've given me an idea," I said, getting out. I opened the gift box and withdrew my flashlight, pliers and jumper cord. Mindful that the next passing car might be an alerted police cruiser, I flung up the hood. There *was* a separate battery! Whether it was of a higher or lower voltage and what would happen when I cut it into the line, I did not know, but I was going to try it. I put the flashlight on my head and bent into the dark interior.

A tense minute later, I slammed down the hood and jumped behind the tiller. We took off at a crawl, with no lights, but at least we moved. I turned down Rowbottom's street. No lights showed in his windows. He probably was not back from taking the others home. I turned into his driveway, stopped at the garage doors and got out. The padlock was in place. Lucy looked on without comment while I rummaged for my picks. With one twist I opened the padlock. The garage was empty. I drove in.

"It looks like he hasn't gotten back, yet," I said. "Come on in. I'll phone another friend to bring us a car."

"Do you have a door key?" she asked in an odd tone.

"Well, sort of."

"All right, Sammy..." She came close and grasped my lapels. "You can level with me. I know jimmies and I know picks, and I know people who wear flashlights on their heads. This car is hot—right?"

Swiftly I considered. For Lucy, it would be the simplest and most convincing story. I nodded embarrassedly.

"A dude heister," she said, patting my lapels, giggling in a girlish way, and shaking her head. "And Ma was trying to tell me you were some kind of nut."

I drew myself up. "I have my methods," I said.

She looked at me admiringly. "You certainly do. And Sammy—" Her hand grasped the back of my head and irresistibly bent it forward; I had the sensation of being plunged into an exhilarating fog of alcohol and perfume, dark hair and red roses. "—I like you," she said, releasing her hold.

CHAPTER TEN
IN THE NOO-WUD

Somewhat dizzied, I groped like the central character in blind man's buff for the garage doors and closed them. But the click of the padlock cleared my head. Bring on your police flashes! I had done it! The electric was safely stashed away and I no longer was liable to arrest. Followed by Lucy with her box of roses, I strode to the back door, where I opened the old fashioned flat case works in seconds. Inside, I saw Lucy to the living room sofa, from where she looked about with interest and approval. From Rowbottom's liquor cache I extracted glasses and a bottle of Scotch. Lucy grasped my wrist, looked at the label and raised her eyes in approval.

"Nothing but the best for you, my dear champion," I said gallantly.

"Thank you," she said. Then, with an odd look in her eyes, she arose, grasped my lapels again and asked: "Did you ever see *My Fair Lady?*"

"Yes."

"Do you remember the young fellow, all dressed up, with the flowers, who kept walking up and down in front of the girl's house?"

"That was Freddie."

"Well, that's how I thought of you at first."

"Oh," I said, deflated.

"But Freddie was a simpleton," she said in a rush, "and you're not, as I realize, now. You're in the racket. Actually, you're smart." She paused and eyed me quizzically. "But here you are, bringing me flowers, like Freddie, like you were in love with me, and yet you offer to try to fix up my marriage." And so saying, her irresistible hand again grasped the back of my head. "There, now," she said at length, stepping back. "And I feel like telling you, after all. Will you keep it a secret?"

"Yes," I managed.

She eyed me earnestly. "Boris was getting up a show for the road. I was to star. Two days ago, he rushed in and said, 'Got'tuh great idea, Kid!'"

"He calls you 'Kid'?"

"Yes. And do you know what he wanted me to do?"

"Wrestle?"

She nodded slowly. "But he wanted me to wrassle, well—" She shook her head unbelievingly, then shot me a sidelong glance. "He wanted me to wrassle without anything on."

"*What!*...You mean, in the nude?"

"In the noo-wud, yes."

I gulped. This Boris appeared to be an undersized monster of some sort. "And then you socked him?"

"Yes."

"This will take some thinking over," I said.

"Won't it, though?" she said, tossing her head. "So go ahead and make your call."

I headed up the stair. In Rowbottom's bedroom I shut the door and dialed Tilborough Street, meanwhile organizing the surprising account I soon would be pouring into Jo's ear.

My narrative, to say the least, held her interest. When I finished, she had news to report from her end. For one thing, she had heard the police flash about fifteen minutes ago. For another, Rowbottom and Teddy, having left Flo with Prudence in Meldonville, had taken off, supposedly for the South Boston police station again, in case anything developed, but actually to a pay phone to call me at Tilborough Street. Being told by Jo that I had not arrived with the electric, they were now on their way to Rowbottom's house, where Jo had agreed to call them the minute she had any news. "And now," she said in a slightly greenish tone, "you're going to take this Lucy nightclubbing?"

"In the line of duty, Jo. So just hop into the VW and drive here. We'll drive you home, and then—"

"O. K.," she said resignedly.

Halfway down the stair, I heard a car in the driveway, then the unmistakable roar of Rowbottom in the role of outraged householder. I bolted on down. Lucy was bending over the television set. Calling cheerily that I would be right back, I dashed out the door.

They were just beyond the foot of the steps. Rowbottom, recognizing me, halted abruptly and Teddy collided with him. From Rowbottom's open mouth came no sound. He stared at me in a baffled manner.

"Hello, Gulliver," said Teddy. "I was so worried. Did Georgette tell you about Norman?"

"Yes."

By now, Rowbottom was breathing fire. "Mr. Gates! May I ask what you are doing in my house? And how, in the first place, you got in?"

"Gully," broke in Teddy, "where is the electric?"

"Come on," said Rowbottom. "We can talk inside."

At this, I raised my hand. "I think not, Mr. Rowbottom."

"*You* think not—!" he roared. "Why—!" He stomped toward me, then stopped, shocked: inside, the television set had blared out, following which the unseen hand of Lucy turned it down. Jaw flapping, he stared toward the door. "You!" he choked. "You have someone else in there?"

I folded my arms and gravely nodded.

"You have the colossal nerve—! Who is it?"

"A lady wrestler," I said, and then, as their two mouths flapped open, quickly added: "Come with me. I have something to show you."

Rowbottom hesitated. Fuming, he took a last look at his violated house, then unwillingly started after us. Leading the little procession, I walked past his car to the garage doors. As I asked for his key, his eyes rolled toward the doors, and I guessed that he suspected the truth. First Teddy looked inside, then Rowbottom. The latter let out a roar.

"Sam! Sam!" cautioned Teddy, grasping his arm. "You'll arouse the neighbors!"

"Get—that—thing—out—of—there!" said Rowbottom in a hoarse whisper. "Of all the idiotic—!"

"This," I said quietly, "is as far as it would go."

"Get—that—thing—*out!*" said Rowbottom, choking.

"Sam," urged Teddy, "it's safe here, for now."

"And it will stay here for now," I added decisively.

"Get—that—"

"Now, Sam," said Teddy.

Rowbottom turned to him and waved his arms.

"This idiot ought to be committed!"

"Now, Sam. I'm sure Gulliver can explain."

Glowering, Rowbottom folded his arms and waited. I closed the garage doors and snapped the padlock into place. Leaning against the doors, I began for the second time that evening to relate my stirring tale of triumph over unexpected obstacles. It was, of course, a longer account than I had told Jo, for this time I had to include the cab driver and the flower shop. But it was, I might add, a story which gripped its audience from beginning to end. Halfway through, I stopped, for to my ears had come the welcome sound of a VW zeroing in to the curb. The car door slammed; then I heard Jo tripping up the walk. I debated going and telling her where we were. Still, she probably would do all right with Lucy by herself. I heard the bell ring. The front door opened and closed.

"That was Jo," I noted, and continued.

"Now, Sam," said Teddy reasonably, when I had concluded. "It appears that Gulliver has done a good job in spite of a great deal of hard luck. Why not leave the electric here in your garage for now? You would be doing me a great personal favor, and I assure you that I shall do my best to reciprocate as to that other matter."

"H'm," said Rowbottom, cooling. He eyed the garage doors. "That means my car has to stand out!" he said in a last burst of anger. Then he turned to Teddy. "Well—"

I now invited them inside to meet my friend Lucy. Rowbottom, after balefully eyeing me, started off. Teddy and I followed. In the living room neither Lucy nor Jo was in evidence. With a cry of anguish, Rowbottom raised and eyed his bottle of Scotch.

"How much of this have you been guzzling?"

"I merely offered it to Lucy. The good host, you know."

He banged the bottle down, strode to the television and viciously snapped it off. In the sudden silence, the sound of girlish voices drifted down from above. I sat on the sofa and Teddy took a comfortable chair. Rowbottom remained standing; from time to time he slowly shook his head. Above, the voices trailed off. A moment later, Jo, alone, descended the stair. I introduced her to Rowbottom. She greeted us rather soberly. "Lucy is so nice, Gully, when you get to know her."

"Oh, yes," I said, relieved at the absence of the green eyed monster in her tone.

"She told me all about herself. How she started out wrestling with her brothers, and how they wouldn't allow a girl on the high school team, and all that. And how she married Boris Kerensky. He's Russian. He started out as a carnival manager in Chicago, but now he operates out of Cincinnati. That's where he insulted her."

"She went into that?"

"Yes."

"Georgette," Teddy interrupted, "this is all very interesting, but hadn't we better be going our various ways? Mr. Rowbottom is driving me home, and I understand that Gulliver plans to take you home and then go out for the evening with, er—, the lady."

"Yes," I said, jumping up. "Is she about ready?"

Jo slowly shook her head. "I'm afraid not. We talked it all over, and after we worked out the answer, she went to sleep."

"What answer?" I asked, in surprise.

"The answer to what we all must do."

"What do you mean?" demanded Rowbottom. "We all know quite well what we're going to do."

"Do you?" asked Jo. Soberly she shook her head and took a chair. "I'm afraid you will have to revise your plans—drastically. Lucy thinks the best answer is for all of us to clear out of here—for good—before she goes home."

"What!" exclaimed Teddy and myself in unison.

"*What*—!" barked Rowbottom, bristling.

Jo looked thoughtfully from one open mouth to the next. Her gaze finally came to rest upon mine. "Lucy likes you. She says you're the first real gentleman crook she ever met."

"Well!" said I, quite touched.

"She assumes that the rest of us are part of the gang and that this is our hideout. So she wants us to find a new one before she returns home."

"Georgette!" said Teddy. "I don't follow you."

"I don't either," said Rowbottom, testily.

"Gully, have you told Mr. Rowbottom and Teddy about Mrs. Stambulov and Al and their gambling joint?"

"Yes," I said.

"And Barney?"

"Yes."

"Well, Lucy has put away quite a bit from wrestling. She used some of it to set up Al's joint."

"That didn't take much setting up," I scoffed.

"Yes, it did. She had to buy the rights to the territory. I didn't inquire into the details, but I can guess. Anyway, she has put considerable money into the venture, and it is paying off. It brings in a good income for all of them—including Barney."

"For protection?"

Jo nodded. A good citizen, I shook my head.

"Barney," continued Jo, "saw you drive off with Lucy in the electric. By now, he certainly has gotten the flash. So Lucy is sure that when she arrives home, Barney will be there waiting to put the arm on her."

"You mean question her?" asked Teddy.

"Yes."

"But if this Barney goes along with a gambling joint," demanded Teddy, "why can't he go along with this?"

"Gambling," answered Jo, "is one thing. Car stealing is quite another."

Rowbottom, beginning to get the picture, groaned and sank into a chair.

"She knows where this house is," continued Jo. "If she doesn't tell Barney, he likely will threaten to arrest her as an accessory."

"Good Lord!" said Teddy.

"First of all, she must protect her investment. So, being fond of Gully, and as a favor to us, she wants us all to clear out of here for good. Then she will take a taxi home."

Rowbottom sprang to his feet. "She's going to tell the police the electric is here?"

"She'll have to," said Jo.

"Mr. Gates!" roared Rowbottom. "Get that thing out of my garage and off my property at once!"

"What good would that do?" I asked, with a shrug. "The police will still know your house was the hideout."

For the first time, he cringed. "Please don't say *hideout!*" he pled.

"Sam!" Teddy, with sudden agitation, jumped to his feet. "When the police find the electric and learn you were involved, Aunt Prudence is going to realize we were trying to trick her, and—!" Helplessly he waved his arms and sat down.

I looked at Rowbottom. His lips were moving but nothing was coming out. Suddenly he sprang at Teddy, who sat with his head in his hands.

"Ted! Do you know what this means? It means that you won't be in a position to recommend B, R & W to your aunt!"

Teddy looked up. "Suppose—" he started, then shook his head. "What if—" Rowbottom started. He then stopped, baffled.

CHAPTER ELEVEN
JO MAKES THE BEST OF A BAD SITUATION

I looked at Jo. She was standing with her arms folded, the small Indian maiden, patiently waiting for the big chiefs to end their pow-wow.

"Jo," I asked, "have you any ideas?"

Slowly she nodded.

An unbelieving Rowbottom and Teddy looked up.

"What?" asked Rowbottom.

"What?" asked Teddy.

"I have a plan," she said quietly, "which I believe will solve everything."

Rowbottom's jaw dropped. Teddy blinked unbelievingly. I looked on admiringly as Jo turned to Rowbottom. There was quite a bit of David and Goliath to the scene, and I for one was betting my shirt on David—Jo, that is. Without having the faintest notion of how, I still had not the slightest doubt that she was going to deliver the goods, right now, air express.

"You, Mr. Rowbottom," she said crisply, "will at once drive Teddy home. There, you will tell Prudence and Mrs. Miller that you are back from the police station with no news. Then you will offer to drive Mrs. Miller home, and also offer to come back early in the morning for Teddy, to drive him to the police station again."

She paused.

Rowbottom looked skeptically at Teddy. I, for my part, looked as skeptically at Jo.

"This is not starting out as much of a plan," observed Rowbottom.

"Well, I don't see—" said Teddy doubtfully.

Undeterred by her cold audience, Jo turned to Teddy.

"Then you will urge that, instead, both Mrs. Miller and Mr. Rowbottom stay overnight—and you, Mr. Rowbottom, will at once say that this is a fine idea. You will say it is especially good because you would be right there to drive Teddy to the station in case the police telephoned during the night—and Mrs. Miller would be there to stay with Prudence. The point is, that way, both of you can deny ever having been here tonight or having seen Gully tonight."

A puzzled Rowbottom shifted impatiently in his chair and shot me a sour glance. "Well," he conceded, "at least that part is good."

"You will not take along any pyjamas, shaving equipment or anything else. That would give it away." Jo turned to me. "At the same time, Gully, you will go out and plug in the charger."

At this astonishing statement, I stiffened and gave her a blank look. "Go out where and plug in what charger?"

"The charger to the electric."

"Oh. Why?"

"Don't interrupt," said Rowbottom.

I stiffened some more. "If anybody thinks for one minute—!"

"Shut up," said Rowbottom.

"Then," Jo continued, "Lucy and I will leave for Tilborough Street in the Volks. In the meantime, Gully, after half an hour's charging, you will start out in the electric."

I shot straight up. "Are you out of your mind? Do you mean to say that you want me to drive that electric home with every cop in Boston on the lookout?" I shook my head hard. "I'd never make it!"

Jo sighed. Slowly she turned her head in denial.

"No, Gully. That is not what I mean."

"Then what *do* you mean?"

"I mean that you must get caught."

The jaws of Rowbottom and Teddy hinged down in unison.

"*What!*" I cried.

"Yes," said Jo. "That is what I mean."

A brief lull in the proceedings now ensued, during which considerable gaping was indulged in by all parties except Jo, and with myself rendering the outstanding performance of the evening.

"Well?" she asked, at length.

I continued to gape. "Jo. Are you serious?"

"Yes. As soon as we get to your place, Lucy and I will turn on your short wave. I won't drive Lucy home until we hear the flash. I'm sure that Lucy will go along with the plan, when I explain. That way, when she gets home she won't have to tell Barney anything at all, because there no longer will be a stolen car. She won't have to reveal where the car was hidden. In fact, once Barney gets the flash, he won't be looking for Lucy any more."

Rowbottom, dumfounded, eyed Jo admiringly. "Perfect!" he exploded. "That leaves me in the clear. And—" He slapped Teddy on the back. "—it leaves you in the clear, too!"

"And me in jail," I added coldly.

"What a brain!" said Rowbottom.

"Yes," said Teddy.

For once, I did not agree. "It's a fat headed plan," I said, "if ever I heard one."

"I haven't finished, Gully," said Jo.

"You've finished Gully!" I shot back.

"Shut up," said Rowbottom.

"So then," said Jo, "after the police pick you up and call Teddy, you will confess how you like to steal cars."

"*I* like to steal cars?"

"Why not?"

"Of course," said Rowbottom.

Jo turned to Teddy. "So then, when you go to the police and learn that the culprit is your friend Gully, you will act surprised and embarrassed. You will say that, since the supposed theft has turned out to be somewhat of a family matter, you wish to drop the charges."

"Yes!" cried Teddy. "I could explain that Gulliver was, well—"

"A harmless kleptomaniac," suggested Rowbottom.

"Yes," said Teddy. "That would make a plausible story."

"A harmless idiotic kleptomaniac," said Rowbottom, warming to the idea.

Biding my time, I said nothing.

"Of course," said Rowbottom to Teddy, that means you'll still be stuck with the electric."

"True," said Jo. "But the important thing is that Teddy won't be in bad with Prudence."

"Yes!" said Teddy, nodding hard.

Rowbottom happily swung his fist into his hand. "Then that's it!" he crowed.

"Good girl!" said Teddy.

"A wonderful plan!" cried Rowbottom.

"Excellent!" seconded Teddy.

A silence then fell, and I became aware of three pairs of eyes studying me. I drew myself up. "There is one little hitch in that wonderful, excellent plan." I announced in an icy tone. "And the hitch is that I am not going along with it."

Words of surprise, indignation and accusation followed, during which period I sat with my arms folded. Jo's manner, however, was mild, and as I looked at her, I saw her left hand slide up to her hip. It was our old signal! Either or both hands on hips meant no; both arms down meant yes. With a thrill, I realized that Jo still had something up her sleeve. She raised her hand for silence. Like two schoolboys, Rowbottom and Teddy at once rang off, and it was clear that neither had any question as to who the leader of the expedition was.

"Gully," said Jo carefully, meanwhile letting her hand slide down again, "you were telling me how, more than anything else in the world, you wanted to see your old friend Christopher Beanfield enter his partnership."

I eyed her in surprise and dismay. Frankly, I had forgotten all about Chris. But she hadn't. And now, for some reason that I could not fathom, she was spilling the beans to Rowbottom that we were pals. Baffled, I eyed her dangling arms. She was calling the play for yes. Well, I had better go along with her idea, whatever it was.

"Yes," I said, nodding and feeling like a ventriloquist's dummy. "More than anything."

Rowbottom's jaw, as I had anticipated, now dropped and he turned to me. "Do you know Christopher Beanfield?"

I nodded.

"Didn't you tell me, Gully," continued Jo, "that Christopher was hoping to borrow ten thousand dollars from Mr. Rowbottom for his partnership?"

"Ten thou—!" exclaimed Rowbottom.

"Chris already has five thousand," I corrected.

"Oh," said Jo. "You mean—"

She then stopped, and I, with one of those thrills which I always experience when she is giving a top speed performance, realized that this was the old seller's trick; you state a steep price to the buyer, then come down, leaving the buyer reeling and eager to grab the sudden bargain. "Chris," I explained, "was hoping to borrow the other five thousand."

"Oh, I see," said Jo, in a deprecatory manner.

But from Rowbottom's agonized movements it was clear at once that no one, not even Jo, was going to sell him on the idea that five thousand dollars, even though marked down from ten, was any trifling sum. "He hoped..." choked Rowbottom. "—from *me*?"

I nodded.

"And that five thousand dollars," asked Jo, "is all that stands in the way of Christopher's partnership?"

"Yes."

"Gully," said Jo earnestly, "if Mr. Rowbottom were to agree to lend Christopher that amount, would you then go through with what we want you to do?"

"Lend that young maniac five thousand dollars!" roared Rowbottom. "Never!"

"Who," asked Teddy, obviously quite in the dark as to this new development, "is Christopher Beanfield?"

Rowbottom swung hard toward him. "He's engaged to my niece. Crazy as a loon. Always has been. Why, once when I was giving a lecture..." And he proceeded to pour out his version of the indignity he had suffered at the hands of fake student Chris.

"Now, now," said Teddy, patting him on the back as he finally ran down. "Can't you dismiss that as only a schoolboy prank? Young blood, let us say, and all that? I'm sure that, like all of us, the years have changed the young man for the better. I'm sure that he will make a fine husband for your niece. And if this matter of the loan is so important—"

"Changed him, did you say?" roared Rowbottom. He stabbed a finger toward Teddy. "You think the years have changed that boy? Let me tell you how the years have changed him! Only this noon, at my club, he suddenly began to explain how he could teach me to swim by some secret Hindoo method. He told me to stand on the end of the high diving board, looking down. And then, yelling like an Indian, he pushed me off!"

"Was that a police siren?" Jo interrupted. All looked up. It hadn't been, of course, but I saw Rowbottom, with a gulp, getting the point.

"Gully," said Jo firmly, "the question is, if Mr. Rowbottom will lend Christopher his money, will you go ahead with our plan?"

Her arms were down. Meaning the answer was yes. I shrugged. "Yes," I said.

Jo turned. "How about you, Mr. Rowbottom?"

Mouth open, he sat back. He stared at me, then at Jo, then turned to Teddy, helplessly shaking his head.

"Sam," urged Teddy, "you must consider what will happen to both of us if Gulliver refuses to go through with Georgette's idea."

"There must be some other way," muttered Rowbottom.

"Sam! If you can overlook these pranks and stake Christopher as Gulliver wants you to, why, I can assure you that, on the other matter, you can count on me."

Rowbottom said nothing.

"Incidentally," said Jo, looking at me in question, "I believe there is a deadline for the loan."

"Yes. Chris has to have it before noon tomorrow or he's out."

"Then how would it be," said Jo, turning to Rowbottom, "if I brought Christopher to your office at nine o'clock tomorrow morning, and you at that time wrote him your check for five thousand dollars?"

Uttering unintelligible sounds, Rowbottom began to twist his shoulders and shake his head.

With sudden anger, I arose. "Then let me tell you, Mr. Rowbottom, how it's going to be. I've had enough. When the police and the reporters come looking for me, I'm going to tell them the truth—that I was a mere pawn in the plot, and that you and Teddy, the principals, conspired to turn in a false report of a car theft."

"*Gulliver!*" cried Teddy.

"Gully!" said Jo. "You *would*n't!"

"Oh, wouldn't I? Who is deliberately going to get himself jailed? And eventually released as a harmless kleptomaniac? Which one of you would like to be labeled a harmless kleptomaniac? Raise your hands," I added.

No one did.

Rowbottom gargled a bit. Painfully his features twisted into a paternal smile. He held out his hands as if to pat my shoulders. "Now, Mr. Gates," he said, straining toward a kindly manner. "Teddy and I appreciate very much what you are doing. And I—well, of course, I will see Christopher in the morning, as you wish. Yes."

"Then it's agreed?" asked Jo.

"Yes," said Rowbottom.

Teddy nodded eagerly.

Jo looked at me.

I nodded slowly.

CHAPTER TWELVE
THE CIGAR-STORE INDIAN

We stood in the doorway watching Rowbottom and Teddy pull away. I snapped into my key case the garage key which Rowbottom had surrendered to me. She shrugged.

"I'm sorry, Darling. It was the best I could come up with. However—" She glanced toward the stair. From above came a faint, ladylike snore. "Maybe we'll think of something. So go out and plug in the charger. And don't you have to rearrange the wiring, first?"

"Yes."

"Don't come in until you hear us drive off. And try not to make any noise. Let her think you've cleared out, too. That's the way she wanted it."

"And in half an hour I start out?"

"No. Stay right here until I phone you." She paused. "And another thing. As soon as you come back in, phone Christopher Beanfield. Tell him to be at Rowbottom's office at nine o'clock tomorrow morning without fail."

"You'll be there?"

"Yes."

"And I'll be in jail."

"Don't tell him that."

"But what if he's afraid to go?"

"Why should he be?"

"Would you push somebody off a diving board on Tuesday and then calmly walk into his office on Wednesday?"

"For five thousand dollars, he will. Tell him I'll wait for him in the lobby."

I switched back the wiring, inserted the charging plug, and sat in the car to take stock. Even now, a faint fragrance of perfume lingered to remind me of Lucy, as did the one red rose in its vase. I toyed with this, re-living how she had put the other one in her hair, and how she had kissed me. She marked my first—and doubtless my last—encounter on the romantic level with a married woman, and the only bright spot in a trying evening. Jo, I must admit, had made the best of a bad situation. Teddy's status with Prudence was saved, and hence his and Aunt Flo's future. And Rowbottom's loan would squelch the Norm-visit. The one great big bad item would be my arrest in a stolen car and my release as a harmless kleptomaniac.

Hearing the Volks take off, I returned to the house, went up to Rowbottom's bedroom and dialed Christopher Beanfield's home.

He sneezed.

"Christopher?"

"Yes. Who..." His tone went from sleepy to angry. "Gully, is that you?" A second sneeze followed.

"Yes. Catching cold, Chris?"

"Gully! Did you wake me out of a sound sleep to inquire about my health?"

"No. Great news! Rowbottom is going to lend you your five grand."

There came a pause. Followed by a sneeze.

"Gully, what did you say?"

"Rowbottom is going to lend you your five grand."

"That's what I thought you said."

"You're a lucky man!" I enthused. "Your worries are over. You'll have your partnership and your Ellen. And your trip needn't be lost. Make it a double wedding, with Randy and Marj. Then you can all go together."

"Where are you?" he asked, at length.

"At Rowbottom's."

"At his house? I don't believe it."

"Well, I am. Listen. You're to be in his office at nine o'clock tomorrow morning for your check."

"You're drunk."

"Chris, it's true!"

"Then let me speak to Mr. Rowbottom."

"I can't. He just stepped out."

"Oh...Just stepped out, did he? And how soon, may I ask, do you expect him back?"

I hesitated. To one unfamiliar with recent developments, my story undoubtedly bordered on the fictional. "The fact is, Chris, he won't be back tonight at all. However—"

"Go back to bed, Gully."

"*Chris*! Wait. Will you hang up, and then dial Rowbottom's number? That's where I am. You'll see when I answer."

"Or I'll see when *he* answers. I'll see that I've fallen for another of your moronic tricks."

"If he answers, you can hang up. You know his voice."

"Only too true...Well—"

The receiver clicked. I hung up and waited. I had never dreamed it would be so hard to hand a pal five thousand dollars. A minute later, the phone rang.

"Hello, Chris!" I said. "Now are you convinced?"

"I'm convinced that for some reason you're in Rowbottom's house. But I won't go to his office alone. Will you meet me outside?"

"No. Unfortunately I'll be tied up."

"Oh, you'll be tied up, will you?" he asked, again in that suspicious tone. "You want me to walk in on Rowbottom, all alone?"

"No. Georgette will meet you in the lobby."

"Who's Georgette?"

"My cousin."

"Unfortunate girl," he muttered.

"Will you be there?"

"All right. But if this is another of your—"

"It's on the level. You'll see."

Twenty minutes later, Jo phoned.

"Do I start out, now?" I asked.

"No. I called about your two liners. Throw me one."

I eyed the instrument blankly. "What are you talking about?"

"Jokes."

"At a time like this you want *jokes*?"

"Yes."

It was crazy, but I tried to give the child what she was asking for: "First goat eats can of film in studio back lot. Second goat asks how did you like it. First goat says I liked the book better."

"H'm..."

I tried again: "Englishman and Italian in lifeboat in Atlantic. Englishman points and asks, 'Is that a *U*-boat?' Italian replies, 'No, that's not'ta *my* boat.'"

"H'm...Well...Possibly."

"Jo! What in the world are you getting at?"

"Just a long shot. Did you phone Christopher?"

"Yes. He'll meet you in the lobby at nine."

"Good. Stay put till I call."

By one A. M. she still had not called. I gave Tilborough Street three rings—our signal—then hung up and waited. Nothing happened. I lay down on Rowbottom's sofa. There, tossing and turning, I dozed off into fitful slumbers in which, with myself at the tiller of the electric, sirens sounded, blue lights flashed, patrol cars screeched through the night and cops poured out with drawn revolvers. At seven-thirty A. M. I tried Tilborough Street again. No answer. Ditto for eight o'clock. At eight-thirty, hearing a familiar beep, I looked out. Jo, in the VW, beckoned impatiently. I went out.

"You didn't phone me," I said.

"No."

"Well, I tried to get you."

"I know. We were busy."

I eyed her glumly. "Is it time for me to start out?"

"Not yet. I'd like you to come along to Rowbottom's office."

"What! Where is Lucy?"

In reply, she turned into a cigar-store Indian, a maddening pose I knew only too well.

As we entered the lobby, a red nosed figure lurking in its shadows came forward to eye me with surprise and suspicion. "I thought you said you'd be tied up," the figure accused.

"Luckily," Jo replied for me, "Gulliver was able to come."

"Is this on the level?" he asked, in the elevator. "I mean, about Rowbottom suddenly having a change of heart?"

"Change?" countered Jo. "As I understand it, you never actually asked him for the loan."

"True. Then who did?"

"Gully did."

"And Rowbottom just calmly said 'O. K.'?"

"Yes," said Jo, although calmly was not the way he had said it.

Jo entered first. I pushed Chris, who had been vying for the number three spot, in ahead of me. Rowbottom glared at him.

"We've brought Christopher in for his check," said Jo.

"So I see." Slowly he withdrew his checkbook from his desk. Then he looked up. "*We?*" he asked sharply. His hard blue eyes now made me out, and as they did, they bulged. He sprang to his feet. "*You!* What are *you* doing here? Why aren't you in jail?"

Jo raised her hand. "I think," she said to Chris, whose head was wildly jerking from Rowbottom to myself and back, "that you might take a seat outside until we discuss certain matters."

"Right!" said he, bolting out.

"Where is Lucy?" demanded Rowbottom. "—gone home?"

"Not yet," said Jo. "After a long talk with her, I became convinced that I could effect a reconciliation. I tried to reach Boris in Cincinnati, but was told he would not be back till noon. I'll try again then. If I succeed, Lucy will go right to the airport, so she won't have to see Barney."

Rowbottom sat back, trying to digest this new idea. I sank into a chair and did the same.

"The electric would stay in my garage?"

"Yes."

"So Teddy wouldn't be stuck with it after all!" I cried.

"No," said Jo.

"And he," asked Rowbottom, pointing to me, and in a tone tinged with regret, "wouldn't go to jail?"

"Only if I fail—in which case we go back to our original plan. However," Jo said in a firm tone, "either way, Christopher must have his check now."

Rowbottom rubbed his chin, ruminated, and finally bent over his checkbook.

"B-e-a-n—?"

"Yes."

Parked across from Rowbottom's bank, I watched Chris Beanfield emerge and happily lope off. A minute later, Jo bounced in beside me.

"I phoned Marj," she reported. "She was very happy. There'll be no trip to California." She then instructed me to drive her to the St. James terminal, as there was just time to catch the bus for Woods Hole.

"But what about—?"

"I reached Boris this morning. They made up, and I drove Lucy to Logan."

I let out a whoop. Then I thought of that cigar-store Indian bit. "But why didn't you tell me?"

"Because you just might have blown your lines. And if Rowbottom had suspected the problem was already solved—no check."

"You might as well go home and get cleaned up," she advised, over a quick strawberry frappe in the station cafeteria. "After lunch, tell him Lucy is on her way."

"But where did the two liners come in?" I asked, as I walked her to the gate.

"Well, when Lucy told me how happy their marriage had been, and about Boris promising to star her on the road, I just couldn't believe he meant to insult her. Boris doesn't speak English very well. Lucy thought he had said, 'Got-tuh great idea, Kid! How you like to wrassle bare?'"

"Jo—!"

"But when I talked with him, I realized that that wasn't what he had meant, at all. You see, he leaves out a's. What he meant was,'How you like to wrassle *a* bear?'"

"He wants Lucy to wrestle a *bear*?"

"Yes. It will be a sensation! She was so happy and excited, she could hardly wait to get on the plane. So long, Darling."

PART TWO
THE MATTER OF THE CARRONADE
Nantucket, September 18-21

CHAPTER THIRTEEN
PAL FIZZO FITZWILLIAM'S PROBLEM

"Read it back."

I did so.

"Good. You will not miss the ten-thirty ferry?"

"No, sir."

"See that you do not. I shall count on you to deliver the materials to Gosnold House at one forty-five tomorrow afternoon. I shall expect you then."

I hung up, leaned back and nursed my ear. The time, for the record, was Monday noon—five days after I had seen Jo off for Nantucket, and from where, just now, Rowbottom had phoned. The place was his office, and what I was leaning back in was his oversize chair. I eyed the portrait on his desk. It was the head of a good looking but rather businesslike young woman, and bore the improbable inscription, *"With all my love—J."* Likely another niece.

I looked at the list he had dictated—plans, Hillcrest maps, the Stubbs file, photographs of plants designed by us, and the plant model which served as our reception room's inartistic centerpiece—and considered. On its own, B, R & W had been making preliminary studies for small-town sewerage and drainage improvements in upstate New York—rumor having it that both state and matching federal funds would soon be available for same. Obviously, we hoped to pioneer a model such project and thus be in the limelight when the gravy was ladled out.

And for that model project, Hillcrest, next door to Kittery, appeared to be the most likely town of all. Also, as I well knew—Jo and his young niece Winnie were pals—Beriah Stubbs, Hillcrest's Town Committee Chairman, was summering on Nantucket. Rowbottom, then, likely had contacted and found Stubbs agreeable to a presentation, and so had run to the phone to bellow for messenger boy Gates to fetch his props.

The thing to do was tell Jo I was coming. In the lobby, I person-to-personed her dormitory, where she now should be at lunch—and she was.

"Perfect, Darling!" she exclaimed, to my news. "We'll do it tomorrow night, then."

"Do *what* tomorrow night?" I asked, aware that Rowbottom would expect me to take the five-thirty ferry back.

"You'll have to stay over, at all costs. It's your big chance, for your bed."

"My bed?" I asked, at once all ears.

"Yes. Allan's uncle is a patent attorney, and—"

"Fizzo's uncle," I corrected, "is a Nantucket insurance broker."

"No, another uncle, Ulysses Quinn. So I'll phone Allan, and he'll see you today. But no matter how crazy the plan sounds, *agree to it*, provided he agrees to ask his uncle to help sell your bed—he could actually show it to manufacturers."

"What plan is this?"

"It's about Winnie and Allan."

"Winnie and Fizzo? You mean—"

"He'll tell you all about it. But whatever you think of it, *agree to it*," Jo repeated, "to get his uncle going on your bed."

I hung up with mixed emotions. On the plus side, nothing was more important than selling my bed. On the minus side, nothing could be worse than anything involving bumbling old Fizz. Too, I was in the dark as to what appeared to be a ripening of the Winnie-Fizzo relationship. In Kittery, in June of Jo's freshman year, I had driven her and Winnie down to Zaza's, above the turnpike exit, for dinner. There, Jo had just noted the nearness of curfew time when, with the clatter of an overturned chair in the distance, then the crash of a bumped waiter's tray, an eager hand clutched my shoulder and I turned to face Allan Fitzwilliam. Hackamore pal Fizz, now an electronics engineer with a Boston computer firm, had been turnpiking home from business in Buffalo and had turned off for the evening calories. I introduced him, a minute of small talk followed, and then we had to rush off.

Next day, back in Boston, old Fizz had appeared on the Tilborough mat to beg for the particulars on Winnie. Glad to oblige, I went up for my address book—and what followed, incidentally, was the last straw which prompted me to propose the already described elevation to separate-but-equal status with Aunt Orpha. Do you recall, in *The Gods of Mars*, how Princess Phaidor, daughter of Matai Shang, accompanying John Carter to the Temple of Issus for her first view of that frightful old lady, trembled and shuddered and paled to a ghastly hue? Well, old Fizz, left unattended in the parlor, apparently had taken out a cigarette with the suicidal intent of lighting and smoking it. For when I returned, a rigid and frigid Aunt Orpha stood in the doorway, directing one of Boston's last lorgnettes extant full upon him, and he was trembling and shuddering and had paled to a hue every bit as ghastly as Phaidor's.

Home from work, I had just gone up to my lab when, out front, in a subsiding whoosh of tires and foreign engine's dying gargle, my ear detected a familiar note. I strode to the window. Below, a venerable Austin Healey, barn red in color, stood at the curb. A stocky small figure, easily identifiable by its trial and error type movements, was attempting to extricate from its interior a large cardboard box. I went down and opened the front door. Box in arm, Allan O. Fitzwilliam tripped, staggered, recovered and jogged up the walk.

"Fizzo!" said I.

"Gully, old man," said he.

Winning through to the front hallway, he eased the box to the floor. I indicated the parlor, then paused for a clinical assessment of the unexplained box. Give your psychologist a boy-with-blanket or man-with-corpse-in-cellar and he is off at a gallop. I tilted the box. It seemed quite light. Hardly a blanket. Certainly no corpse. Released, it righted itself with only a faint, dry rustling from within. A dead parrot at most.

I entered the parlor. Old Fizz, the room's period-piece surroundings obviously having recalled the fearful association just described, was staring wildly about.

I smiled reassuringly.

"It's all right, Fizzo, about my aunt. The Magna Charta has been signed, the Bill of Rights pushed through, the Emancipation Proclamation proclaimed. In a word, franchisement—but enough of the local struggle for power. What's all this about a plan?"

He squirmed, and I detected the straying of a guilty eyeball toward the hallway.

"It's about Winnie."

"So you've been seeing her," I said indulgently.

"Constantly. We're going to be married."

I blinked. "Married, did you say?"

"Married, yes."

Gravely I shook my head and gave counsel. "Listen closely, Fizzo. High school seniors in general have a tendency to go wildly romantic. Give it another month, and you will find that, as fall and the whirl of college set in—"

He sprang to his feet. "But Gully! Right after our first date she started studying Portuguese!"

"Portuguese?"

"Day and night. How many girls would do that?"

The answer, I conceded, was not very many.

"You can bet your life, not!" he cried, eyeing me triumphantly.

"Fizzo," I said, baffled, "let us take the scene from the top: 'Enter Fizzo, bearing box.' O. K.?"

"O. K., then. Excelsior."

Nonplused, I waited for more.

So did he, eyeing me apprehensively.

"You're supposed to raise your arm," I said. "Shades of night. Alpine village. Banner with strange device. Then up with your arm and out with your punch line."

"Oh." He shook his round head. "No. This is the small 'e' kind."

"Small 'e'?"

"Small 'e' excelsior, yes. The kind my company ships computer parts to Brazil in. And that," ended Fizzo soberly, "is where, in just eight days, they're shipping me."

"You're going to Brazil?"

"For two years. My big chance."

"Well! Congratulations! But wait a minute. Isn't that where they speak Portuguese?"

"Yes."

"So that's why Winnie is studying Portuguese?"

"Yes. It's Greek to me, so she'll be a big help."

I eyed him with new approval. I mean, take the average girl today. You ask her to marry you, and she doesn't even go out and learn how to boil an egg, let alone Portuguese.

"Have you set the wedding date?"

"No. There's a hitch. Winnie's only seventeen and a half, and Beriah Stubbs won't give his consent."

"But he's only her uncle."

"True. But also her legal guardian."

"Then wait six months."

"No, Gully. We want to leave for Brazil together—face the unknown together. Anything could happen during those six months. We're together now, and we intend to stay together."

"But why won't he consent?"

"Because of Leroy."

I sat back, puzzled. During a brief stop with Jo at the Stubbs' small mansion in Hillcrest, Leroy, a thin, restless squirt with glasses and singed eyebrows, had skittered in, smelling of carbide, to ask if I knew how to make fulminate of mercury. I firmly denied any such knowledge, whereupon he skittered offstage again to where, from the occasional booms, he apparently was experimenting with a carbide cannon.

"What has young Leroy to do with it?"

"He asked what the 'O' stood for, and I said 'Obed', so Stubbs wanted to know if I was an Islander."

"Naturally," I agreed, for there is a dash of whaleblood, as they say, in my own family. Thus, back at Hackamore, when old Fizz first attempted a touch until allowance time, identifying as surety his uncle and guardian, John Jared Kettleworth, I at once asked if the latter was an Islander. Jared, Obed, and the like are the tipoff.

"So," said Fizzo, "I said yes."

"And you told him about your Uncle John?"

"Yes. Then he threw me out."

"Did he give any reason?"

In the manner of one contemplating pounding his head against it, Fizzo stared at the wall. "It seems," he said, "that back in whaling days, Beriah's great, great grandfather ate my Uncle John's great, great grandfather."

It would be accurate to say that Fizzo's statement surprised me. But not if you threw in an "astounded," or even a "shocked." Granted, it was not a nice thing to do. But in those days of sail, shipwreck and men long adrift in open whaleboats, it was simply an accepted hazard of the trade, and there is the Island story of the young stranger calling upon the retired Nantucket seacaptain to inquire if by any chance the latter had ever known a certain relative of the former's, and the old fellow's cackling reply: "*Know* him? I *et* him!"

"About the plan," I prompted.

"Well, in principle it was to set up a danger to Beriah so deadly, then stage a rescue by myself so heroic, that he, overcome by gratitude, would consent."

"Sound," I conceded. "So—?"

"So we went down the list, and—" Fizzo paused, regarded me in a peculiar manner, and took a long breath. "So finally we came to the burning house."

"The burning—!" I shot out of my seat. *"Excelsior!"* I cried.

"Gully, old man—"

I shook my head hard.

"I won't have anything to do with it!"

"Gully, old—"

"No!"

"But Georgette was sure you would, if I would get my Uncle Ulysses to do something for you. She wouldn't say what."

CHAPTER FOURTEEN
THE BACHELOR'S FRIEND

I pulled myself together. *Agree to it*, Jo had said, no matter how...I leaned forward. "Fizzo," I said, "I have an invention ready for market. I thought you might prevail upon your uncle to help me interest a manufacturer."

There was an interval of flow, then a visible flash as, somewhere back in Fizzo's head, the two ideas connected.

"You mean, if I can get my uncle to help place your invention, you'll—"

"That's it."

"Why, of course he will!" Fizzo sprang up. "I'll get him on the phone right now—but first you'll have to tell me what it's all about."

I arose. "Follow me," I said.

In the open doorway to my laboratory, he stopped in amazement, for the sight within was easily one to startle the uninitiated.

"Do you remember Pugston Pendlebury?" I asked.

"Pug? Sure. Stupid as they come. Flunked out."

"The point is, he was run over by a bicycle—on the Common, by the Frog Pond. By getting run over, he saved a little child's life, and this little child's mother happened to be the wife of the vice president of a big company in New York City. She was so grateful that she made her husband get Pug a junior executive's job there." I paused. "All clear, so far?"

"I guess so," said Fizzo, with a baffled look.

"Now, get this. The evening before he was to report, Pug went down to New York. In his hotel lobby, he met two old Army pals. They did the town, and Pug turned in about four A. M. He was supposed to report at eight, so he asked the clerk to call him at seven. But when the clerk phoned, Pug picked up the receiver and said 'Thanks,' and then rolled over and didn't wake up until one o'clock that afternoon. He arrived at his new office about two, and his supervisor fired him."

"Served him right."

"But here is the point," I said. "Pug lost the opportunity of a lifetime because he couldn't get up in the morning."

"Even if he had, I don't think he'd have made it."

"But let us give him the benefit of the doubt," I said. I picked up a large box, set it on the workbench and removed the cover. "And let us give him this, *The Gates Automatic Bed—The Bachelor's Friend—* an invention which fulfills a human need."

He looked at it in silence.

"This," I said, placing Mister Jenkins, an old doll of Jo's, on the bed, "is Pug, turning in at four A. M. He wants to be sure of getting up at seven. So he sets this electric clock." Carefully I made the setting. "Then, without a worry in the world, he sleeps." I turned the hands around to ten minutes of seven. "Then—"

"Why the red light?"

"That represents a coffee maker. Pug should have black coffee ready and waiting at seven. So at ten of, the coffee starts to brew." I turned the hands again, and the bed began to go into action. First it bent in the middle, the head-half rising. Then it twisted to the right. Unfortunately, it was set a little too fast.

"Flat on his face," observed Fizzo.

"No," I said, picking up Jo's doll. "In actual practice, if you were raised and twisted, you would put out your arms and place your feet on the floor. You would end up on your feet. And you can't crawl back into bed afterwards. Watch." The bed straightened and began to rise, until it had folded up flat against the wall like a wall bed. "Now," I instructed, "press this button."

Fizzo did so, and the bed came back down.

"All you have to do," I said, smoothing the mattress and the covers, is take this to your uncle—"

"Take?" asked Fizzo, in surprise.

I nodded. "—tell him the story of Pug Pendlebury and press the button. Then you ask him how many hotel rooms there are in New York City alone. Do you have any idea?"

"No."

"There are thousands upon thousands."

"But Gully! My uncle lives in Los Angeles."

"Los Angeles—!"

I looked at him in dismay. I had assumed his uncle lived in Boston.

"That's why I said I'd phone him. I could tell him the idea. He's coming to Boston later this week. I'll make an appointment for us to show it to him."

I considered. The important thing, as Jo so wisely had said, was to get Fizzo going with his uncle.

"O. K., Fizzo. Let's go."

I sat in the parlor while he placed his call. During the ensuing conversation, however, I made out only the name "Aunt Polly."

"That was my Aunt Polly," said Fizzo, re-entering. "My uncle has gone to San Francisco, but she'll tell him to phone me at work, tomorrow. O. K.?"

Well, he had done his best. The wheels were turning.

"O. K.," I said.

"Now, about tomorrow night," said Fizzo briskly. "I'll catch the six o'clock ferry and be there by eight forty-five. You can bunk with me at my Uncle John's. I'll phone him and tell him you'll be arriving first, and to put you up. O. K.?"

"O. K.," I said.

He took a long breath. "About the fire, Gully. Here is what we planned. You know those picket fences? Well, about midnight, you casually stroll past with the box of excelsior, set it against the fence and strike a match to it. Then you stroll on."

"*Casually?*" I asked, with all the sarcasm I could put into it.

"Yes. Then I happen to be coming along. I spot the fire, rush in, wake up old Stubbs and save him. Meanwhile, you rush back, turn on the hose and keep the flames from spreading, just in case. How does it sound?"

It sounded crazy, but I did not say so.

"—and you could run Winnie down."

"Winnie's in Boston?"

"Yes. She came over to shop. Will you?"

"Why, of course."

"Good. I'm going to see her now. I'll tell her."

As the Austin Healey roared off, I was struck by an odd incongruity: having just spiked Christopher Beanfield and Randolph Reichenbach Bohr's trip to Brazil, I now was committed to sending Fizzo and Winnie there.

At bedtime, with the relaxing warmth of a shower, my thoughts turned, as they often did, to Leonardo da Vinci. Like myself, he had had an idea for an automatic door. Like myself, he had dabbled in locksmithing, and had, as one biographer delicately put it, "designed instruments to open a dungeon from the inside." And like myself, in order to be able to carry on his investigations, he had served under a succession of titled patrons whose aims and interests were as remote from his own as were mine from Rowbottom's. And then, as also often happened, up from the depths arose an idea re my present problem: the thing to do was pump Winnie about Beriah. We would be together for two hours on the road, then three hours on the boat. During that time, I could learn from her the whole story of the Stubbs-Kettleworth feud. And then, with all the facts at hand, I would try to come up with some sounder scheme than Fizzo's.

It often happens that the night-conceived plan upon which one happily sails off to the land of nod shows in the dawn's cold light as full of holes as a colander. But not this time. For when I rolled out at an early hour Tuesday morning, I was filled to overflowing with the determination that today, in our five hour, uninterrupted tete-a-tete by land and by sea, I would elicit, extract and extort from Winifred the Stubbs-Kettleworth history in all its details and come up with some sounder plan than that of setting fire to a picket fence with excelsior.

It was only after I pulled up at her hotel that I received my first intimation that this tete-a-tete might not, after all, be achieved without difficulty. This difficulty appeared in the form of a scrawny but well dressed squirt standing beside a smart suitcase at the curb. I got out and approached him with a sinking heart. Sure enough, it was the Carbide Kid.

"Hello, Leroy," said I.

"What a crummy car," said he.

More and more, on the journey through life, the conviction has struck me that, in the case of the twelve year old, the only really effective conversation-opening gambit is a good bat on the ear; but I stayed the eager hand.

"Crummy, did you say?" I asked indulgently.

"You heard me, Big Boy. Capital K-rummy."

And so saying, he backed into a TV-gunfighter's stance, whipped out a cap pistol with a scrap of white paper stuck into its hammer-pan, and pulled the trigger. The report, ten times the expected magnitude, caused me to jump with a will.

"I thought that would stop you!" he crowed.

"What's the white stuff?" I queried, ears ringing but professional curiosity aroused, for the paper had disappeared.

"Bugsy makes it."

"Bugsy?"

"Bugsy Wilson. He uses iodine and something. Do you know how?"

"No," I said, and from his expression it was clear that I again was a disappointment. "I see they've about grown back," I added, indicating his eyebrows.

"Ah, that." He tossed his head. "How about gunpowder?" he asked eagerly. "Do you know how to make gunpowder?"

I considered. In my own day, logically following the carbide phase, I had made gunpowder. The old Chinese formula. Gunpowder was easy. But would it be wise to tell him? As I debated, his manner suddenly changed from eager to reserved, and, turning, I saw that Winifred Stubbs was approaching.

At Zaza's, only three months ago, the small blonde with Jo and myself had struck me as rather plain and on edge; now she was smartly dressed, radiant and sure of herself. Babbling pleasantries, I shifted the back seat's cargo to make room for the unexpected Leroy. Why had Fizzo not mentioned that he was along? The likely answer in this instance, as it had been in many others, was that he simply hadn't thought of it. We plunged down into the Southeast Expressway, veered into Route 128, and soon were bowling along the straight ribbon of the Cape Highway. Determined, despite the presence of Leroy, to get going to some extent on the business at hand, I asked as to their house.

"It's typical—old as they come," said Winnie. "Uncle Beriah's grandmother lived in it to a ripe old age. She willed it to him."

"I suppose," I asked casually, "it's insured, and all that?"

"I suppose so," she said, with an uneasy glance at me; so I rang off.

It was only after I drove the VW into the hold, Winnie and I took chairs in the lounge above, and Leroy disappeared—that I began to hit pay dirt. Mayhew Stubbs' eating of Captain Hezekiah Kettleworth had sparked a feud and business rivalry between the two families. The crux, presently, was that Beriah wanted to join the Cachalot Club, but Kettleworth, its president, had blackballed him.

"So *that's* it!" I exclaimed.

"Yes," said Winnie.

I sat back. Old Fizz, as usual, had missed the point.

"Does Kettleworth know about you and Fizzo?"

"No. At least, we've tried to keep it from him."

At Vineyard Haven, we went outside to watch the colorful business of arrival. As we pulled off again, Leroy, as promised, returned to verify that he still was aboard, then disappeared again. We took chairs outside. The sky was clear, the sun bright, the air invigorating, the sea whitecapped but fairly smooth, and seagulls screamed and wheeled above. In this fittingly nautical atmosphere, I at last drew from Winnie the Mayhew story as she knew it.

At that time, an Island proposal of marriage by a young man who had yet to account for his first whale would ordinarily have been considered an affront. But in the case of rich young scion Mayhew Stubbs, the lady apparently waived that requirement. Afterwards, husband Mayhew determined to go into the whaling business. To learn it from the bottom up, he signed on as cabin boy of the whaleship *Desdemona*, under captain and part owner Hezekiah. Three years later, homeward bound, they were captured by a French privateer. The privateer impressed the *Desdemona's* captain and crew and put a prize French crew aboard the whaleship to sail it with its rich cargo of oil to France. But an American man-of-war surprised the pair and gave chase to the French warship. Crippled, the French warship went down during the stormy night. Next day, the American ship, finding no survivors, recaptured the *Desdemona* and convoyed it back to Nantucket, where the missing crew's families were given those effects not pilfered by the French and paid their lays.

"But," I objected, "you say the French ship went down and the American ship found no survivors, so how—"

"I'm coming to that."

CHAPTER FIFTEEN
THE CARBIDE KID

A year later—Winnie continued—another whaleship returning to Nantucket delivered a letter from the American consul at Valparaiso. The letter reported how a ship, heading for Valparaiso, had picked up a lone, half-dead Kanaka—one of the *Desdemona's* ill-fated crew—long adrift in a lifeboat. This Kanaka, crazed by hunger and thirst, soon died. But before he did, he managed to tell how Mayhew, Captain Hezekiah and himself had been the last survivors. They finally had shaken dice, and Hezekiah had lost. So cabin boy Mayhew Stubbs and the Kanaka ate him, and a few days later Mayhew went mad and jumped overboard.

"Was your Uncle Beriah born on Nantucket?"

"Not exactly. That's the one point which allows John Kettleworth's blackballing to stick. My uncle's family were Nantucketers all the way back, but he was born while his mother was visiting relatives in Hillcrest. She returned with him when he was two months old, and he grew up on the Island."

"I see," I said gravely, for I knew what sticklers Nantucketers were on this point. Legally, Beriah was an off-Islander, and that was that.

"He left the Island as a young man, and made his pile in construction. Last summer, when the house became his, he decided upon semi-retirement, summering on the Island and wintering in Hillcrest. But when he applied for membership, he was turned down. He didn't give up: this spring, he caused his company to bid on an Island job at a certain loss, just to bring him into contact with Island officials. Some of them belong, and he wanted to win them to his side. Then he tried for membership again, and Kettleworth blocked him again."

"And that was when your uncle threw Fizzo out?"

"Yes."

"And yet you manage to see each other?"

"Thanks to Jo. Allan writes to her, and she gives me his letters. Weekends, when he comes over, he sees her and she arranges our meeting place."

We long since had sighted the old black water tower and the gold church dome. Now we could see the white beach and the low cliff with its line of mansions. I sat back. Up to now, Jo had said not a word about Fizzo and Winnie or about her secret activities in their behalf. She really could keep a secret. There had been no need to let me in on it, and she had not.

"Romeo and Juliet," I mused. "The Montagues and the Capulets. Except that the Montagues, to wit, old Kettleworth, don't know what is going on."

"Not so far."

We were standing at the rail; our ship had entered the channel between the jetties and was swinging around Brant Point. And I, with the facts of the feud before me, was studying the situation and trying to come up with a sound scheme, but without result. Suddenly she stiffened and grasped my arm.

"Don't look now," she whispered, "but that tall man who just passed is John Kettleworth."

Here, at last, was to be my first view of the number one villain of the piece. Fizzo's uncle John, who was to be my Nantucket host, was about sixty, with a long, weatherbeaten face and an autocratic air. He strode forward as far as the rope across the bow allowed, and stood staring straight ahead. Winnie, meanwhile, pressed against me to keep out of his sight; and I had just become aware of a silent and intently watching Leroy beside us when, from somewhere on the waterfront, a cannon boomed—and this, to my surprise, prompted old Kettleworth, still at attention, to remove his hat, revealing a weatherbeaten bald midway. He remained thus for another minute, when the cannon gave a second blast. Whereupon he slightly bowed, replaced his hat and turned, displaying wide dark brows, a long thin nose, a small mean mouth, and a long pointed chin. Looking neither to left nor right, he strode past us and inside.

"The Wicked Witch of the West is gone," I said, sounding the all clear. "Why! He acted as if they were shooting off that cannon in his honor."

"They were," said Winnie. "It belongs to the Cachalot Club. When a boat is due, someone on the porch watches with a spyglass. If they see a member on deck, he gets one welcoming shot."

"But he got two."

"The president gets two. And every time my uncle hears it—!"

Leroy tugged at my coat. "I want to show you something," he said earnestly. "—something private."

I glanced at Winnie; she shrugged. "All right," I said, and followed him to where he stopped in a deserted spot and secretively took out what appeared to be a ballpoint pen.

"This is a very special pen," he informed.

"Oh?" I held out my hand.

He drew away. "No! You mustn't handle it until I explain."

"A trick pen, eh?"

"It's not a pen at all," he said shortly. "Bugsy Wilson made three, and the other two worked, so if you'll tell me how to make gunpowder, I'll give it to you."

"What does it do?"

"It starts a fire."

"Starts a fire—!"

"Yes. Don't you ever watch TV?"

I eyed him apprehensively. By now, I was acquainted enough with Leroy's pyrotechnic proclivities not to scoff. Also, I suddenly had the giddy premonition that I was about to open the oyster with the pearl inside.

"Starts a fire, you say? How?"

Holding it carefully, he made out to twist and pull the cap, but did not. "Turn it as far as you can, pull the cap off, and lay it in the street. In one minute, it bursts into flame."

I blinked, and it hit me. Over and over, I had re-pictured my demanding role in tonight's script. Stopping to set down that box, lighting a match, setting the excelsior on fire—and then casually walking on! That was the part that always got me: *casually walking on!* Sure, anybody could abandon a box of excelsior by a picket fence and casually walk on. But to stop, strike a match, set fire to the excelsior and *then* casually walk on—well, that was something else again.

And here was the answer, if the devilish thing this child held in his hand really worked. Just before setting down the box, I would twist and pull the cap, insert the pen in the excelsior, and casually walk on, secure in the knowledge—or belief, at least—that I had a whole minute to get out of the neighborhood before the fire started. And if it didn't work, I simply would have to go back and strike the match, after all. I couldn't lose by giving Leroy's pen a try.

"It looks interesting," I conceded, trying to keep the excitement out of my voice.

"Do you want it?"

"Why, yes, I suppose. I might try it on the beach."

"All right. Tell me how to make gunpowder."

I thought for a moment, and it all came back. "You'll have to get some sulphur, some charcoal, and some potassium nitrate—they call it saltpetre. Or if you can't get saltpetre, you can substitute—"

"Write it down," he pled.

I produced paper and pencil and did so, sketching out the theoretically workable range of proportions, then adding, at his insistence, the details of my own favorite mix. This done to his satisfaction, he gingerly surrendered the pen, which I as gingerly took.

"Clip it inside your coat pocket with the cap up," he directed, "and it'll be safe enough."

"All right," I said, carefully doing so.

"You won't tell?"

"No. But don't go blowing your head off," I advised with a dash of camaraderie.

"We won't. Don't burn yourself," he added in like manner, and took off.

"About the cannon," Winnie remarked as we started down, "it's really a carronade."

"Oh," I said knowledgeably, for like every Quincy schoolboy who has been shepherded through the frigate *Constitution* over in Charlestown, I knew that the Long Toms went below, while the stubby infighters, the carronades, were placed on the top deck.

"It was on the *Desdemona*. When the ship was finally broken up, it went to the Kettleworths, and when the Cachalot Club was founded, they donated it."

The Stubbs' house, a two story box with a narrow one story projection at the rear, was only a few blocks from the center of town. The hose, I noted, was hitched up in front.

"Four windows above," I said, eyeing the structure hard.

"The two on the left are my bedroom. The others are the landing and a closet," said Winnie.

I carried her bag to the door.

"That hose, Winnie. See that it stays there."

"I will," she said.

As I took off, I thought how close the Cachalot Club was, and how Beriah Stubbs must dream of strolling down there of a summer's day and plunging into its round of activities with kindred spirits of his own age. An impatient Rowbottom waited at the Gosnold House curb. He carrying the papers, I the unwieldy model, I followed him up to his room and down again, he instructing me to return at four. In the lobby, his manner suddenly changed to that of beaming salesman, and he abruptly left me for what, just entering, I made out to be the salty and unappetizing figure of old Beriah Stubbs. Surmising that he had invited Stubbs to lunch, after which, above, he would make his sales pitch, I headed for the home of the man who blocked Stubbs' dream.

He still was wearing the Homburg when, to my ring, he opened the door. And while this hat's brim width and crown height, on close inspection, fell short of the Wicked Witch's, his manner did not. He looked down at me disapprovingly, then at my suitcase in surprise.

"Mr. Kettleworth?"

"I am Mr. Kettleworth, yes," he rasped.

"Gulliver Gates," I said hopefully. "I suppose Fizzo—Allan, that is—phoned you about me?"

"Allan? My nephew has not phoned, to my knowledge. I have only just returned from the mainland."

With a shock, I realized that Fizzo had not even known of his uncle's trip. He probably had called, all right. And getting no answer, he had decided, in his usual undeliberative manner, to leave it to me to ingratiate myself upon my arrival. By now, however, it was clear that John Kettleworth did not ingratiate easily.

"Well," I stammered, "I was to stay over with Allan, tonight. He was going to phone you."

"I see," he said, taking a long and unfriendly look at me from head to foot and back again. "Tell me, young man, did I not just now see you at the Stubbs' place?"

"Why, I was there. Yes, sir."

"I take it you are a friend of the Stubbs?"

"Why, yes, of course."

"I see. In that case, I will inform Allan, upon his arrival, that you are staying elsewhere. Good day, sir."

My mouth opened, but it is hard to keep up much of a conversation under such circumstances, and nothing came out. As for old Kettleworth, where a less aristocratic man at this point doubtless would have slammed the door in my face, he did not; he closed it slowly. But when he had finished, it was shut. And all this, from the uncle of a nephew whom I, for four long years at that home away from home, Hackamore U., had nurtured to my bosom, instructing and guiding him in the social graces.

I picked up my suitcase and headed back to the car.

"*Well*—!" about summed it up.

One who, at season's height, arrives on Nantucket without reservations, or who, as in my case, experiences a last minute cancellation, is likely to be up against it. As I re-stowed my suitcase, a large truck approached. I glanced idly at the driver as it passed, then whipped around.

"Homer!" I cried.

The truck slowed and stopped. I trotted up. Hackamore pal Homer Hart, as thin and hornrimmed as ever, extended a long arm and happily peered down.

"Gully, old man. What are you doing here?"

"Looking for a room."

"A room? I can put you up. Hop in."

CHAPTER SIXTEEN
THE HOUSE WARMING

After Pug Pendlebury was run over by the bicycle, he phoned from the hospital to ask me to take his date to our alumni dance. Loretta Clemholtz-Browne left me cold, but not, it appeared, Homer. I had not even noticed him there—which sums up Homer Sudbury Hart in a hurry—but next day he asked to meet her. I counselled that she was a dynamic and ambitious female and not at all suitable for a slim pursed young professor-to-be, but he would not listen, so I arranged the date.

Homer had been graduated with honors in architecture, and had stayed on, a teaching assistant, for his master's. At the time of the Loretta interlude, he had been expanding his thesis, *Early Homes of Sippewisset*, into a book which included such intriguing items as the puzzle of high, glazed panels on *interior* doors—were they to check on fires or on ardent suitors?—and secret rooms of smuggling and abolitionist days. But when Loretta learned that only university presses would go for such a volume, the no-dough angle cooled her. Her parting crack—that he was utterly impractical—had inspired Homer to switch to, and to succeed in, that most practical of fields, construction. He had just been taken on by Stubbs & Corio, and except for one piece of bad luck—he had not properly moored a small workboat and it had broken up on the rocks—was coping well.

"How is Ethel?" I asked, as he ushered me into his third-rate rooming house, for soon after the Loretta bust I had produced for him a far more likely partner, leggy and bosomy Ethel Claire Montgomery, a sorority date of our Hackamore days.

He sighed, and an agonized squirm rippled down his long frame. "We've had a row over my job. She says it's dirty work and doesn't take any brains. She wants me to go back to the university life. She pictures me becoming a full professor, a department head, and finally university president." He shrugged. "The way it came up, I received an offer of an instructorship, and I have to say yes or no by Friday."

By now, he was changing from workman's to businessman's attire, for Stubbs had ordered him to fly to Hyannis on company business. "—so for tonight, at least, it's all yours," he said, and took off.

At four o'clock, as I entered the Gosnold lobby, a little procession passed, outward bound. Its leader, old Stubbs, was stomping along in a huff, deaf to the entreaties of the Rowbottom who followed, his arms spread in appeal and uttering such would-be conciliatory cries as "I don't know how—" and "I can't imagine—!" and "But if you'll only—!"

I proceeded to his room, where to my surprise the model's small wooden cylinders—representing digester tanks and the like—lay scattered over the floor, along with pieces of broken glass. I looked up: somehow the ceiling fixture had been shattered. A heavy tread now sounded and I turned to face a livid Rowbottom.

"*You*—!" he roared.

"Whatever happened?" I queried.

"It exploded! And you—" Shaking with anger, he extended a rigid arm toward the door. "—you are fired, F-I-R-E-D, fired! Get out!"

I got.

During the brief hour that Jo had off for supper, we reviewed the day's disasters. The matter of the model was clear. En route to Woods Hole, young Leroy, sitting next to it for two hours, had not been idle. He had boobytrapped it with his explosive white paper. And Rowbottom, tapping with his pencil as he lectured to old Stubbs, had sent a salvo of cylinders skyward.

Against my idea of telling Rowbottom the truth, however, Jo pictured the aftermath: Leroy confessing to his crime, but in retaliation revealing the transaction of the incendiary pen. Afterwards, it would not require the keenest of minds to postulate some connection between that pen and tonight's house warming. In short, any public announcement that I was the proud possessor of an incendiary pen would force me to resign from my role for tonight. As to which I asked:

"Will I see you afterwards?"

"No. You and Allan had better be on your own. I'd like to see the fire, but Beriah just might wonder."

"Jo, the whole idea is crazy!"

"Just remember your bed," she counselled. "That is number one. Make your decision when you meet Allan. If it looks like he's going to come through with his Uncle Ulysses, go along with it. If not—not."

"How," asked Fizzo, stumbling down the gangway at nine P. M., "did you make out with my Uncle John? I tried to phone him but—"

Leading him to the car, I sketched out the encounter.

"And he pushed you out in the snow! Where'll you stay?"

"Right here," I said, pulling up at Homer's. "What about your Uncle Ulysses?"

"Great news! His secretary called me. He'll be in Washington tomorrow morning. He's going to phone me right here, and I'll put it up to him then."

I paused. It was now my last chance to reconsider. Actually, Fizzo had not yet even talked to his uncle. Still, he had pushed the matter as far as he could.

"I was going to meet Winnie at the Circus," he shot in, meanwhile. "You might as well come along."

"No, Fizzo. I'll stay right here, out of sight."

"Then you won't be needing your car?"

"No," I said, floored by this opportunist.

"So how about letting me borrow it?"

I sighed.

"All right, Fizzo."

It was twelve-fifteen, and I was wagetty to the core, when he returned. "By the way," I asked, getting behind the wheel, "do you know the fireman's carry?"

"Oh, yes." He jerked his arms about. "I know...Gully, did you ever have a feeling like there were butterflies flying all around in your stomach?"

"I know it well. Once we get moving, it will go away."

Two blocks from the Stubbs', I quietly parked and drew out the box of excelsior. Fizzo, at the curb, gazed up at the moon.

"If only we could turn it off," he said.

"Well, we can't, so casual does it. All set?"

"I guess so."

All the houses we passed were dark. There was a gentle breeze; the night was balmy, the sky clear.

"Perhaps," said Fizzo, "we should have waited for the fog, tomorrow night. On the boat, they were saying—"

"Forget it." We came to the corner and stopped. The Stubbs place was up the side street. "Now," I said, "what do you do?"

"I wait here till I see the blaze. Then I rush up."

"Good," I said, and took off. It was hard to hit that casual stroll; I wanted either to sprint or to stop dead still. I looked back. I saw Fizzo's dark shadow, and thought I could make out his encouraging wave. I resumed my march, feeling utterly alone. I passed the Stubbs' gate, then stopped and set the box against the fence. Now came the crucial business of the pen. I twisted and pulled at the cap. It came off easily. I inserted it in the excelsior. Then, though wanting to run, I casually moved on.

An age or so later, I reached the next corner. Casually I stopped and turned. Back down the street, all was dark. Would Leroy's—or rather Bugsy Wilson's—pen prove, after all, a dud? I felt in my pocket for my matches. I would count to ten, then casually stroll back for the disagreeable business of igniting that excelsior by hand. The flash came before I even started to count. And before I realized it, my feet had taken over and I was flying through the air. As I drew near, I saw that the fence was crackling merrily. At the edge of the yard, I vaulted the fence and headed for the hydrant. I then stopped in dismay.

At the sound of another's rapidly approaching footsteps, I turned. A dark figure clambered over the fence. As it reached my side, I pointed to the bare faucet.

"Fizzo!" I said hoarsely. "The hose! It's gone!"

"No!" he wheezed.

He bent, gave the handle an unbelieving twist, resulting in a rush of water, and turned it off again.

He straightened up.

"No hose," he affirmed.

We eyed each other blankly, then simultaneously turned to view my blossoming handiwork. This was the point where he was supposed to dash in while I played the hose, but the lack of a hose and the enthusiasm of the blaze clearly called for revised plans. As one, we turned again, exchanged looks of dismay, then eyed the faucet again. The leaping flames, which made the house front light as day, showed the faucet indisputably bare of hose.

"It was there when I brought Winnie home," I said.

"Well, it's not there now."

"I'll try next door," I said.

"Yes!" said Fizzo. "And I'll run around back. It may be there."

As he disappeared around the house, I leaped over the dividing fence to the next yard. At once, thanks to the flames, I spotted this good neighbor's hose, hitched up and ready to go. I turned the faucet on full and pulled the hose over the fence as far as it would reach. Meanwhile, I kept an eye out for the reappearance of Fizzo, for it would not do to put out the fire too quickly, before he barged in for the rescue. Tentatively I played the stream on the end of the blazing portion of the fence. A shower of steam, smoke and sparks shot up.

I looked around. No Fizzo.

By now, the breeze was carrying sparks against the house wall and up onto the roof. Indeed, the fire seemed to give a reinforcing chimney-effect to this breeze, the rising current of hot air arching up and over the house, and, en route, wafting eager sparks onto the shingles. It would be wise, it now occurred to me, to wet the roof and front. Accordingly, I aimed the stream of water toward the roof, but found that even after a judicious fiddling with the adjustable nozzle, it scarcely carried to the eve.

A minute later, I was only keeping pace with the determined little streamers of fire that licked up the shingles and trim, and by now, one question was uppermost in my mind:

What had happened to Fizzo?

Another question bothered me, too, and that was as to the neighbors. Our whole project depended upon the element of surprise. Minute by minute, we were losing that element; it could not be much longer before some light sleeper with a front window became aware of the bright blaze. The inevitable now happened. Across the street, a window shot up and a man shouted, "Fire!"

From somewhere behind him, a woman screamed. Soon, I was conscious of lights in more windows and more calls of fire. With a sigh of regret for old Fizz and Winnie, I decided to aim at the fence and turn off the show before the thing got entirely out of hand. But no sooner had I done so than, glancing back at the house, I saw that two separate spots along the eave were on fire. Quickly I aimed at these, even as a streak of flame hopped onto the roof.

The Stubbs' front door now opened, and young Leroy, in pyjamas, emerged, followed by Winnie in nightgown and robe. Leroy stopped and eyed the fence.

"Wait outside, Winifred," he said. "I'll phone for the fire department." And with this sound resolve, that astute child ducked back inside.

"Hullo, Winnie," I said. "Nice evening."

"Gully!" she cried, making me out. "Where is Allan?"

"That," I said, "is the burning question."

"Gully! This is no time for puns!"

"Sorry. He went around back to look for your hose. It's gone as you can see. Lucky your neighbor's was handy. Hope he doesn't mind. Watch out your gown dosen't catch. Looks nice," I added.

I then raised my hand for silence.

CHAPTER SEVENTEEN
MAYHEW STUBBS' DIARY

From the distance was coming what I must confess was the welcome clang of a bell and roar of an engine. Apparently, somebody had gotten to the phone before Leroy. A chemical truck, red toplight flashing, pulled up and men jumped off.

"All right, Buddy," called one of these toward myself. "Enough of the hose. Get out of the way. We'll give it the old bubble bath."

Obediently I retreated, hose in hand, over the fence again, glad to be out of the limelight. I turned off the faucet and reeled in the hose. When I looked up again, Stubbs' house and fence were a swirling mass of detergent, the fire was out, and the street was dark except for the flashing red light.

Old Stubbs, in a bathrobe, now strode out, his feet disappearing eerily into the blanket of bubbles that gradually was sinking and drifting away.

"What's going on, here?" he roared.

The small crowd of neighbors who, in various stages of undress, were gathered in the street, volunteered the information that his fence had been on fire. I went around by the walk and stood at the edge of the onlookers. Some of these, now that the peril was past, were seizing upon the occasion to renew old acquaintance, and I felt rather out of it. Meanwhile, I observed old Stubbs talking with the fire chief, and the persistent efforts of two volunteer firemen to gain Stubbs' attention. At a sound behind, I turned and made out young Leroy climbing about in the rear of the truck.

Winnie came up to me.

"Where in the *world*," she asked, "is Allan?"

I shrugged. By now, it did not matter where he was. One simple answer occurred to me: he had panicked and run off. But I just could not believe it, and I did not say it.

"He was here. He went back to look for the hose."

Winnie snapped her fingers.

"Oh, the hose. I remember, now. Leroy and Bugsy were running water into the well."

"Running water into the well—!"

"Yes. They were testing gunpowder. I told them to put it back, but they must have forgotten."

Then it hit me.

"Good Lord!" I cried. "The well!"

"You don't think—"

"Of course," I said, and took off.

As to where old Fizz was, I now had not the slightest doubt, and as I rounded the corner of the house I silently reprimanded myself for ever harbouring the suspicion that he had panicked and run off. For Fizzo Fitzwilliam was not the type that panicked and ran off. He was the type that fell into wells.

At the end of the kitchen addition, I slowed and cautiously looked ahead. Near the house, I made out a round spot darker than its surroundings. I went to the edge and peered down.

"Fizzo!" I cried.

He looked up, then clapped a hand to his head.

"Oh!" he groaned.

"How did you get down there?"

"It was easy. I fell down."

"Did you hit your head?"

"Yes. Get me out."

I looked around. If I reached down for him, I might end up down there with him. Then I made out the line of the hose, leading from the rear hydrant down into the well.

"Just grab hold of that hose, Fizzo. Hand over hand, and up you come."

He took hold of it and pulled. There sounded a sharp, metallic snap at the house and a splash from the well. Old Fizz, sitting in the water, gave vent to some choice words.

"It broke," I advised.

Fizzo uttered more of the same.

"Let go your end," I now instructed, "and I'll lower it doubled."

"Do you know there is water in this well?"

"Yes. Winnie tells me that Leroy and his pal Bugsy borrowed the hose to run—"

"Just get me out."

"Right! Here," I said, lowering it double. "Get the loop under your arms."

He did so, and at length clambered over the edge. I grabbed his arm. Muddy and dripping, he got to his feet.

"What happened in front?" he asked.

I sighed and shook my head.

"It's all over, Fizzo. The fire truck came."

He rubbed his head. "Then there *was* a bell?"

"A bell? Yes. On the fire truck."

"Oh. I thought it was in my head," he said relievedly.

"Allan!" cried a small female voice.

We turned.

"Oh, Allan!" Winnie, her robe billowing back, ran toward him. "Are you hurt?"

"I guess not."

"I'm glad."

"But I'm afraid we blew it," said Fizzo.

I drew myself up and opened my mouth to ask where he got that "we" stuff. I then hesitated and thought better of it, for a billing and cooing had set in which called for my retiring to a decent distance.

At length, they parted. I looked toward the street. None of the curious had come around the house. "I think," I said to Winnie, "that the best thing for Fizzo and me to do is mix with the crowd, drift around to the sidewalk, and shove off."

"Yes," said Winnie, patting Fizzo lovingly.

By the time we rounded the house, the crowd had thinned, and those who remained had closed in around old Stubbs and the two volunteer firemen. These, I gathered from their argumentative conversation, were rival carpenters, and were bidding against each other for the job of repairing fence and house. One proposed to cover the damaged parts with canvas which he had available, in case it rained, while the other insisted that it was not going to rain.

Leading Fizzo, my arm firmly in his, we edged to the street and set off, his water filled shoes squashing noisily at each step.

"What did Beriah say to Allan?" asked Jo, as, Wednesday morning, over breakfast, I outlined the disaster.

"Nothing. He didn't even know we were there. What a show!" I exclaimed, struck by our small billing in spite of all our efforts.

Jo then asked that we return to the scene of the crime, as she wanted to see Winnie before Winnie and Leroy left for school.

The front of the Stubbs' place was a scene of considerable activity. Two light trucks stood at the curb. Most of the picket fence had been pulled out by the roots, and a scaffold had been erected across the front of the house, on which two carpenters sawed and hammered away, and two gaping new holes showed in the roof. Considerably taken aback by the trouble and expense our efforts of the night before had caused old Stubbs, but reflecting that we at least had contributed our bit toward the Island economy, I parked behind the trucks and prudently remained in the car while Jo went in. A minute later, I was surprised when one carpenter beckoned to me.

"They're in the attic. They want you to come up."

I went inside and climbed the steep stair: the Nantucket economy type with a rope siderail and another knotted rope that just dangled—a detail rather disconcerting at first sight, but which, particularly in making the descent, was comforting to have hold of.

"Hello!" I said, at last reaching the plank floored attic. "Where is everybody?"

"Down here," came Jo's muffled voice.

Near the thick central chimney, a small trapdoor was open. I peered down. A steep ship's ladder led down toward the chimney trunk, which was split and arched to form a tiny room. In this cramped space crouched Jo, Winnie and Leroy, he holding a flashlight over what appeared to be a small seachest.

Jo clambered up.

"It's a secret room," she said excitedly. "Leroy found it when the carpenters moved a lot of stuff."

"Where is Mr. Stubbs?"

"Out taking his constitutional."

"Look what Leroy found," said Winnie, emerging and holding what appeared to be an old diary or sea journal. "It was in a secret tray in the lid."

Far below, the front door slammed and a seacaptainish voice demanded to know the whereabouts of Winifred and Leroy.

"Up here," called Winnie.

"Time for school!" boomed the voice.

To Winnie's command, and loudly groaning his objections, Leroy emerged, gave me a perfunctory glance and disappeared down the stairway.

"Can we stay a minute and read it?" asked Jo.

"Of course," said Winnie, and started down.

As Jo intently read, I peered down the secret opening.

"Old Homer Hart would go crazy over this, Jo."

She did not answer. Outside, the carpenters beat a tattoo on the wall. I chose a box and sat down. Many times had a much younger Jo and I sat thus, re-reading some gripping Barsoomian passage before staging it. I chuckled.

"Do you remember how we used to—"

Abruptly, holding it open, she handed me the book.

"Read this," she said tautly. "It's Mayhew Stubbs' diary."

"What! The one who ate—?"

"Yes. Although it ends before that."

Curiously I examined it. The pages were dry and crisp. The ink, whatever its original color, now was brown. Ruled lines which, because of the writing's regularity, originally must have been there, had disappeared. I read: *"Weds. 11th., An exciting day, culminating in the foregoing bill of sale.""*

"What bill of sale?" I asked.

"Read this, first."

"All right," I said, and read on:

Our three boats lowered early at the call, cook, cooper and self remaining as usual. I being at the wheel, watched the larbut boat far aport. It appeared to be signalling. Then came a fearful shock. Cooper shouted: a rogue whale has rammed us! He called for cook to come below with him, but ordered me to remain. Soon cook ran up for canvas. He said we were stove at the water line but thought they could staunch it, and to send up the red flag.

I did so, then spied the monster resurfacing. It lashed about angrily and circled toward the ship. I fixed the wheel, ran for powder and ball, and rammed Old Betsy. The whale charged in. I sighted as best I could judge, aiming for the eye. A bullseye! Whale sank and was not seen again. Soon Captain Kettleworth came on, later the others.

We shifted cargo, rigged overside and patched. Captain Kettleworth said: had I not stopped the whale's second charge with "the machine"—his Quaker talk—there would have been no Desdemona to come back to: that he and the crew owed their lives to my marksmanship; that I was to name my reward.

I replied: my comfortable circumstances, and being beholden for his ever shipping on such a landlubber, precluded my naming any monetary reward. In jest I added that I had long envied how our brave harpooners proudly carried their weapons ashore, and that I should like to do thus with the machine of my own first kill.

Captain Kettleworth then said heartily that "the machine" forthwith was mine to have and to hold and to bear witness to my descendants forever of a feat that no man to his knowledge had ever performed before.

But later, as festivities began, cooper privately came to me and counselled that, as time passed, the captain's fervor would cool; that once safe in port, he might prove reluctant to vouch for my claim to Old Betsy against his partners' objections to his impulsive generosity.

Accordingly, I surrendered present book to cooper, who took it to our law-versed second mate, who wrote down the foregoing proper bill of sale—the ship's carronade to me, in exchange for my dollar to the captain; the second mate advising that a court of law would hold this dollar's change of hands more convincing then any setting forth of the captain's present gratitude.

I looked up to Jo's excited but puzzled eyes.

"So," I said, "Mayhew Stubbs shot a whale."

"And bought the *Desdemona's* carronade!"

"Why, Jo!" I exclaimed, as it hit me. "By rights, that carronade belongs to Beriah Stubbs!"

"Yes! But why doesn't anybody know about it?"

"Because," I explained, "the crew never had a chance to tell anybody."

Quickly I outlined the *Desdemona* story.

"Gully," said Jo, when I had finished, "it's too bad that Allan couldn't have discovered this. It might have won Beriah." She sighed. "Now, there's nothing to do but go down and turn it over."

CHAPTER EIGHTEEN
ROWBOTTOM REVEALS UNEXPECTED DEPTHS

Beriah Stubbs, wearing gold rimmed spectacles and smoking a long cigar, sat in his parlor in a high backed rocking chair, reading The *New York Times*. He looked up tolerantly as Jo entered, apparently having grown accustomed to her presence. Me he ignored.

"Here is the book Leroy found," said she. "It's Mayhew Stubbs' journal."

Stubbs sat upright. "Mayhew, did you say?"

"Yes."

He swallowed hard. The *Times* slid unheeded to the floor. Carefully he placed the book on the table and opened it. A minute or two later, he stiffened, and I judged that he had arrived at the bill of sale. His head jerked up. "Why—!" His head lowered again. A page later, his eyes bulged. "Mayhew shot a whale!" he exclaimed.

"Yes," said Jo.

He read on; then, red faced, he looked up. "Why!" he exploded. "That cannon's mine!" He stood up, trembling with excitement. He tapped the book. "The bill of sale! It's all there! It's mine!"

"Yes," said Jo.

He paced the room. At the front windows, he slowly nodded in the direction of the Cachalot Club. There was an ominous glint to his eyes as he took his chair and began to read the journal again.

"Look at this, Georgette!" he cried. "Read that."

"*—to have and to hold and to bear witness,*" Jo read.

Someone rapped on the door.

"I'll answer it," I said.

"My cousin, Georgette Gates," I said civilly, "and Mr. Beriah Stubbs, both of whom I believe you know."

"Yes, indeed," said Rowbottom, nodding hard. By now, the bulging eyes, speech impediment and helplessly waggling eyebrows with which, at the invitation of myself, the perfect host, he had crossed the Stubbs' threshold, had returned to normal.

Stubbs, in response, said nothing. Busily I proffered a capable chair and took Rowbottom's hat. I then looked first at Stubbs and then at my former employer with some concern, for the show was not going over. Stubbs slowly closed the journal and eyed it thoughtfully. Rowbottom eyed Stubbs uncertainly.

"I was out for a stroll," Rowbottom tried at length. "Looking at the repair work, outside, I saw your nameplate, and thought I would just drop in."

Stubbs did not respond.

"There was a fire, last night," Jo volunteered.

"A fire, you say?" asked a grateful Rowbottom.

"Yes. That's the reason for the carpenters and all."

"I see. Well—" Suddenly, as if putting two and two together and arriving at the answer *Gulliver Gates*, he stared hard at me.

I stared back noncommittally.

"I'm sorry to hear it," said Rowbottom, turning to Stubbs, "but bad luck occasionally happens to all of us—as yesterday, in the case of my firm's model. I cannot imagine how it happened, but I am truly sorry."

Stubbs still said nothing, and Rowbottom began to redden. Then, suddenly, Stubbs sat up. He smacked his palm onto the journal.

"The cannon's mine!" he thundered.

Rowbottom blinked. "The cannon is yours?" he quavered.

In reply, Stubbs sat like a statue.

"Yes!" said Jo, nodding hard.

Again, a grateful Rowbottom eyed her.

"Technically, it's a carronade." I said brightly.

"A carronade? Indeed!" exclaimed Rowbottom, just as brightly.

"Do you know, Mr. Stubbs," Jo said happily, turning to him, "last night's fire was actually lucky for you. Without it, Leroy would never have discovered the journal."

Stubbs, to whom Jo always seemed to get through, had been paying her his close attention; now her infectious smile finally took hold. "Why, of course!" He slapped his knee and and let out a happy roar.

Rowbottom, without knowing why, joined in.

I glanced at Jo. There was an alert look in her eye, and I saw what she was thinking: reinstating Rowbottom with Stubbs could mean reinstating me with Rowbottom! Enthusiastically I joined in the laughter.

"I'm afraid," said Jo to Stubbs, as they subsided, "that Mr. Rowbottom doesn't know just how this all came about. Shall I tell him?"

"Go right ahead, my dear."

Jo started in. Toward the end, Stubbs held out the journal to her to hand to Rowbottom for a first hand look. And having looked, Rowbottom said what was expected of him.

"There is not the slightest doubt, Mr. Stubbs, that this carronade is rightfully yours."

"Yes!" Stubbs rolled his head. "But what about the matter of actually gaining possession?"

"That will take some doing, I would say. It will have to go through the courts, unless the Cachalot Club voluntarily—"

"Ha!" said Stubbs.

"It would be simpler, of course, if you had possession, throwing the burden onto the Club to try to disprove your right."

"True enough," grumped Stubbs. "But impractical. Can't just walk up and—"

"No."

For some reason, I glanced at Jo. Sure enough, she was quietly having an idea, though what, I could not imagine, and, if I had, doubtless would have run screaming from the room.

"No," Stubbs repeated, but rather to himself, and I realized that Rowbottom was losing him again. Stubbs now eyed the ceiling, drummed his fingers on the rocker arm, and glanced out the window: in the practiced manner of some businessmen, he was indicating that the interview was over.

Rowbottom at once arose. So did Jo and I.

"Well!" said Rowbottom. "I enjoyed talking with you, and I'm certainly happy about your discovery. Perhaps later—"

"Yes, later," said Stubbs brusquely. "Meanwhile, I would appreciate your keeping this matter in confidence."

"By all means. Certainly."

I was not surprised, when, as we went out, Jo offered Rowbottom a lift. En route to the Gosnold, he intently listened to her account of the feud and how the carronade meant revenge.

"Mr. Rowbottom," she concluded, "I was thinking about what you said—how it would be so much simpler if Mr. Stubbs had possession."

"Of course. But he can't just—"

"Suppose," Jo said quietly, "that someone who knew he legally owned the cannon were to take possession for him."

"Why, what do you mean?"

"Gulliver was telling me how your firm hoped to secure a certain award in Hillcrest, and how Mr. Stubbs—"

"Yes, indeed. But—"

"Once you got the cannon to the mainland, you could store it in some safe place, then phone Mr. Stubbs that it was on its way to Hillcrest. You would not actually deliver it to him there until you were sure of the award."

As Rowbottom digested this, he regarded her with the expression of one who, not for the first time, has come to realize that there is more behind the smooth forehead of Georgette Irene Gates than appears to the naked eye. At length, he gave a harsh laugh.

"Well! Thank you for the idea. Do you happen to know of anyone with a car who steals cannons?"

"Gully would be glad to help."

"I would not!" I cried.

For the first time, Rowbottom turned to me. "Now, Mr. Gates. Under stress, we have uttered harsh words. But that is past. Indeed, as a loyal member of the firm, undertaking such a venture in its behalf, you could expect an immediate advancement from your present position of senior engineering aide to that of junior engineer."

I considered. He was treating my recent firing as if it never had happened. Well, that was all right with me.

"Assuming I would," I said, "the carriage is too big for this car."

"You would not take the carriage," countered Jo. "That would be stealing. It has been replaced several times. The present one was built by the Cachalot Club. It's only the barrel that matters. If you took out the right front seat, it could go on the floor."

"So," I said sarcastically, "we calmly drive up to the Cachalot Club and load that barrel into this car?"

"No. It's not there. It's at the Music Circus—or will be, before long, for the Peter Pan matinee. Yesterday, for rehearsal, a truck brought it. They left it on the walk behind the big tent. After the scene, today, they'll probably roll it right back to the same place. You could drive up beside it, pry the keepers off the trunnions, and lift the barrel into the car."

"With people all around?" I scoffed.

"Everybody is busy inside. There are storage sheds at both sides of the walk. With the car at the curb between them, you would be cut off from view."

"Yes," said Rowbottom, turning to me. "As I see it, we casually drive up, as if waiting for someone. You get out and pretend to be curiously examining the cannon—while actually prying off those keepers. And then, and only if the coast is clear, we give the barrel the heave-ho and are off."

I eyed him in surprise. I would not have believed that he would consider being an active party to such a thing. In the background, yes; but lifting the cannon, no. He was revealing unexpected depths. I considered. Fizzo's Uncle Ulysses still was an unknown quantity— and with last night's failure, Fizzo had no *quid pro quo* to prod him to further effort in my behalf. And if I chose not to go along with Rowbottom now, he would, I was sure, fire me again, bringing on the final horror of disfranchisement with Aunt Orpha. I sighed.

"All right," I said.

At three o'clock, I drove to the Gosnold. A waiting Rowbottom climbed into the rear—the front seat not being there—and said nothing. Neither did I, for our relationship's swift shift to fellow conspirators had the aspect of a nightmare from which I soon might wake. I drove to the Circus, and past where the cannon should be. A small panel truck was parked between the shacks.

"Not there," said Rowbottom agitatedly. "And that truck! Right in the way!"

I circled and parked half a block away. As I did so, the tent flaps parted and three men struggled out with the carronade. Rowbottom gasped, and I think that only now did the enormity of our undertaking strike home.

"Look here, Mr. Gates. I suggest that we get out and stroll by. You may be able to release the trunnions while I conceal your activities with my back. Then, when the truck leaves, we'll be ready."

"O. K.," I said.

We were halfway to the tent when, from out of nowhere, young Leroy Stubbs and a short, stout companion passed us, walking fast and holding their heads down. I turned to look after them.

"That was Stubbs' son," I said uneasily.

"What about him?"

"I don't know, but—"

There came a thunderous explosion.

The peak of the big red-and-white-striped tent settled five feet, then stopped. People began to pour out. Rowbottom gripped my shoulder.

"The shot must have cut a rope," he said. "Don't run, whatever you do."

"No," I said, seeing the wisdom of this.

Quickly the walk filled with people, a few frightened, but most of them laughing. A crowd formed around the cannon. A truck with a crane appeared, and, honking, backed up to it.

"Well," I said, "I'm afraid that's that."

At the car, as I opened my door, the blanket on the floor moved and an excited young face peered out.

"Hi, Big Boy. Could you run me into town?"

"All right."

Rowbottom opened his door. "This is Leroy Stubbs," I said, as he stepped over him. I pulled away.

"What happened to Bugsy?" I asked toward the blanket.

"We thought it best to split up. Then I saw your car. Do you think father will be pleased? He always wanted a salute."

I gasped. "You wanted to give your father a salute?"

"Yes. Did you like it?"

"It was fine," I breathed. "Just fine." In the middle of town, I stopped. "How about here?"

"O. K. We tried your mix. What do you think?"

"Good," I breathed.

"Did we put in too much?"

"Possibly."

He scrambled out. I headed for the Gosnold, feeling Rowbottom's burning gaze upon the back of my neck.

"Mr. Gates," he rasped, "did you tell that boy how to make gunpowder?"

There was not much to say except yes, and I did.

A strangling sound came from the rear, then:

"Mr. Gates, you are F-I-—"

I held up my hand.

"I know," I said.

CHAPTER NINETEEN
HOMER HART INSPECTS THE SECRET ROOM

To my surprise, Fizzo sat on Homer's step.

"Where in the world have you been?" he asked.

"Stealing cannons. How do you feel?"

"I'll be all right. How do you mean, 'stealing cannons'?"

I sat down and brought him up to date. It took some doing. At the end, he shook his head.

"Gully, you'd never have made it. When anything disappears, here the first thing the police do, they search outgoing ferries. You'd have needed a private boat." He then let out a cry and grabbed my arm. "Gully! I've got it! The *Skipjack!*"

"The *Skipjack?*"

"Stubbs and Corio's workboat. I was walking along by the pier and I saw Homer Hart tying up."

"What are you getting at?"

"Gully! It's just what we need—Stubbs' own boat! And the fog is coming in beautifully! What a night to steal a cannon! We'll put it on Stubbs' boat. Then I'll tell him. All he has to do is run it over to the mainland. We'll be waiting. We'll drive it to Hillcrest. He'll be so grateful that he'll consent."

I did not respond to his enthusiasm.

"Fizzo," I asked, "any news on your Uncle Ulysses?"

"Oh, that," he said impatiently. "A telegram came. He's in Boston."

"He's in *Boston?*" I cried. "For how long?"

"He'll board the *Senator* for Washington at twelve-fifteen tonight. From there, he goes to Japan."

"Japan?" I asked in dismay. "Why Japan?"

"Something to do with transistors, no doubt. I phoned his hotel right away, but he was out."

"I see," I said through gritted teeth. Here was my golden opportunity! "Look, Fizzo! Let us pass up the cannon for tonight. This is our big chance to demonstrate my bed. We can take the five-thirty ferry, get the model and actually demonstrate it before he leaves."

Fizzo's face screwed up in anguish.

"But Gully! Your bed can wait. The cannon can't."

My jaw hardened.

"Fizzo, my bed is a matter of life and death."

Fizzo's jaw also hardened.

"So is the cannon," he said stiffly.

I sighed. We had reached an impasse.

"Gully, old man—"

"Fizzo—"

He frowned and turned away, shaking his head. Then suddenly he smacked his hands together.

"Gully! I've got it! *I'll* go to Boston and show your model to my uncle—while *you* steal the carronade!"

"—while *I* steal the carronade? Alone?"

He nodded hard.

I reflected. When it came right down to stealing a cannon, old Fizz, judging from past performance, would never pull it off. But could I? Immediately, I saw the answer. Jo's philosophy still applied: the important thing was to get Fizzo going with his uncle on my bed. If the cannon proved too tough, I simply would back out. By which time Fizzo should have accomplished my purpose with his uncle. But would he actually have time?

"So what do you say?" he asked eagerly.

I raised a hand. "Let us check out the timing, Fizzo. You propose to take the five-thirty boat, arriving at Woods Hole at eight-thirty."

"Yes!"

"Where you left your car?"

"Yes, yes!"

"You drive to Boston, arriving at Tilborough Street easily by ten-thirty—?"

"Easily, yes."

"Where you enter, go up to the attic, get my model and take it downtown to your uncle at his hotel."

"Yes! Then—"

"You then have till twelve-fifteen to demonstrate it."

"Sure, sure," said Fizzo, starting a one-legged jig. "So is it a deal?"

Again I raised my hand. "Fizzo, how am I to lower a cannon barrel weighing, say, five hundred pounds, from the dock to the deck of the boat?"

"Easy! It's moored right under one of those little derricks with the windlass and crank."

We drove to the pier. Right below the derrick, with a shanty of a cabin and a short mast, sat the ugly little *Skipjack*. Bricks, blocks, boxes and canvas were strewn over its deck.

"You can hide the barrel under all that," said Fizzo. "I was to see Winnie tonight," he added, as we headed back for the steamship dock. "Tell Jo to tell Winnie, will you?"

"I will." I handed him my front door and attic padlock keys. "Don't lose them."

"I won't."

At the gangplank, the last passengers were getting on.

"It's all in the box," I said with last minute haste. "Doll, mattress, everything—and a cord. Just plug it in."

"Don't worry. But you'll want some tools along, you know, to unfasten the barrel from the carriage. A hammer, maybe a screwdriver—"

"I know. But can you remember about Pug Pendlebury?"

"I remember. Old Pug walking along by Frog Pond—bicycle slammos—saves kid's life—dad VP—gets NY job. But you have to pry the holders off the pinions. Then it lifts right out. Be sure—"

"I can handle that. What's the red light?"

"Coffee for good old Pug. But you could use a couple of planks for leverage, if you can find—"

"Good idea. But the hotel rooms. How many—"

"Thousands and thousands—you can roll that barrel, you know."

"I know. But what's the special catchy name?"

"Bachelor's Friend. But if you can get the muzzle-end up—"

I pointed. Two attendants were laying hold of the gangplank. He stumbled up.

"Good luck, Fizzo," I called.

Jo being off for the evening, and the heist set for midnight, we suppered leisurely, then scouted the route. As we passed the Cachalot Club, she gasped and pointed.

"Look! The chain!"

I stopped and backed. Beyond, at the far end of the deliveryway, barely discernable in the fog, the carronade sat on its carriage, pointing seaward. But the street end of that deliveryway was barred by a heavy chain. In the headlights' beam, I studied the padlock.

"Old and simple," I said at length.

I then drove her to the Stubbs', and waited in the car, but hardly had she entered when she reappeared and motioned for me to come in. In the parlor, I was greeted by a delectable Winnie in a frilly party dress, obviously all set for a date with the one and only.

"To make it worse," said she, "this is the one night I could have had Allan in."

Beriah, she informed, for the first time in his life had taken not only Leroy, but Bugsy Wilson as well, to the movie. At this, Jo and I exchanged a look: Beriah had been told of the salute and was standing treat.

"They won't be back until nine-thirty. So why don't you stay until then? I know," added Winnie, "that you two are up to something."

At this, Jo eyed me thoughtfully, for we had agreed to keep our plan secret. "Gully, when and where will Allan phone you?"

"Why, I suppose from South Station, about midnight."

"But where?"

"Why, at Homer's."

"But you won't be there."

"No. So then he'd probably try your dorm."

"And I won't be there," Jo pursued.

"Then there'd be nothing to do but try Winnie."

"Right. He'll end up calling her, so I think she should be prepared."

Briefly I considered, then nodded. "Spill it," I said.

I suppose I never again will see a small blonde's blue eyes widen so much, or for so long, as did Winnie's during the ensuing account. The old banjo clock on the entry hall wall was striking nine when she jumped up.

"Show me the part about the carronade."

"Where is the journal?" I asked.

"Probably in his desktop—and probably locked."

"No problem," I said, following her to Stubbs' study, where, with a bent paperclip, I worked the snap type lock and lowered the lid. The journal lay there.

"Wonderful!" said Winnie, grabbing it.

There came a timid knock at the front door.

"Your uncle!" I said. "Put it back, and I'll lock it."

She shook her head. "He wouldn't knock. And certainly not like that."

I had hardly digested this well reasoned observation when I heard Jo at the door, then the flighty voice of Homer Hart.

We went out.

"You must be the Homer Hart," Jo was burbling, "that Gully has told me so much about!"

"Hello, Homer," I said. "What brings you here?"

"I was to meet Mr. Stubbs. Is he in?"

"No, but he'll be back shortly."

"Oh..." His voice trailed off as he eyed the stair.

"That's it," I said. "A real, live rope rail."

"Gosh!" he said, moving toward it as if drawn by a magnet.

Jo, meanwhile, stood transfixed in the front doorway, eyeing something outside. She now went to Homer's side, and turning, gave Winnie and myself an electrifying look.

"Gully told me you were writing a book called 'Early Homes of Sippewisset'—secret rooms, and all that."

"Why, yes," admitted Homer, blushing pleasurably.

"This morning, we found one in this very house!"

"What—!" He looked around wildly.

"That's true, Homer," I put in.

"Would you like to see it?" asked Winnie, instinctively getting into the spirit of the thing, for Jo was signalling full speed ahead.

"Very much!" said Homer. Then he hesitated. "But I'm not sure Mr. Stubbs would approve my poking around."

"That's true," said Jo—to my surprise, since she seemed so bent upon promoting the idea. But a moment later, it all fell into place. "He might not," she went on, "so the thing to do is whip up there before he arrives. Winnie, why don't you take him up, right now?"

"Of course," said she. "I'll get Leroy's flashlight."

"You'd better hurry," said Jo, reaching for the journal. "I'll put this back. It's too bad that Gully and I have to rush off."

Winnie started up the stair. Homer followed.

"Be sure and show him the old sea chest," Jo called up. She dashed into the study; I heard her slam the desk top. "Come on!" she said, dashing back. "And give me your car key."

I did so. Outside, I saw Homer's truck at the curb, headlights on, engine running.

"Would you mind telling me—" I started.

"Get in that truck," she said, "and follow me. When I start up the Volks, I'll make it as loud as I can. But when you start up, be as quiet as you can. Try to coast down to the corner."

"But Jo, I've never driven a truck!"

"You start now," she said, and strode to the VW.

I climbed into the cab. By now, I reflected, Homer would be letting himself down through the trapdoor into the secret room, where he would hear nothing from out front. Which, of course, was what Jo was counting on. Ahead, the VW roared, its lights flashed on, and Jo took off. I let off on the brake. The truck started to roll. At the corner, I clashed into low. I thought of the crane behind, and it hit me! Jo wanted this truck to pick up the cannon! I followed her to the site of the new junior high which Stubbs & Corio, thanks to Beriah's college try for Cachalot Club membership, was building at a loss. She turned in, stopped behind the main building, jumped out and ran back.

"Douse the lights, lock it up and come along."

I did so. In the Volks, we headed for town.

"Jo," I said, "you're out of your mind."

"But think how much easier—"

"Homer will tell Stubbs we stole his truck!"

"No. It was still there when we left in this car."

"But Stubbs will tell the police. They'll look for it."

"Not too hard, though. The idea of anyone trying to steal a truck on this island is ridiculous."

"Ridiculous is right!"I seconded.

"And that," said Jo, "is why we'll get away with it."

In a drugstore downtown we had frappes; then Jo entered a booth to phone Winnie. Emerging, she reported that Beriah and Leroy had returned, after which Homer had left with Beriah to look for their stolen truck. And Winnie wanted us to come back. This being the most innocent thing we could do, and still having over two hours to kill, we did.

CHAPTER TWENTY
FIZZO AND THE WARLORD OF MARS

In the parlor, Jo asked Winnie if she and Homer, while up in the attic, had heard anything unusual.

"No," said Winnie. Then, as Jo silently stared at her, she let out a yip. "You! You and Gully—!"

Jo laid her hand on Winnie's. "That truck was heaven sent. It has a crane—just the thing for making off with a cannon in a hurry."

"But what if you're caught in it?"

"We'll say we found it. You told us someone had stolen it, so we were bringing it back."

"Jo," I put in, "what were we rushing off to? Old Homer may ask me."

"Why, the Circus phoned my dorm. There was a chance for me tonight for a small understudy's part. But when you rushed me there in the Volks, I was told I wouldn't be needed, after all. So we came back here. And that was when we learned that the truck, which we had seen here as we rushed off, had been stolen."

"Sounds good," said Winnie.

I sighed—the child is quick on these—and added my approval. Their conversation now drifting into immaterial female concerns, my mind took up the important subject of Fizzo and his likely progress. The boat had pulled out with him aboard at five-thirty. Of that I was certain; the rest was speculation. But if he had not gotten off at Martha's Vineyard by mistake, he should have disembarked at Woods Hole at eight-thirty and arrived at Tilborough Street before ten-thirty. I glanced at my watch. It was just ten-thirty.

The phone, located in the rear entryway beside the back stair, rang. Winnie jumped up to answer it. She came back.

"It's for you, Gully. Person to person."

I grasped the dangling receiver and completed the formalities of a person to person.

"Gully, old man—"

"Fizzo! Where are you?"

"At your place."

"How did you ever—"

"I tried your rooming house, then Georgette's dormitory, and finally Winnie's."

"Good thinking, Fizzo," I said. Actually he had followed precisely the course that Jo had predicted.

"Ouch!" said Fizzo.

"What's wrong?"

"Burned my finger again," he muttered.

"Anyway, you made it," I said, though puzzled by that last. "How's it going?"

"Well," he said rather petulantly, "I've been having a little trouble."

"Trouble? What?"

"For one thing, I lost your key."

Silently I shook my head. "But you managed to get in?"

"Yes. I, —er, Gully, you know those little side lights by the front door?"

"The side lights? Oh, yes," I said with a gulp.

"Well, I kicked one in. Considering the urgency, I hoped you wouldn't mind."

"Oh, no. Quite all right. You had to get in. Good thinking again, Fizzo."

It was a time to accentuate the positive and not quibble over a few smashed window panes, though what my Aunt Orpha was going to say on her return was something else again.

"And then I reached in and turned the knob."

"I see. Clever. So you got in."

"Yes. But I had trouble with the lights."

"The lights? You mean the switch? It's behind the door. Not the usual place, I suppose, but that's where it always has been."

"I realize that now, Gully. But it doesn't work."

"You just flick it. Did you flick it?"

"Yes. Only I knocked over a sort of lamp, first."

I put my hand against the wall and braced myself. I hoped it was not the one I was sure it was, my aunt's prize astral dangler.

"Knocked over a lamp, did you?"

"Yes. In the dark. I'm sorry."

"Quite all right. But the switch. I don't see—"

"Well, I finally felt along the wall and found the switch and flicked it, and there was a blue flash from this lamp on the floor—I'm afraid it's smashed, Gully—and that was all. I tried the other switches.

I must have blown the main house fuse."

I put my hand to my brow and tried to think. The fuse box was in the basement, but he could break his neck trying to find his way down there in the dark.

"So you haven't made it up to my lab, yet?"

"Oh, yes. I got there."

"Do you have a flashlight?"

"No. Matches."

I gave a silent gasp. "Fizzo, you want to be careful with those matches. Might burn the house down, you know."

"I know. And—Ouch!"

He apparently was sitting at the hall phone in the dark, striking a match from time to time.

"Just be sure they're out," I said. "Do you have plenty?"

"Oh, yes. I stuffed my pockets, last night, in case you ran out. I think that's how I lost the key—took a pack out with the key inside. Anyway, I made it up to your lab and opened your padlock with the other key."

"Wonderful! and you got the model?"

"No, Gully. I didn't get in."

"Didn't get *in*?"

"No. I still can't open your lab door. There's some weird thing that appears to be another lock. That's why I came back down and phoned you."

Again I grasped my brow. I had forgotten entirely that I also had re-set my electronic lock, and I had not explained to him how to work it.

"Fizzo, I forgot to tell you about that. And by the way, instead of any more matches, reach into the drawer of the telephone table, right where you are, and you should find a flashlight."

"Right. Hold on."

I heard several loud sounds, like those of someone in the dark pulling a drawer too far out and letting it crash to the floor.

"Got it, now," he said. "Mightly weak, though."

"Keep snapping it on and off—conserves the power."

"I know."

"About that lock, Fizzo. Pay close attention. It's a photo-electronic combination lock, and it's tricky."

"Never heard of such a thing."

"Of course not. It's an invention of mine."

"Oh," he said, in a resigned tone.

"It operates on the same principle as those on Mars."

"How's that, again?"

"It's because of my cousin, Norman Miller. Come to think of it," I added, recalling the equal ages and similar traits of Norm and Leroy, "you may be needing one like it, later on."

"Gully, are you drunk?"

"No. But to open that lock, the flashlight you have won't do."

"You open it with a flashlight?"

"Yes. Facing you is a cylindrical end, and in that you will see a pinhole. You have to tap out the combination in light flashes, at that pinhole. It has to be a red and white flashlight."

"A red and white flashlight—!"

"Yes. You'll find it in the middle drawer of my desk, up in my bedroom."

"I see. Well, what's the combination?"

"You'd better write it down. You'll find a pencil and pad right in front of you, and—"

Hearing a grunt, I stopped, deducing that these writing materials by now were not in front of him, after all, but on the floor, and he was searching for them.

"All right," he said, "let's have it."

I opened my mouth, then shut it in dismay. I was so rattled by Fizzo's large and small accidents that I could not, for the life of me, remember that combination.

"Don't you remember it?" he asked, at length.

"No," I admitted, "I don't."

"Maybe if I just tried it at random—"

"You'd never hit it in a million years."

In fact, though I did not tell him so, it would need a little luck on his part to hit it even if he *did* have the combination. I thought fast.

"Fizzo. I'll tell you what you do. Go up to my bedroom and look in my shelves for a book called *The Warlord of Mars*. The combination is in there, somewhere. Bring it back down to the phone, and I'll help you find it."

"*The Warlord of Mars*, you say?"

"That's it."

"Hold the phone."

I stood and waited, feeling rather weak in the knees. I was

relieved to hear no further dismaying sounds in the receiver. It was only a simple matter of going up one flight, entering my bedroom, finding the book, and coming back down the stair.

"Got it right here," came his voice. "Now what?"

"I think it's about the second chapter. John Carter and Woola—"

"Woola?"

"A kind of monstrous dog. I'll explain it some other time. They've rowed up the River Iss from the Lost Sea of Korus—can you spot that part? And they fight their way through the tunnel under the Temple of the Sun."

"Looks interesting. Where in the world do you get these books?"

"They were Jo's father's."

"I see. Um—um—um," he mumbled, presumably reading.

"Under this temple," I said, "is a great hollow shaft that slowly turns, and in its base is a small door with nothing to open it except a tiny pinhole. That's where I got the idea."

"What idea?"

"For the radium lock."

"Radium! Gully, radium is dangerous! Are you really using radium in that thing?"

"No. It's just the idea I used—the radium flash torch. Mine is a selenium cell job."

"Oh," he said relievedly.

"What you want is the part where John Carter overhears the two therns talking."

"Therns?"

"There's no time to explain. Your Uncle Ulysses will be on the train before you get that lock opened. Just accept the therns. These two therns were in the party with Thurid and Matai Shang, and they inadvertently reveal the combination—that's the point."

"All right," muttered Fizzo.

I waited, realizing that I could not expect him to make much speed reading a strange novel with a weak flashlight.

"What about my red and white flashlight?" I asked. "Did you find that?"

"Didn't look," he muttered. "Get on way up."

"O. K."

"Here!" he said. "Got it! 'Let the light shine with the intensity of three radium units for fifty tals, and for one xat let it shine with the *intensity of one radium unit, and then for twenty-five tals with nine units.' Is that it?"*

"Yes" I cried, as the combination came back to me.

"But what are tals and xats?"

"Seconds and minutes, Martian time. But don't let that bother you. Here's all you do. Write this down. Ready?"

"Ready."

"First you give a long blast, right into the pinhole, with the white light. That simply erases any stray impulses."

"I see. Long white. Right."

"Then you turn the flashlight around and give it three red taps."

"Three reds, right."

"Then turn it around for one white tap."

"One white."

"Then around for one red."

"One red, right."

"Then nine whites, and finally, twenty-five reds."

"Nine whites, twenty-five reds. Right. Got it. And then it opens?" I sighed.

"Well, it should. But if it doesn't, you tap it a little. If it still doesn't, you give it a long white, to erase everything, and you start over."

"I see," he said dubiously.

"You'll get it, all right," I said encouragingly. "And Fizzo—"

"What?"

"After you get in and get that model, will you phone me here again?"

"O. K., Gully."

"Do you think you have it straight?"

"Sure. Don't worry. I'll call you when I come back downstairs."

Damp and undone, I staggered into the parlor.

"That was Fizzo," I said.

"Any trouble?" asked Jo.

I sank into my chair.

"He was having trouble with the electronic lock. He'll call again when he brings the model downstairs."

I then leaned back and went into a coma, while Jo and Winnie chatted merrily. When I glanced at my watch again, it was a quarter of eleven.

"Give him time," said Jo.

I lay back again, trying to picture his progress. Had he failed to find the red and white flashlight? Or was he having trouble with the lock? I looked at my watch again.

"What time?" asked Jo, noting my anxiety.

"Just eleven."

"So call him back," said Winnie.

I jumped up. There was no use making it person to person. I dialed, quoted Stubbs' number, and waited.

And waited.

CHAPTER TWENTY ONE
DISASTER

"I think it's all right," said Jo, on my return. "I think he was in such a hurry to get to his uncle that he decided not to take the time to call."

I sank back into my chair again.

"I hope you're right," I said.

"Gully, about the Club lock. I think we should make that our first move, while we're still in the Volks. That way, there'd be no truck engine to attract attention."

I considered, then nodded.

"Yes. That way, we can drive right in. Good idea."

I sat back again. I tried to picture Fizzo's progress. By now, he should be at his uncle's hotel, with the model set up and plugged in. I could see the bed, the red light flashing on. Would he forget to emphasize the number of hotel rooms in New York City alone? And would he remember the catchy name, *The Bachelor's Friend*? A heavy tread sounded, the door opened, and old Stubbs entered.

He stopped in the doorway to the parlor. His hat and clothing were wet from the fog. What, earlier, must have been an actively angry face, now showed only dull anger and bafflement.

"We were just leaving." Jo said quickly.

"Well, I'm turning in."

He clumped up the stair.

"Go ahead, then," whispered Winnie. " I'll stay awake and listen for the phone. If Allan calls, and if it will keep till morning, I won't try to call you."

Half a block past the Club, I parked, got out and walked back. The heavy old shackle was easy. I lowered the chain to the ground, then re-snapped the padlock onto the end, so that no one passing might have the bright idea of re-fastening it.

"That was quick!" said Jo, as I rejoined her.

"A breeze. Early training does it."

At the junior high site, the big truck stood where we had left it. In it, we rolled into town without incident. At the Club entrance, I slowly ran over the chain.

"One of your best ideas, Jo, doing the chain first."

I drove on out. Ahead, I made out the form of the carronade. I brought the truck around so the crane would swing over it, then turned off the lights and engine. I jumped down. Steel wedges held the half-round trunnion covers in place. I tapped them out and swung back the covers, tossed the wedges onto the back of the truck, and figure-eighted the rope sling around the barrel. Then I jumped up into the back, freed the hook and swung the crane beam out.

"Pull down on the hook when I start the winch, Jo."

"O. K."

I entered the cab, started the engine and eased forward on the winch control.

"It's coming," she called. "A little more. Good!"

I jumped out. The hook dangled beside the cannon; I caught the doubled rope into it.

"Stay away, Jo. You could get squashed."

"Right."

I climbed back in. Leaning over to watch what happened, I eased back on the control. The hook tightened. The sling slid together a little, then held. In a moment the barrel was gently swaying, free of the carriage. I raised it to clear the level of the concrete blocks, jumped out, climbed up onto the back and swung the cannon and boom around over the nest I had cleared. Then I jumped down, got into the cab again, and, watching through the rear window, gently lowered the cannon.

"Get in, Jo! We'll leave it just like that."

We headed for the pier.

"You're leaving it hanging?"

"It's half on the floor. You'd have to be above the level of the blocks to see it. The point is, we won't have to use that derrick on the pier. I can lower the cannon to the *Skipjack* right from this crane."

"Wonderful!"

At the pier, I headed for the gallows-like derrick and brought the wheels against the timber stoplog. Jo got out. Watching through the rear window, I hoisted the cannon again. When it was high and clear, I climbed up onto the back and swung the crane and its dangling cannon out over the boat.

"Good," said Jo breathlessly.

"O. K. Now, down we go."

I climbed back into the cab, placed my hand on the lever and looked back.

"Gully! It's tilting!"

My hand froze. I did not know what to do. The barrel, not quite balanced, was tilting, the muzzle going down. And the more it tilted—the more it tilted. Gently I eased over on the lever, then back. It was, I realized at once, the worst thing I could have done. With a scrunching sound, the sling's loops slid together. And as they did, the muzzle tilted more and more until it was pointing straight down. By now, the rope loops were hung up on the trunnions. There came a pop, which was the rope snapping; a jolt, which was the truck's bounce as it was relieved of its twisting load; and a shattering, splintering explosion, which was the cannon hitting the deck.

I got out. Jo stood at the edge, staring down. She pointed to the ugly new hole in the deck.

"It went right through!" she gasped.

There sounded a rushing and splashing, like that of a fire hydrant opened for the kids on a hot summer's day.

"It's leaking—!" I said.

"Leaking—! It's pouring in! The barrel must have gone right on through the hull!"

Before our eyes, the boat was settling in the water. Already, the cannon had probably buried itself in the mud below.

I heard the taut scrape of a rope.

"Come back!" I cried, grabbing Jo's arm. "The mooring ropes—they're tightening!"

Seconds later, one snapped, then the other.

We went to the edge again. With a great gurgling, the deck went under, then the cabin and the mast. Now there was no boat at all, only bubbles. We stood there, fascinated.

It was Jo who first came to life.

"Let's get out of here! Fix the hook!"

I climbed onto the back, swung the beam in and caught the hook. Glancing back, I saw Jo unfastening the end of the mooring rope from its cleat. She tossed it into the water.

"Might as well leave no trace," she said, as I jumped down. "Let them think it drifted away."

"Good idea. Do the other one."

She ran forward to the other cleat. I climbed into the cab. Jo climbed in beside me and we headed for the junior high.

The alarm clock rang; from my army cot I quickly shut it off.

Homer stirred but did not awaken. He lay just as he had when I came in, on the bed that had been mine. Quietly I went down the hall. Shaving, I tried to make real the enormity of the night. We had stolen a truck and a cannon. Now, the cannon lay in the harbor mud and the sunken *Skipjack* lay on top of it. When I returned, Homer sat on the edge of the bed, looking beat. He stretched, then groaned.

"All night, looking for that damned truck."

"Truck? Oh, yes," I dissembled. "When we stopped by afterwards, Winnie said your truck was gone."

He eyed me thoughtfully.

"When you went out, was it there?"

"Yes—lights on, engine running."

He shook his head.

"That was my big mistake. You see, when I went in, I thought Mr. Stubbs would be ready."

"Ready for what?"

Homer looked puzzled.

"He never did tell me. He just said to be there with the truck at nine-thirty."

"What did the police say?"

"That's funny too. He said, 'Never mind the police! We'll find it ourselves!'"

"And he never did explain why he wanted the truck?"

"No. He phoned me in Hyannis and said, 'Homer, you've cost the company a boat. Do you want to get in right, again?' And I said, 'Of course.' Then he said, 'Good. Get right back over here and don't ask a lot of fool questions.' So I didn't."

Over breakfast, Jo listened without comment to my second hand report of Beriah Stubbs' strange deportment. Out in the car again, she sat back and eyed me.

"Gully, wasn't it a great piece of luck, for anybody wanting to steal a cannon, to look out Stubbs' doorway and see a truck with a crane waiting at the curb?"

"Very lucky, yes."

Jo shook her head.

"It wasn't luck at all. Stubbs was planning to snitch that cannon himself."

I sat back, flabbergasted.

"I think that's the way it was, Gully. I was puzzling over why he didn't want to report it to the police. If he had, he wouldn't have dared go ahead with his plan, even if they had found it for him."

"Good thinking."

She sighed. "We'd better get along, if we're to catch Winnie before she leaves. And we'd better not tell her what happened. We'll just say we failed, and will tell her the details later."

I agreed, and we headed for the Stubbs', where, I hoped, Winnie at least would have good news as to Fizzo's uncle Ulysses and my automatic bed.

The truck stood in front where I had left it. A sober Winnie let us in, her expression giving me a sinking feeling that any news she might have was bad.

Jo silently indicated the truck.

Winnie nodded. "I noticed it there when I got up."

"What did your uncle say?"

"He hasn't seen it, yet. He's still asleep."

We went into a huddle in the parlor.

"How did you make out?" Winnie asked Jo.

"Not good. We'll have to think of something else."

"Then I guess that makes it unanimous," said Winnie.

"You mean Fizzo—?" I asked.

"Gully, Allan is in jail."

It was a time for clapping the hand to the brow, and I did so with a will.

"In jail!" asked Jo. "Where?"

"In Boston. After you left, he phoned me. He said they would only allow him one call. He'd been booked for breaking and entering."

"Breaking and entering—!" I exclaimed.

"Yes. He was up in your attic in the dark, trying to open your laboratory door, when the police came. He told them he was getting something with your permission, but they wouldn't believe him. He said not to tell anybody but you, Gully. He wants you to take the first boat and get him out. All you have to do is tell them that he was entering your home with your permission."

"Poor Allan," said Jo.

I sat down, dejected. Poor Allan, indeed! It would be a simple matter to explain the facts to the police, and he would be free. But he, by his bumbling, had destroyed my last hope. By now, his Uncle Ulysses, no doubt idly wondering what had happened to his no-show nephew, would be nearing Washington, from where he would take off for Japan. For me, for the immediate future, Fizzo's Uncle Ulysses was out of the picture.

At a timid but insistent rapping, Winnie went to the door. It was Homer.

"I came to see Mr. Stubbs on an urgent matter," he wheezed, panting as if he had run all the way from town.

"He's not up yet."

"Well, even so, I would appreciate—"

"Certainly," said Winnie.

She started up the stair, and Homer leaned against the door jamb, breathing hard and looking utterly baffled.

"What the devil is it now?" boomed Stubbs, as, in bathrobe and slippers, he padded down the stair.

"The truck," said Homer, holding out the keys.

"You found it! Where?"

"Well, no, I didn't exactly find it."

Homer pointed. Stubbs looked out.

"It's here! You brought it back?"

"No. I was coming—running, in fact—to tell you something else, and the truck was here."

"It was here when you got here?"

"Yes. But I didn't find it. I came to tell you the *Skipjack* is gone."

A pregnant silence followed. Then Stubbs slowly asked: "Can it be that I heard you correctly? Can it be that I heard you say, 'The—Skip—jack—is—gone'?"

A blistered Homer silently nodded.

"I don't believe it," said Stubbs. "Come on."

CHAPTER TWENTY TWO
JO ACCUSES JOHN KETTLEWORTH

From the windows we watched Stubbs, followed by Homer, pad out to the truck.

"He's going to believe it," I said.

Five minutes later, I heard the truck and looked out. Beriah Stubbs, alone, was coming up the walk, shaking his head; he entered the hallway and started up the stair.

Some minutes after that, I was surprised to hear voices outside. I looked out.

"Jo!" I quavered.

She came to my side. A police car was parked behind the VW. A large and elderly policeman crouched in the back of Stubbs' truck, inspecting its floor with interest. Below stood Kettleworth, as autocratic as ever and needing only a broom to complete the picture.

"It looks like we've had it," I said.

"Not necessarily. Sit tight."

The policeman eased himself down and talked with Kettleworth. Then they headed for the house. Although I knew it was coming, the sharp rap sent my heart into my mouth.

"Answer it, Gully."

The big policeman outside gave me a friendly smile. Old Kettleworth, behind, did not.

"Captain Nelson," the former announced briskly. "Is Mr. Beriah Stubbs at home?"

"Yes, sir. He's upstairs. Dressing, I believe."

"I see. Would you ask him to come to the door?"

"Yes, sir."

Trying not to act like a guilty suspect, I climbed the stair. As I did so, the sound of a razor being stropped grew deafening, and with an odd feeling of kinship, I realized that old Stubbs, like my Uncle Roscoe Miller, belonged to that fearless, hold-out group of straight razor shavers.

"Mr. Stubbs?" I called toward the bathroom door.

"What is it, now?" he rasped, in the tone of one convinced that everything that possibly could have happened to him, already had.

"A Captain Nelson is at the door. He asked me to ask you to come down."

"Captain Nelson?"

"Yes, sir."

A thoughtful silence issued from the other side of the door, lasting for about the time it would take a perspicacious contractor to conclude that, although he had intended to commit a crime, he had been rather thoroughly prevented, by persons unknown, from even getting to first base, and therefore was guiltless of the charge.

"Tell him I'll be right down," he growled.

"Yes, sir."

As I started down the stair, I saw that Winnie had gone to the door and was ushering Captain Nelson, whom she appeared to know, into the parlor, followed by a reluctant John Kettleworth. By the time I as reluctantly joined them, Jo had been introduced, whereupon I was identified to Captain Nelson as her cousin. This left Kettleworth, and as I hastened to note that we had already met, he curtly nodded. I then announced that Mr. Stubbs would be right down, and Winnie said that she must excuse herself. She no sooner had left the room than old Stubbs padded down and in.

"Well," he said. "Captain Nelson."

"How are you, Beriah?" the other said easily. "I believe you know Mr. Kettleworth, here?"

"Harragh!" said Kettleworth.

"Harragh, yourself!" retorted Stubbs.

"I'm afraid this is not exactly a social call," said Captain Nelson, still smiling.

"No?" growled Stubbs. "Well, sit down, anyway."

"Beriah," said Captain Nelson, "I'll lay my cards on the table. The Cachalot Club's cannon is missing."

"Stolen," snapped Kettleworth.

"Probably stolen," conceded Captain Nelson. "And I have reason to believe—"

Beriah Stubbs' jaw dropped.

"The Club cannon? Stolen?"

"Yes. The barrel, that is—not the carriage. And I have reason to believe that your own truck, out there, was used."

"*My* truck?"

Captain Nelson nodded.

"Well," said Beriah, "I didn't steal the cannon!"

"I'm sure you did not. Nevertheless, I must ask you about the truck. How long has it been standing there?"

Stubbs hesitated.

"I'm not sure," he said. "Last evening, a bonehead employee of mine parked it in front with the keys in the ignition and someone made off with it."

"You didn't report this?"

"No. I suppose I should have. But later, whoever took it, returned it. And to top it off, a few minutes ago, one of my men came to report that my company boat, the *Skipjack*, is missing. We drove to the pier, and sure enough, it's gone."

In spite of himself, Captain Nelson cracked a smile.

"You're rather hard on boats, Beriah."

"Hah!"

"I'm sorry to hear about the boat, but getting back to the truck, here is what happened. Early this morning, the Club janitor reported to Mr. Kettleworth that the cannon barrel was missing. Later, as the news got around, a friend of the janitor's told him of catching sight of a truck something like yours pulling out of the Club driveway sometime after midnight."

"There are other trucks here that look like mine."

"True. But before we came to the door, I climbed up on the back of your truck and had a look around, and I found these."

And Captain Nelson held out the two wedges which, I now regretfully recalled, I had tossed onto the back of the truck.

"Never saw them before," said Beriah.

"Mr. Kettleworth has identified them as the wedges that hold the barrel to the carriage."

Kettleworth gave a corroborative nod.

"I don't know a thing about them," snapped Stubbs.

"Now, Beriah," said Captain Nelson. "When would you say you returned from looking for your truck?"

"Before midnight," said Stubbs.

He then turned, as Captain Nelson had, toward Winnie and Leroy, who, ready for school, stood in the entrance to the parlor.

I got up. So did Jo.

"Ready to leave?" I asked.

"Yes," said Winnie.

"We were going to drive them," said Jo to Stubbs.

"Wait!" said he. "I would like you to stay, Georgette, if you will. And you, too, Mr. —ah, Gates. There's plenty of time for them to walk."

"All right," said Jo.

Stubbs turned to me.

"Mr. Gates, I asked you to stay in order to bear me out. You were here last evening rather late. You saw me come in, did you not?"

"Yes, sir."

"At what time?"

"It was before midnight."

Stubbs eyed Captain Nelson in triumph.

Captain Nelson was silent.

"You can have your men search my house," Beriah burst out. "I give you my permission. Go out to our job site and search that, too. Also, there's a secret room up in the attic of this house which my son Leroy discovered, thanks to the fire of the night before last. Search that, too. Perhaps you'll find your cannon. Perhaps my boat is there too," he ended sarcastically.

"A secret room, you say?" asked Captain Nelson.

"Yes, although I haven't been up there, yet. Georgette, here, has."

Jo nodded eagerly.

Captain Nelson turned to Kettleworth.

"Getting back to the cannon. I am of the opinion that someone took Beriah's truck, and, sometime after midnight and without his knowledge, used it to lift the cannon barrel from its carriage."

"Well, now," said Stubbs. "I don't deny that that is possible. The question is, who?"

"Of course," said Captain Nelson.

Kettleworth glared at Stubbs.

"Harragh!" he said.

Stubbs, red with anger, arose.

"Are you inferring that I stole your damned cannon?"

"Now, Beriah, the answer likely is trippers," said Captain Nelson, referring to the despised over-and-back one-day excursionists. "Don't you agree, John?"

In reply, Kettleworth gave Stubbs a black look.

"Harragh!" he said again.

Stubbs glared and took a step toward him, and it appeared that a fight was imminent.

At this point, Jo, who had sat immobile for some time, suddenly leaned forward.

"Captain Nelson, may I say something?"

He turned, grateful for the diversion.

"Go ahead, Miss Gates."

"Captain Nelson," she said earnestly, "I know of only one person who would have a motive for stealing that cannon."

"Well! And who would that be?"

Jo sighed.

I looked at her, without the faintest notion of what was coming next. And when it did, had you given me a thousand guesses, I would not have guessed the name she named.

"Mr. Kettleworth," she said.

John Kettleworth blinked in surprise. There was, in fact, considerable blinking all around.

Captain Nelson leaned toward her.

"What is this, Georgette? Do I understand you to say that the only person who would have a motive for stealing the cannon is Mr. Kettleworth?"

"Yes."

Old Kettleworth stared at her incredulously. So did Captain Nelson and Beriah Stubbs. And so did I.

"Ridiculous!" said Kettleworth. "The girl is either joking or crazy."

"Mr. Kettleworth!" said Jo sharply. "You know very well that Mr. Stubbs is the rightful inheritor of that cannon. You know very well that he presently is instituting proper legal proceedings for its recovery. And you know as well as I do that, in a foolish attempt to forestall Mr. Stubbs' proceedings, you engaged your own nephew, Allan Fitzwilliam, to spirit that cannon away."

The following silence was punctuated only by John Kettleworth's staccato "What—! What—! What—!"

Beriah Stubbs sat down again and eyed Jo in puzzled surprise, and Captain Nelson and myself sat in silence. For my part, you could have knocked me over with a very small feather.

At length, Kettleworth left off and turned to Captain Nelson in protest.

"The girl is talking pure nonsense!"

"Perhaps," said Captain Nelson. "But let her explain."

"Do you deny," asked Jo of Kettleworth, "that your nephew showed you the sea journal of Mr. Stubbs' great, great grandfather, Mayhew Stubbs, containing a bill of sale for the carronade from Captain Hezekiah Kettleworth to Mayhew Stubbs?"

John Kettleworth's only reply was a hanging jaw and a blank look. Stubbs sprang to his feet.

"What is this, Georgette? Who has my journal?"

"Allan Fitzwilliam."

Stubbs whirled around and strode out of the room and into his study, from whence issued first the sound of a desk top being roughly opened, and then a roar of anger. He stomped back in, his face livid.

"The journal!" he roared. "It's gone!"

"Of course," said Jo. "Allan took it."

"But my desk was locked!"

With a knowing smile, Jo nodded.

"Allan is very clever at opening desks. Also at stealing trucks. And even, it would seem, at stealing boats."

John Kettleworth sprang to his feet.

"A pack of lies!" he cried. "I won't have any of this said about my nephew!"

"John! John!" said Captain Nelson. "Sit down. One thing at a time. First of all, I would like to know about this journal."

"This *alleged* journal," said Kettleworth.

"Ha!" said Stubbs.

"Leroy found it," said Jo. "You see, yesterday morning, when the carpenters came, they moved some things in the attic, and Leroy found a trapdoor to a small room in the chimney. In that room was an old seachest, and in a secret tray inside, Leroy found the journal. Gulliver, here, and myself read all of it. So did Mr. Stubbs."

Stubbs nodded.

"Tell them what it said, Georgette."

Her audience was silent as Jo recounted the story of Mayhew and the whale, the carronade and the bill of sale. At one point, when she used the name "Old Betsy," John Kettleworth, who had been listening with an expression of utter disbelief, gave a start, then re-froze. In conclusion, Jo offered to take Kettleworth and Captain Nelson up to the attic.

Both declined.

"And what," scoffed Kettleworth, "would the secret room prove?"

"Do you still deny," Jo shot at him, "that Allan showed you the journal? Do you still deny that you caused him to steal and hide the cannon so that Mr. Stubbs could not rightfully reclaim it, thus saving your club and yourself from public ridicule?"

"I deny that, yes!" said Kettleworth, hotly. "And I deny everything you have said about Allan. Allan has never picked a lock in his life. He has never stolen a truck in his life, or a boat, or a cannon, or anything else. He has never been accused of any wrongdoing whatsoever in his whole life!"

Jo smiled wickedly.

"Oh, no?" she asked.

"Just what do you mean, young woman," demanded Kettleworth, "by that impertinent, 'Oh, no?'"

"Do you mean to say that you don't know where Allan is, right now?"

"Why! I assume he's in Boston, at his work."

"Ha!" said Jo.

"Miss Gates," asked Captain Nelson, "do you know where Mr. Kettleworth's nephew is?"

It was time for her punch line. She sat straight up and delivered it.

"Right now," said Jo, "Allan Fitzwilliam is in jail in Boston, charged with breaking and entering."

And it brought down the house.

CHAPTER TWENTY THREE
BERIAH STUBBS STILL REFUSES

"Captain Nelson," said Kettleworth, at length, "I don't believe this girl. Her whole story is an utter fabrication from start to finish, its only purpose being to divert suspicion from Mr. Stubbs and throw it onto myself."

"What do you mean?" roared Stubbs.

Captain Nelson flung out his arms.

"Wait!"

He turned to Kettleworth.

"John, I can easily check on her final statement. I mean, as to the whereabouts of your nephew."

"The worst lie of all!" snapped Kettleworth.

"Do you want me to check it?"

"Yes! By all means."

Captain Nelson turned to Stubbs.

"May I use your phone to call Boston?"

Stubbs looked at Jo. She nodded emphatically.

"Go right ahead," said Stubbs.

It was something like sitting in a courtroom, waiting for the jury to file back in with the verdict—guilty or not guilty. It shouldn't have been, of course. I mean, even if it turned out to be true that old Fizz was in jail, charged with breaking and entering—which he was—that did not prove he had stolen the journal, the truck, the cannon, or the boat. On the other hand, old Kettleworth had rather staked his nephew's guilt or innocence on all counts on his guilt or innocence on that one.

Some minutes later, the jury—or rather Captain Nelson—reappeared. In sober silence he walked to his former chair and sat down.

Kettleworth watched him agonizedly.

"Were you able to reach them?" he asked.

"Yes, John. And I am sorry to report that what Miss Gates stated is quite true."

"No!" said Kettleworth.

"I'm sorry John, but there it is."

"No!" said Kettleworth, wilting.

Beriah Stubbs, exuding virtue, pursed his lips and shook his head.

I looked at Jo. She was regarding Kettleworth with great interest. I then looked at Kettleworth. His head was bowed and his autocratic air was draining out. Jo had played Dorothy to his Wicked Witch, and the latter at last was melting away. Suddenly Jo jumped up.

"Mr. Kettleworth," she said brightly, "I have an idea."

I might have commented that she already had had enough for the season, but did not.

Kettleworth looked up dully.

"I would like to have a word with you," said Jo. "—in private."

"All right," said Kettleworth.

Lifelessly he got up and followed her through the dining room. I heard the door to the back entry close, and then another: she had taken Kettleworth back into the kitchen.

Captain Nelson now remarked upon Mayhew Stubbs' feat of shooting a whale with a cannon, and Beriah, relaxing, recounted the tale. Captain Nelson appeared familiar with the old cannibal story of Mayhew and Hezekiah, and painstakingly, with Stubbs' eager help, began to fit the newly discovered events of the journal into it. For Captain Nelson, I could see, this was going to make a jewel of an off duty conversation piece.

They were so engrossed when, ten minutes later, Jo re-entered, respectfully followed by John Kettleworth. The Kettleworth who took his chair again was a new, shoulders back Kettleworth, a let bygones be bygones Kettleworth. He gave Jo a large smile, his first I so far had witnessed. Captain Nelson eyed him in surprise, Stubbs with alert suspicion.

"Well!" said Kettleworth, thoughtfully massaging his knee, "Georgette, here—" He nodded approvingly in her direction. "Georgette and I have been having quite a talk. It seems that, after reconsideration, she is willing to withdraw her flat accusation that I, or my nephew Allan acting at my instigation, stole the carronade. True, Allan is in jail, but he has not been convicted of any crime."

"That's right, John," said Captain Nelson.

"And it may all be a ridiculous mistake."

"Of course."

"Possibly, and possibly not," said Stubbs, the only discordant note.

John Kettleworth raised his hand appealingly.

"The circumstances of the missing *Skipjack*, considering that, only recently, another Stubbs and Corio boat was lost due to the simple carelessness of an employee, may have no connection. What we both now think most likely," Kettleworth went on, with a glance at Jo, who nodded brightly, "is that it was a tripper's prank, and that, before long, the carronade's barrel will be found in the trunk of a tripper's car."

"Of course!" said Captain Nelson.

"Georgette has admitted that she believes me when I say that, up to now, I never saw or knew of the existence of Mayhew Stubbs' journal."

"Yes," said Jo.

"I, on the other hand, wish to apologize for my unwillingness to believe in the existence of this journal. I have never in my lifetime heard the carronade called 'Old Betsy,' but I do recall seeing that name in some very old family letters. And so, to me, that one name out of the past, which Georgette could have seen nowhere else, is the final proof of the legitimacy of the journal. I am sorry," he said, turning to Stubbs, "if I appeared to doubt your word."

"Ha!" said Stubbs.

"And this has suggested to her—I must say—rather keen young mind, another possibility. And that is that Allan, without my knowledge, and with a quixotic but shortsighted sense of loyalty toward myself and the Club, and wishing to prevent Mr. Stubbs from legally obtaining possession, took it upon himself to spirit the carronade away."

And at this point, for all my studied air of indifference, my mouth fell open, for young Jo had topped by far all previous performances.

Kettleworth turned to Captain Nelson, who shrugged.

"If this proves to be the case," he continued, "I assure you that I will prevail upon him to return it at once."

"Good enough," said Captain Nelson.

Kettleworth turned squarely to Stubbs.

"And now, assuming that, one way or the other, the carronade soon turns up, I am faced with a new problem. As I say, I do not doubt that Mayhew Stubbs' journal exists, that it contains the bill of sale which Georgette has described, and that the carronade is rightfully yours by inheritance."

"Wh-what?" said Stubbs.

"My new problem is that I dread, quite as Georgette has suggested, the public notice which the press would give to any such proceedings as you appear to have in mind."

"Hmph!"

"Particularly when there would be no need for you to go to all the trouble and expense."

"No need?" stammered Stubbs.

"Mr. Stubbs, I shall call you Beriah, if I may—"

"Go right ahead," said Stubbs, truculently.

"Beriah, once the processing of your application for membership in the Cachalot Club is completed, as it will be shortly, your fellow members are certain to look askance upon your proposal to remove what is probably the organization's most well known and most cherished symbol."

"Did you say," Jo piped up, "that Mr. Stubbs' application was soon to be approved?"

"At the next meeting, without a doubt."

"How wonderful!"

I looked at Stubbs. Sometime previously, he had risen to his feet. He now was swaying, as if in a heavy sea.

"Long ago," said Kettleworth, toward no one in particular, "my family, under the impression—now revealed erroneous—that the carronade was theirs, donated it to the Cachalot Club. And I can think of no finer gesture, upon the Club's conceding to Beriah's claim, than for Beriah, in his turn, as a respected member of the Club, to donate the carronade to the Club."

"Wh-what!" said Stubbs, still swaying.

"Would he get a salute?" asked Jo.

"Of course!" said Kettleworth.

"Still, if he is donating the carronade, why shouldn't he get *two* salutes?"

"Two?" faltered Kettleworth.

During the recent Kettleworth-Georgette tete-a-tete, this touchy point apparently had not been brought up. A silence fell. I thought that Jo had gone too far: Stubbs would have settled for one. I looked at Kettleworth. He was in agony. I turned to Stubbs. He had stopped weaving and was giving Kettleworth a hard eye.

"Why not two?" he rasped.

Kettleworth sat back.

"All right," he said. "Two."

Beriah Stubbs, head high, hands clasped behind his back, stood at the windows until the police car, with Captain Nelson and John Kettleworth inside, pulled away. He then nodded approvingly.

"I must say, Georgette, that you handled matters admirably."

Jo smiled.

"Thank you, Mr. Stubbs. Winnie told me how you always had wanted to belong to the Cachalot Club. I'm so happy for you. And, just think—two salutes."

Stubbs chuckled.

"That really ground him into the dirt, and I want to thank you again. However, when the time comes, I believe that I shall choose to be, ah—"

He paused.

"Magnanimous?" I offered.

He turned in surprise, apparently having forgotten that I was still there, and, having been thus reminded, not thinking too much of the idea.

"I shall choose," he said gruffly, "to have only one salute, like any other member."

"That is," said Jo, "until you become president."

"Well, now," said Stubbs, stifling a smirk.

The purpose of this bit of buttering up became clear when Jo sighed and shook her head.

"I'm sorry, though," said she, "that I was forced to paint Allan Fitzwilliam in such dark colors."

"Hah! Solid black is the color for that lad."

Jo pursed her lips and arose.

"On the contrary, Mr. Stubbs."

"What? Why, you said yourself that he stole my journal, stole my truck, stole my cannon, and stole my boat to take it away in. You said he was an accomplished lockpicker, and even now is in jail for attempted burglary."

Jo stiffened.

"Mr. Stubbs. Allan did forcibly enter my cousin Gulliver Gates' house in Boston, but he was following Gulliver's own instructions. Allan's arrest was because of appearances, a mistake which Gulliver will clear up just as soon as he returns. What Allan knows of lockpicking, he learned from Gulliver, who is a graduate of an accredited locksmithing school."

I gave a start. I had not taught Fizzo any such thing. Nor would I ever have tried. By now, however, old Stubbs was eyeing me in surprise, and so, wondering what Jo was up to, I quickly nodded.

"I do not know," continued this daughter of Ananias, "whether or not Allan succeeded in stealing the carronade. But he did tell me that he was planning to, and why. His reason may surprise you."

And so saying, Jo sat down again.

Eyeing her warily, Stubbs settled into his rocker.

"Go ahead."

"He knew that the carronade was rightfully yours, and he knew, just as Mr. Rowbottom suggested to you yesterday morning, that it would be easier if you had possession during the proceedings. And so Allan intended to take it to your home in Hillcrest."

"What!"

Gravely Jo nodded.

"Allan has been desperately striving to win your approval, Mr. Stubbs. He is deeply in love with your niece, and she with him. He has a promising career ahead of him in a booming industry, and his present earnings already are well into the five figure range."

Old Stubbs briefly squinted, no doubt while making this out to be twenty, probably thirty, possibly forty grand—not bad for a youngster like Fizzo, not yet dry behind the ears.

"And in a few days," continued Jo, "his firm is sending him to Brazil for two years."

"Glad to hear it," snapped Beriah.

"Winnie and he want to marry and go there together."

"What? Ridiculous!" roared Stubbs. "Winnie marry that young idiot? Not so long as I have anything to say about it. A cannon stealer! Hah!"

"But the fact remains that Allan was acting entirely in your behalf, and that, as a result, you instead have achieved something much more desirable to yourself than mere possession of the carronade."

"It did work out that way," said Stubbs, gruffly.

"Too, as fellow members of the Cachalot Club, you and Mr. Kettleworth—Allan's uncle, former guardian and closest relative—will be seeing considerable of each other. You will be friends."

"Fellow members," corrected Stubbs.

"But he will be forced to live with the fact that you, a fellow member, refuse to allow your niece to marry his nephew. Won't there be a certain amount of ill feeling?"

"It may bother *him*. It won't bother *me*."

"So you still will not permit Winnie to marry Allan?"

"Never!"

"I see," said Jo, with a sigh.

She gave me the eye. I got up.

"Well," I said, "we'll be shoving along."

CHAPTER TWENTY FOUR
GULLY MUST BURGLE FOR WINNIE TO MARRY

I stood in the hallway as Jo arose, tucked her bag under her arm and received a tardy outburst of thanks from Beriah Stubbs. She had, I thought, made a magnificent final pitch in behalf of Winnie and Fizzo. Indeed, of all our recent efforts, it was the only one that had even come close. But this would be small comfort to poor Fizzo Fitzwilliam when, in Boston, I accomplished his release and made my sad report.

In the middle of the parlor, Jo paused.

"The only thing that rather worries me, Mr. Stubbs, is your journal."

"Yes," said he. "I would appreciate your instructing that young idiot to return it immediately."

"I wish it were that simple."

"What do you mean?" cried Stubbs, in sudden alarm. "Why isn't it that simple?"

Jo shrugged. "Because he doesn't have it."

"He doesn't have it? Why, when Kettleworth and Captain Nelson were here, you said—"

Jo shrugged again. "I know I did. But it wasn't true. I was merely trying to protect you."

"Protect *me*? What do you mean?"

"I didn't want Mr. Kettleworth to learn where the journal really is. I was afraid—"

"My journal!" cried Stubbs desperately. "Where is it?"

"When Allan phoned, I thought to ask if he had it with him. He said no, he had left it on top of his dresser in his bedroom here."

"At the Kettleworths'?"

Jo nodded. "Allan also said that he had just mailed a letter to his uncle, saying that he would not be able to make another trip to the Island before leaving for Brazil, and asking his uncle to pack and send along what belongings he had left there."

"Good Lord!" I exclaimed, getting the picture. "Why, when John Kettleworth goes into Fizzo's bedroom, he's sure to spot that journal. And when he does, do you know what he'll do?"

Jo nodded. "He'll burn it," she said flatly.

"Burn it?" cried Stubbs, aghast.

Jo shrugged. "Why not? I gather that, up to now, you and Mr. Kettleworth have not been the best of friends. He has, has he not, singlehandedly blocked your Cachalot Club membership?"

"Yes!"

"And still would, if he could?"

"Yes! Like a shot!"

"Except for the hold your journal gives you over him?"

"Yes."

Jo sighed. "So that is why I think, Mr. Stubbs, that when he sees your journal on Allan's dresser, he will burn it and then deny ever having seen it."

"I'll—I'll phone him," said Stubbs, wildly.

"And tip him off that it's there?"

"No!" said Stubbs, drawing back. "No, that won't do."

Abruptly, the wind gone out of his sails, he sat down and held his head in his hands.

"It could happen any minute." I remarked.

"Gully!" scolded Jo. "Don't say that! Besides, the mail isn't delivered till around noon." She stood up and raised her hands to her hips. "Mr. Stubbs," she said, "you must get that journal back at once, before Mr. Kettleworth is aware it is there."

He smiled wryly.

"Of course. And perhaps you can tell me how?"

"Why—" Jo's right hand came out toward me, then returned to her hip. "—have Gulliver steal it."

"Hey!" I exclaimed.

"What do you mean?" asked Stubbs. "How could he steal it?"

"In the first place," said Jo, "we would have to get Mr. Kettleworth out of his house. Then Gulliver simply would go to the door, pick the lock, enter, and take the journal from Allan's dresser."

"Hey!" I said again.

"You really think he could get in?" asked Stubbs, ignoring me.

"I think so," said Jo.

"In broad daylight?" I asked incredulously.

She nodded.

Stubbs eyed me appraisingly, then turned back to Jo.

"But assuming he can," he asked, "how do you propose to get Kettleworth out of the house?"

"You could phone him, right now. Tell him you have to fly to Boston on business, but that first you would like him to meet you downtown for an early lunch, to talk over your membership, and all, and—well, to celebrate the start of a new friendship."

Stubbs gulped hard. "*Me* invite *him* to lunch?"

"You wouldn't be willing to invite him to lunch?"

"Why—" Stubbs twisted in protest. "Well, I suppose it's the only way. All right, I will."

I shot a quick look at Jo. She had let one arm down, keeping the other up. Here she was, proposing that I do something, yet signalling "No," unless I was very much mistaken. Well, I was going to say no, anyway.

"Just a minute!" I cried, turning to Stubbs. "If you think I'm going to jail so you can belong to the Cachalot Club, you're badly mistaken."

"Wait," said Jo. "No one is asking you to take such a risk for nothing."

"What do you mean?"

"Gully, you were saying to me that if there was one thing in the whole world you wanted, it was to see your old friend Allan and Winnie happily married."

"Why—" I gulped, noting that both of Jo's arms were down. "Yes," I said, obediently. "I did say that."

"Well, then—?"

"Wait a minute!" cried Stubbs. "Who said anything about my letting Winifred marry that—that boy?"

"And who," I retorted hotly, "said anything about me doing your burglarizing for you?"

Beriah Stubbs clamped his jaw shut and breathed audibly through his nose. At length, he shot a cautious glance at Jo.

"Five figures, did you say?"

She nodded. "While he's in Boston. But while he's abroad, this automatically increases by twenty-five per cent."

Stubbs' eyes raised, as if calculating the minimum new total. At length, he nodded a grudging approval. "And he's in electronics, you say?"

"Yes. Monster computers."

Once again, Stubbs considered.

"I suppose, when you come right down to it, the only thing I really have against the boy is his being related to the Kettleworths."

"Of course," said Jo. "And as a Club member, you will have to see considerable of John Kettleworth."

Stubbs sighed and turned to me.

"Do I understand that, if I consent to my niece Winifred's marriage, you will attempt to break into the Kettleworths' house and get my journal?"

"Why—" I looked to Jo for guidance. She was eyeing me hard— and both arms were up again! I did not get it. Here she finally had worked up the deal: I to burgle in return for Stubbs' consent. But now, loud and clear, she was calling the play for "No." I thought hard. And then it hit me!

"Mr. Stubbs," I said, "before I consider your offer, I would like to call my Boston office."

"Go ahead," he said.

I did not mince words with Rowbottom. I was prepared, I stated, to deliver the Hillcrest award in return for reinstatement at the junior engineer level and no questions asked; and after a period of gargling, he agreed. I then strode back into the parlor and stated to Stubbs that if, in addition to his consent, he would agree to favor my firm with the Hillcrest award—I would attempt the burglary.

Stubbs looked at Jo. She nodded. "I think that is fair, Mr. Stubbs. Gulliver's firm is nationally known in its field. Hillcrest could not engage a more capable and experienced firm of consultants."

"I suppose not."

"And there is the matter of urgency. The quicker you phone Mr. Kettleworth and get him out of that house, the less are the chances of his discovering and destroying your journal."

Stubbs arose and turned to me. "All right, young man. I will see to it that your firm gets the job."

"Thank you," I said. "Hillcrest will not regret it."

He headed for the dining room, then stopped.

"But Georgette, what if he won't come?"

"I think he will. Besides, you can now hint that there is another matter needing discussion between you—the matter of his nephew's impending marriage to your niece, as to which he is completely in the dark."

"He is?"

"Yes. Allan and Winifred thought it best to keep it that way."

A wry sparkle lit Beriah Stubbs' eyes.

"I see," said he, and took off.

Two minutes later, he gleefully strode back in. He smacked his hands together. "He agreed! He'll meet me downtown in half an hour."

"Good!" said Jo.

"I think I will be able to keep him at lunch for an hour."

"Time enough," said Jo.

I looked at her annoyedly. Who, I could have asked, was doing the burgling? But I did not.

"Darling," said Jo briskly, as we pulled away. "Listen carefully."

"I have been, most of the morning."

"I would like you to drop me at the bank. Then go to your room, pack and clear out, all ready to leave, and meet me at the ferry— O. K.? And hurry, Darling."

En route to Homer's, I thought of her shapely head and the Super-X brain it contained, thanks to which old Fizz and Winnie soon would be wed and leave for Brazil together as they so ardently desired. Too, soon the senior Capulet and Montague, like two wrestlers at the gong, would be cautiously edging their chairs closer across the luncheon table, the former with the delightful secret thought that by this clever maneuver the latter's house was being burgled by myself. Old Stubbs, as he so ardently desired, shortly would become a full-fledged member of the Cachalot Club, sitting out on its veranda in sight of his great, great grandfather Mayhew's carronade. That is, when, as sooner or later it would be, the sunken *Skipjack* was discovered and raised, and someone, noting the accurate vertical alignment of one gaping hole in the deck with another in the hull, surmised that some heavy object, plummeting through, had caused the sinking, and still lay below. And I would be a junior engineer, freed from the threat of disfranchisement—all, of course, contingent upon the success of one event, my daylight burglary.

"Going somewhere?" I asked, as a happy Homer straightened up from the half-packed suitcase on his bed.

"Yes, Gully, I'm flying to Boston. Stubbs fired me."

"So what will you do?" I asked, not very surprised.

"I've already done it. I phoned and accepted the offer I told you about."

"Good. I always felt that was your field. But what about Ethel?"

"I phoned her, too. Now that I am abandoning a doubtful career in construction, the one point of difference between us has been removed. She has agreed to become my wife."

At the ferry, Jo jumped in.

"Here's your ticket. Get in line."

"But Jo! You seem to have forgotten the most important item on the agenda!"

"The journal? It's in a safe deposit box at the bank."

"*What*—!" Flabbergasted, I tried to think back. "Jo! You told Kettleworth and Captain Nelson that Fizzo had it. Then you told Beriah it was on Fizzo's dresser. But all the time—" I thought again. "When you took it from Winnie last night, you didn't put it back in Stubbs' desk!"

She nodded. We had come to the gate. She gave me a quick kiss, got out and stood beside me.

I'm going to tell Beriah you were successful, but that you refused to give it to me, and took it with you to Boston to keep until Winnie and Allan are married, and also until the Hillcrest award was approved—so long, Darling."

PART THREE
CONCERNING ONE PR. ITEMS
Kittery, October 11-13

CHAPTER TWENTY FIVE
SAMPSON ROWBOTTOM'S TORCH

"Where *are* you?"

"At the bus station."

"In *Boston?*"

"Yes, Darling. Can you pick me up?"

I headed the old VW up Boylston Street. The Saturday after the Thursday I left her on Nantucket, I had driven down a final time to Woods Hole to drive her in to Quincy. That Sunday, I had driven her with her school gear up to Kittery.

It now, for the record, was seventeen days later—three P. M. Wednesday, October eleventh—and why this jill-in-the-box was back, I could not imagine.

As I pulled up opposite the station, a trim small figure, clad in the standard campus garb of knee length socks, pleated skirt, mangy trenchcoat and moldy tennis sneakers—worn there even in deepest snow—darted across the street, tossed a suitcase onto the rear seat and bounced in beside me. She had, she informed, hoped to find Aunt Orpha home, and had been pleased but surprised when I answered the phone.

"Sick?" she asked knowingly.

I nodded: the hard fact about office sick leave today is that, if you don't take it, you don't get it.

"But what—"

"I'm to collect at the Tilton dinner."

I shot her a look of impressed surprise. I knew about tonight's dinner, for this year, Kittery College's energetic fund raising committee had left no aunt or cousin unturned. Both Aunt Orpha and self had received illustrated brochures re the hoped for new campus buildings, together with reservation forms for tonight's fifty dollar a plate dinner. Mine, because of straitened circumstances, I had ignored. As had my aunt, who, though she has it, holds onto it with grips of steel. At any rate, while Kittery's chancellor and deans

144

exhorted the diners to greater heights of tax deductible generosity, Jo would be one of the evening gowned girls who scurried about with pledge forms and ballpoint pens—a role not ordinarily filled by a mere sophomore, as I now observed.

"One of Juliet's gang sicked out, so she asked me."

"Oh."

At Tilborough Street, she proceeded to bathe, finally emerging, robed and exuding freshness, to patter across the hall to my bedroom.

"You'll have some time to kill," I said, from my perch on the stair.

"No, I won't. I have an appointment, right now."

"With whom?"

"With Mr. Sampson Rowbottom."

"*What*—!"

From the half open door came small, busy sounds.

"Jo—!" I demanded. "How come?"

"He phoned me in Kittery, and asked if I could come down to Boston. When I told him I already was, he asked me to take a taxi to his office. He said he would pay for it and for another to the Tilton."

"Well!" I exclaimed, surprised by this outburst of spending on the part of old Rowbottom. "But what does he want to see you about?"

"He didn't say."

"How did he sound?"

"Sound?" She paused. "Well, he sounded lovesick."

"*Lovesick*—!" I scoffed. By now, I knew Rowbottom in all his obnoxious moods, and lovesick was not one of them. "No, Jo. He probably had something stuck in his throat."

At her request, I called a taxi, then returned to my former perch, where a faint odor of perfume wafting down the stairway indicated that the end was near.

"How do I look?" she asked, in the doorway.

She wore a cream-white gown of a Chinese cast, and grown-up heels; around her dark hair was a white band. Her taxi now sounding off, I held out her black cloak—which by its contrast produced a stunning effect. She eeled into it.

"You look beautiful," I said.

"Thank you, Darling. I'll call you if I can."

After that, the day was a total loss. What urgent business could Rowbottom have with Jo? Up in my lab, I did nothing but listen for the phone. It never rang. We had agreed that I would look for her in the Tilton lobby after the dinner and either drive her back here to change, if there was time before her bus, or, if not—not. At eight-thirty, dressed my best and with Jo's effects behind, I parked at the station and walked to the stately old Tilton. Inside, I had negotiated no more than a dozen yards of expensive carpeting when, catching sight of a trio dead ahead, I made a Tarzan-like leap for the nearest marble column.

I peered around it. There stood Rowbottom in black bow, hard shirt, dinner jacket—the works. Beside him, in the manner of young niece beside rich uncle, was Jo. The third party, a trim figured woman of thirty-five, could have been the portrait on Rowbottom's desk ten years later. And Rowbottom's normally fierce physiognomy, to my amazement, was contorted into precisely Jo's expression: lovesick. He appeared to be pleading some cause—and a lost cause, for the third party's head was swiveling in a dignified but firmly negative manner. And I was thinking how it would be prudent to retire to some far corner, when over my shoulder spoke a well modulated female voice, one filled with friendliness and a hint of humor:

"Mr. Gulliver Gates, I believe?"

At bay against the column, I whipped around.

"Juliet Lawrence!" I exclaimed, and, regaining my composure, grasped her proffered hand—which, I might add, led on back to one of nature's best efforts to date.

"You remembered my name."

"How could anyone forget your name—or you?" I said gallantly.

She smiled. "Georgette said you'd be around. She's over there with the Dean and—"

"I know. I prefer to keep my distance at the moment."

"A childhood fear of deans?"

"Not of deans, no."

"Of Georgette's family friend, then?"

"Family friend—!" I started, and then, realizing that Jo as usual was up to something, I dissembled. "Oh, yes. The trouble is, he also happens to be my boss."

"I see. Well, he certainly would be a good friend to have around. I happened to be the one to sign him up, and I must say, he is most generous."

I opened my mouth to repeat her word "generous" and to follow through with a couple of question and exclamation marks, but did not, for I had become aware that she was not alone.

"...Peter McGlue," said Juliet, and I recognized her companion as the gorilla whom Jo had pointed out as Kittery's football hero. While Juliet chatted, he stood in an apelike manner, contributing an occasional grunt and at length announcing his intent to "go get the scooter."

"You're driving back with Pete McGlue?" I asked, puzzled, as we strolled toward the entrance.

And indeed I was. At the welcoming dance, I had seen her dancing with (a) Dr. Washburn, head of the infirmary, and (b) James Williams, president of Alpha Alpha Fraternity and her campus steady— this being at least partly political, for Gams and Alphas traditionally had been socially close. Whereas, (c) Pete McGlue presided over Zeta Nu, the Alphas' bitter rival for Greek surpremacy.

"There's your answer, nosey," she replied to my query, indicating a foursome by the open door of a black limousine. They were, she informed, the Dean; Austen Stuyvesant, a tall, white haired multimillionaire; Chancellor Fogwell, also distinguished looking and white haired but shorter and rounder; and a balloon-busted small girl with a pout—Stuyvesant's only child and Kittery's prize freshman.

The trouble, she explained, had started when Jim Williams at the last minute broke a date and then was spotted with Babs. Incensed, Juliet had accepted longtime admirer Pete's invitation to drive her here. And only this morning had she learned the truth: that Jim Williams had acted under a supersecret directive from Fogwell himself, the Chancellor's practical thought being that a happy Babs could mean a generous Austen.

"What a fix!" She grasped my hand as a beaten up Sprite crowded in. "Tomorrow night, the girls are giving me a birthday dinner at the House. Drop in and straighten it all out, won't you?"

"I wish I could," I said. "Anyway, happy birthday."

A moment later, Jo came up.

"You never phoned," I accused.

"I didn't have time. Is Aunt Orpha home?"

"Yes."

"Then let's talk in the station."

As to myself, the bombshell in Jo's ensuing account was that the Dean had just been elected chairwoman of the Hillcrest Town Committee. Beriah Stubbs—along with all our recent efforts—was out. And a curt letter to B, R & W from the Dean, in her new capacity, had informed that, following delivery of our "Phase A" report, the Hillcrest project would be shelved. How Dean Jewel Van Eyck came to chair such a committee was as follows.

As a graduate student in Cambridge, she had once been Rowbottom's pupil in municipal sanitation, where he had fallen hard. She had coolly accepted his attentions until receiving the highest grade in the class, and then as coolly had broken off. But even now, he carried a futile torch. Hillcrest resident Jewel, following Chancellor Fogwell's dictum that faculty members should broaden themselves by participation in civic affairs, had made known her desire to become a public servant. And just now, with the important matter of the drainage & sewerage project brewing, she—and because of her special qualification, namely, that top grade—had been elected.

In his office, Jo continued, Rowbottom had outlined his resulting peculiar situation. The lady he loved, but who long had spurned him, was to be forced to meet with him Friday. How would it go? Answer: probably not well. How, then, could he make it go better? Pondering this, his eye had fallen upon an item in the morning paper: Kittery College's chancellor and deans were to attend an alumni fund raising dinner tonight in Boston. His Jewel was coming to Boston! How, then, to meet her socially and melt her icy heart?

Like a flash had followed the association: Kittery College meant Georgette Gates. If, somehow, he could cause Jo to attend the dinner—at this point, he did not know that she already would—accompanied by himself posing as a "friend of the family" interested in Kittery College and a prospective donor—? In his office, with the facts before her, Jo had judged the plan worth a try. She then had done some sticky, high level phoning—sticky because Jewel must be bypassed—to squeeze in a last minute reservation. To Rowbottom's big-donor billing, Juliet Lawrence had attested; and from behind the column I had witnessed the hoped-for meeting in a social atmosphere where Jewel was forced to be at least civil. Thus far had Jo been able to bring him, but no farther.

"He wanted to drive her back to Kittery," said Jo, having stowed away her usual strawberry frappe. "He kept pleading with her, and she kept saying 'No, Sam,' until he looked as if his heart would break." The loudspeaker now announcing the departure of her bus, she laid her hand over mine. "I'll write, Darling."

There was just time for a quick visit to the Copley Library's patent room. When I returned to Tilborough Street, an unfamiliar new white Thunderbird stood squarely at our walk. And our parlor lights were ablaze, indicating that the Old Party had hooked onto a client of some means. I therefore entered quietly and without a glance through the parlor's open doorway. I was passing the hall telephone when her voice stopped me in my tracks.

"Is that you, Gulliver?"

Her tone was strangely amiable and come-hitherish.

"Yes, Auntie."

Laying my just renewed *Life of Edison*, in two volumes, on the table, I dutifully returned to the parlor doorway. Inside, and displaying what, at least in my direction, was a rarely exhibited smile, Aunt Orpha sat in her high backed Victorian easy chair in a Whistler's-motherish pose. She at once glanced meaningfully across the room, and I, turning to view her visitor, was astonished to see that it was not a client at all, but gangly old pal Bunnington Wood, whom I had not seen or heard from since graduation.

"Bunny!" I exclaimed.

"Gully, old man," said he.

CHAPTER TWENTY SIX
BUNNINGTON WOOD FALLS AGAIN

Pumping away, I eyed him in disbelief. Below his sandy hair was the same pale, equine face, but the smile was more assured and his whole manner more relaxed and confident than that of the Bunny I remembered.

"I caught sight of you in the Tilton," he said. "Then you disappeared, so I thought I'd drop by."

"I'm glad you did."

"Yes, indeed!" seconded Aunt Orpha, emphatically.

I looked at her in surprise. All though the preliminaries she had sat smiling and nodding with wholehearted approval—this being the exact opposite of her reception of, and attitude toward, all other pals of mine who had dared cross her threshold. To top it off, her lorgnette, which she was wont to wield with death ray effect against their slightest impropriety, lay forgotten in her lap.

"Since when," I asked, "did you become a Kittery alumnus?"

"Not me. My Aunt Hattie."

"Hattie Boxford," my own aunt put in brightly. "Of the Brookline Boxfords."

As to whom these might be, I had not the foggiest, but one thing suddenly was clear to me, and that was the reason for my aunt's strange deportment. For it is a well established fact that Mrs. Orpha Illingsly Albright can smell money five miles downwind.

"She now lives in Springfield," Bunny informed. "—with my father. Our headquarters is there, the main factory, head office and all."

"The Thomas Wood Industries?"

"Yes."

During the above back-and-forth between Bunny and the aunt, I again observed the latter with surprise. Her eyes were shining, and I sensed that only by the greatest self-control was she refraining from rubbing her hands.

I then looked hard at Bunny. He had entered Hackamore a shy, tongue tied washout, and in spite of continuous effort on my part exited without noticeable improvement. I recalled how he had switched from engineering to business administration, explaining that his father's furniture business was "doing rather well," and that there could be a spot in it for him. At the time, I had pictured this spot as that of a store clerk, prodding mattresses for a prospective customer or stammering out an invitation to try the sofa.

But this was not the self-assured young man who, impeccably clad in grey, sat at his ease, responding with an easy laugh and deliberate statement, and with no trace of the former tied tongue, fidgits and blushes.

"Bunny, is that your Thunderbird, out there?"

He nodded matter-of-factly.

I blinked in surprise. What a far cry it was from the beaten up old Chevvy he had always supplied for our painful double dates!

"You must have made your first million," I said with a laugh.

"No, but my father recently did."

With my mouth half open, I paused. He was not laughing over his quip, as, frankly, I had hoped, but sat with the air of one who simply had stated a fact.

"You're kidding."

"No."

I gulped. The philosphers say that one's first reaction to news of a friend's success is far from that of joy. And taking inventory of my own present symptoms, I realized how true this was. Helplessly I glanced at my aunt. Her eyes were shining ecstatically.

"Well, I'm certainly glad to hear it," I choked out. I sought for some appropriate follow-through. Nothing came. "But," I tried inanely, "You aren't living in Springfield?"

"No. I head up our small Boston office...I had a time locating you."

"Did you? That's right. You probably didn't know we had moved from Quincy."

"No, I didn't. You name wasn't listed, and I couldn't for the life of me recall Mrs. Albright's, so I phoned Randy Bohr, but no one answered, so I thought of Marjorie Miller. Randy was there and answered the phone."

I nodded, surprised by Bunny's temerity. Too, his statement for some reason caused me to eye the table-lamp that stood within range of his arm. Then, recalling the reason, I gave a reminiscent laugh.

"I had forgotten you knew Marj," I said, although I had not.

"You introduced me," he said, without a tremor.

"Oh, yes," I said, marvelling at his manner.

My final effort with Bunny, just before graduation, had been to try him out on the pre-Randy Marjorie. She, up to that time, although highly eligible, had disdained to cultivate the wiles that win the males, causing concern and the letting drop of hints in family council that "something should be done about Marjorie." And so, pitching in, I had lugged old Bunny Wood across the Miller mat. But there, to my dismay, the introductions were scarcely cool before arm-waving Bunny sent a prized Miller lamp crashing to the floor. Later, as was my practice, I stopped by alone to ascertain Marjorie's reaction, and her eyeball-to-eyeball comment had been: "If you *ever* bring that jerk around again—!"

I wondered what had brought him to Tilborough Street. Considering his determined efforts to locate me, and in particular his daring to phone Marjorie, I was sure that he, like the recent Rowbottom, had some urgent problem. But he had let drop no hint of it in his conversation to date, and by now it appeared likely that so long as my aunt remained with us, he would continue not to do so. She now arose.

"It is past my bedtime," she observed, "so I will have to leave you."

We got up.

"I should be getting along, too," said Bunny, in an unconvincing tone.

My aunt raised her hand.

"Oh, no, Mr. Wood. By all means, stay. I am sure that the two of you have much to talk over. You must see more of Gulliver," she added archly, in the manner of an adult talking over the head of a child. "He has become rather a stay-at-home."

And with this parting shot, she left the room.

I stared after her, irritated to the core. She well knew that my hard-won franchisement left me without means for stepping out, even if I had wanted to. And she well knew the prime reason for my staying home, but persisted in acting as if it did not exist.

"A stay-at-home?" exclaimed Bunny. "Why, you were always—" He flapped a long arm.

"Not any more," I shot back, meanwhile searching for some clue to his present objective.

I reviewed our association at Hackamore, where, datewise, most of my pals had, after a few carefully coached dual flights, soloed off on their own. But not Bunnington Berkeley Wood. He had never gotten off the ground. With shy Bunny, it always went like this. Seeing me in company with girls A and B, say, he at the time would keep his distance. But next day, blushing hard, he would sidle up to me to confess his love at first sight for girl A or B, as the case might be, and his burning desire to meet her. Because of his always supplying the car, and also being quicker than most at picking up the check, I would set up the date. And that night, at the sorority house steps, he invariably would freeze, calling for all my experience and ingenuity to get him inside. Afterwards, he would rave about the girl and I would coach him through the business of phoning her for another date. And invariably the answer would be no.

I arose and closed the door, then turned to smile quizzically at Bunny, who had lapsed into an odd silence.

"So here we are again," I said, taking a shot in the most likely direction. "I suppose you've gone and fallen for another girl."

"Well—" He swallowed hard. Jaw down and glassy-eyed, he stared at me. "Well—" he tried again. He squirmed. He wound his legs together and raised his arms. "Gully—"

Did you ever see that old movie where, before your eyes, the respectable Dr. Jekyll changes into the horrendous Mister Hyde? That was what Bunny was doing before mine.

Suddenly I made a grab for the lamp. And just in time.

"Sorry," said Mister Hyde—Bunny, that is.

As he untangled his feet, I eased the lamp over to the far side of the table, oddly thrilled. For the Bunny Wood who now sat opposite me was no longer the sure, self-confident head of the Boston office of Thomas Wood Industries but again the blushing, tongue-tied washout of our undergraduate days.

"I suppose," I hazarded, "you are going to ask if I still believe in love at first sight."

"How did you know?" he stammered.

"All the symptoms, Bunny."

"Well—" He leaned forward, his long face that of a perplexed horse with indigestion. "—do you?"

"It depends," I said delicately. "In your case, it always turned out that the experience was—shall we say—one sided."

"Puppy love!" he retorted with sudden heat. "This is different! This is the real thing!"

I settled back, sure that the coming consultation would take some time. In the past, it always had.

"That first sight, Bunny. Where, when and how?"

He clenched his hands together. Intently he stared into space.

"I was sitting with my Aunt Hattie. Chancellor Fogwell was speaking, and some girls were going up and down between the tables with pledge forms, and the Chancellor called for those who would go to a thousand, and my Aunt Hattie raised her hand."

I swallowed something jagged.

"She pledged a thousand dollars?"

He nodded. I took a breath. "Go on."

"So when Aunt Hattie raised her hand, a girl—"

He leaned back, overcome.

"*The* girl?" I asked gently.

He gave a slow and reverent nod.

"She came up?"

"Yes."

"And handed your aunt a ballpoint pen?"

He frowned and considered.

"I don't know if it was a ballpoint or not."

"Anyway, a pen?"

"Yes."

"And then?"

He wound and unwound his legs.

"Well, while my aunt was making out the form, she stood there. She—" He shook his head in wonderment. "—she just stood there."

"I see," I said understandingly.

You will note that I did not push and I did not joke, for I had served in my present role enough times to know that here, pressure is resisted and wit wasted.

"And finally, Gully—"

He stopped, open mouthed.

"And finally—?"

"Well, I looked at her."

"Ah!" I said, for I judged we were about there.

He paused, as after a hard climb.

"And then, she looked at me."

"I see," I said, eyeing him gravely. True, the total of the facts elicited so far was that, (a) Bunny Wood had looked at a girl, and (b) she had looked at him. But there is only one thing to do, following such a sacred moment of revelation, and I did it: I eyed him gravely. "You looked at each other," I said, summing it up.

"Yes," he confirmed, breathing hard.

"What did you say to her?"

"Say?"

"You didn't speak to her?"

His face screwed up agonizedly.

"Gully, I *couldn't!*"

"All right," I said quietly. "Did she speak?"

He pondered this.

"Well, not exactly."

"How do you mean, not exactly?"

"Well, Aunt Hattie had forgotten her glasses and couldn't make out where to sign her name, so she showed her where."

"I see. And—?"

Wide-eyed, Bunny raised his hands.

"Her voice, Gully!"

"Heavenly?" I suggested.

He nodded and sank back, overcome again.

"I see. And then?"

He shook his head.

"Well, then she went away. I tried to catch sight of her, but Aunt Hattie told me to stop twisting around. On our way out, I looked, but no luck. But then, outside, I saw you with her!"

"That was Juliet Lawrence," I informed, "a Kittery senior of great natural charm, the type that, in later years, becomes the capable ladies' club president. Presently, she is president of Gamma Delta Sorority. She hails from Buffalo, New York."

"Juliet Lawrence..." said Bunny, fervently. "And you know her," he breathed, his manner that of a pal about to get down on his knees at my feet.

"Yes," I said. "And you want to meet her?"

"Yes."

He closed his eyes, and I turned away, for Bunny's facial contortions when newly in love never were good for my digestion. Too, I was thinking of how Juliet Lawrence looked at people. The chances were good that Bunny had gone out of her mind—if he ever had been in it—the moment she turned away. It would be a case of starting from scratch, although it would not do to tell him so.

"Are you positive," I asked, "that you've found the most wonderful girl in the world?"

"Yes!"

"O. K., then. As a matter of fact, she may very well be. So we'll do it right."

"Do it right," he parroted, nodding eagerly.

"A double date."

"A double date, yes! When?"

"I'll get right to work on it. But it won't do to rush into something as serious as this. You'll need a little buildup, first. Then the casual date."

"You'll phone me?" he asked anxiously, as I ushered him to the door.

"The minute I have any news," I said.

In the doorway, watching him pull away on cloud nine, his wheels scarcely touching the pavement, I brushed away a small twinge of conscience. For the fact was, I did *not* intend to get going on his problem right way. That I could cause Juliet Lawrence to date him once, I did not doubt. For although I was sure she would not remember him from Adam, I also was sure that when I described him as the only son of a millionaire, she at least would want to meet him. A ride to Kittery in his Thunderbird, he outreaching me for the tab as of old, would not be hard to take; but at the moment there was the matter of dangerous Pete McGlue, though he soon might blow over. Meanwhile, Bunny could sweat it out.

CHAPTER TWENTY SEVEN
SALESMAN GULLIVER GATES

Sampson Rowbottom's square jaw hinged down to speak, then clamped shut again. He arose, stalked to his window and stared out into the crisp autumn morning through which, half an hour earlier, I had been swinging along, idly wondering what the mood of a man, frustrated both in love and business the night before, would be. He turned.

"You are familiar with the Hillcrest Phase A?"

"...yes, sir."

He bent to a drawer and piled upon his desk a number of identically bound reports.

"It is necessary that a representative of the firm formally turn over to the representative of the town six copies of this report—" He tapped one. "—together with a seventh, which, after your going through it page by page and answering any questions, the representative of the town will initial and return to you."

"You mean that I—?"

Ignoring this, he handed me a form.

"The town representative to whom I refer is the new chairwoman of the Hillcrest Town Committee, a Miss Jewel J. Van Eyck—" I noted how he lingered over her name. "—who is Dean of Women at Kittery College. She will sign that form, acknowledging receipt of the six copies."

He eyed me in question.

"Sign the form," I said. "Yes, sir."

"Dean Van Eyck, as you will address her—"

He paused and eyed me fiercely.

"Dean Van Eyck. Yes, sir."

"—is to meet you in the Hillcrest Town Hall at ten o'clock tomorrow morning. You will leave this afternoon." He produced a large, empty manila envelope, addressed to himself and generously postage stamped, and handed it to me. "After your meeting you will place in that envelope the initialed copy of the report, together with the signed receipt. You then will seal the envelope and immediately mail it. Is that clear?"

"Mail it immediately. Yes, sir."

"This procedure is to protect the firm's interests, in the event that, for example, on your way back—" He ended the sentence with a vague wave of his paw and a faint smile, apparently happily envisioning myself in some fatal catastrophe of the highway.

"I see," I said, with a gulp.

"After securing Dean Van Eyck's signature upon the receipt, you will suggest that the firm be authorized to proceed with final plans and specifications as recommended in the report," He produced another form. "This is only an 'agreement to agree,' the detailed terms to be worked out later, but in practice it amounts to an order." He arose and turned to the window again. "There is, however, little prospect of the agreement being signed. If it is not, the firm will be forced to reduce its work force at once, and you, along with others, will receive two weeks notice."

Head in hands at drafting board, I pondered the situation. Why was Sampson Rowbottom, tireless wooer of Jewel Van Eyck, sending me to meet with her in Hillcrest instead of going himself? Answer: because last night she had made it abundantly clear that there was no use in his seeing her again either for personal reasons or as to the Hillcrest deal. So he simply was sending me as the necessary delivery boy, following which the horror of disfranchisement would be only two weeks off. Well, at least I would see Jo. Then I thought of Bunny, and it hit me! I headed for the lobby to dial his office.

"Gully, old man! I was hoping—"

"Are you still serious about Juliet Lawrence?"

"Absolutely! Have you—?"

"Can you wind up at your office and take off?"

"For this? Any time!"

"Bunny, I'm not promising a thing, just yet. You'll have to take a chance. Can you meet me at Tilborough Street in half an hour?"

"Right! I'll be there."

I strolled through the Common and the Garden toward home, well pleased with myself: my inspired present plan could not fail. As I neared our old brownstone-quoined brick front—my aunt's long-time goal, in which she now took fierce delight—I reflected that the half of its expense which I now endured the humiliations of a wage slave to supply, soon would, instead, be effortlessly supplied by my royalties. She, upon investigation, proved to be out. Five minutes later, I ushered Bunny into the parlor.

"I wonder, Bunny," I began, "if you can face the fact of your one-date record. I would get you a date with a girl. Then you would ask her for a second date and she would say no—remember?"

He grimaced and wryly nodded.

"So this time," I said in a businesslike manner, "it has to be different—right?"

"Right!"

"And you will be guided by me?"

"...yes."

"Good. Tell me," I asked casually, "do you know how Thomas Alva Edison proposed to his second wife?"

"I didn't even know he had two."

"The first one died. At any rate, he was deaf, and he and his wife-to-be were in a roomful of people. So he tapped out his proposal in Morse code on her wrist."

Bunny stared at me in consternation.

"You mean, you want me to—"

"No. I was simply showing you how love may require invention, and how Edison found a way. I was, in fact, leading up to the general subject of inventions. There is something I would like to show you, up in my attic lab."

"Lab? You have a laboratory?"

"Yes."

"But about Juliet—"

"It all ties in," I said, rising. "Follow me."

I led the way to the attic. As had Fizzo Fitzwilliam, in the doorway he gaped in astonishment.

"Gully, are you an inventor?"

"Yes. But I keep it a secret, because the attic inventor is considered a nut—until he hits. Then he's a hero."

"But by now, isn't the individual inventor about out of the picture? Corporations have big laboratories—"

"The day of the individual inventor is *not* over, Bunny! And it never will be. Do you know what I do when I'm stumped? I study these."

And so saying, I pointed to the wall, hung with framed copies of historic patents—Danny Kaye's nose tickler, Hedy Lamarr's secret communication system, Lillian Russell's trunk, Cornelius Vanderbilt Junior's shoeshine kit, Houdini's diver's suit, Lin Yutang's typewriter, and finally, in its central place of honor, Abraham Lincoln's manner of buoying vessels. I then launched into the story of Pug Pendlebury and demonstrated the resulting automatic bed. We had come to the red light when I stopped, struck by a profound thought.

"It's funny, Bunny, how all the little experiences of one's past suddenly can fuse into a great new idea. For instance, take my cousin Georgette's appendicitis. At the hospital, I naturally experimented with the electric beds. And all that experience was stored up in the old brain cells." Significantly I tapped my head. "And then, when Pug was fired, why—bang! That's all there is to genius: the unrelated experiences and then the flash."

"I suppose so."

"All right. Now, press this button."

Gingerly he did so. The bed lowered.

"Now turn the hands through twelve hours."

With some fumbling, he did so.

"Now put Pug to bed."

"Oh *damn* it, Gully!"

"Go ahead."

Finally he did so.

"Now turn the hands to ten of seven."

Resignedly he did so. The red light came on.

"Now—what's the red light?"

"Coffee."

"Right! So turn the hands."

He did so. As the bed started to rise, I bent the doll's arms and legs as one would naturally do, and made it end up on its feet.

"It leaves a better impression if you do," I said.

"If *I* do? Say, what—?"

"I'm coming to that."

"Gully!" he exploded. "Are you trying to make a bed demonstrator out of me?"

Unwittingly, he had hit it on the nose. Fixing him with a look, I indicated a stool. He seated himself and eyed me warily.

"Bunny, I can hire a patent attorney to patent this bed, I can engage a patent broker to offer it to his client-manufacturers, or I can contact manufacturers myself. Being busy with other ideas, I don't like to spend time on the business end, and, in any event, one likes to do business with friends rather than strangers. So I thought of your father."

"My *father*—!" His face whitened. He gargled and flapped his arms. "I hardly think—"

"All you have to do is place this box on your father's desk, tell him the story of Pug Pendlebury, and press the button. Then you ask him how many hotel rooms there are in New York City alone. This is the plan, Bunny. I'm working on our date for tonight. Also, I'll have to find some pretext for getting off work."

"Well, I certainly—"

I waved my hand depreciatingly. There was nothing to be gained by telling him I had to go to Hillcrest anyway.

"So I thought you could take this box and breeze off to Springfield. Show it to your father, get his reaction, and then phone me at the office—by noon at the latest. If he wants to talk it over, I'll drive right there. And afterwards, we'll head for Kittery."

His Adam's apple worked overtime.

"But Gully! You don't know all the trouble we have with inventors. We have a research and development department; they work on furniture ideas all the time—and they resent outsiders. The rule is, ideas go through our R & D experts first. That takes months. And, frankly, outside ideas don't stand a chance."

I smiled.

"But this one does," I said firmly. "And it isn't going to take months. Because right now, this morning, you're going to carry it in and set it down on your father's desk and demonstrate it."

He squirmed.

"You wouldn't consider my putting it through R & D in the regular way?"

I shook my head.

"Bunny, I've learned to go right to the top. Sidestep the underlings. Go right to the head man."

"But what if he says no? Then you won't—"

"Bunny!" I said, shocked. "We're pals. I'm doing all I can for you, and you're doing all you can for me—that's all. We're doing all we can for each other."

"Oh," he said, relieved. "Well, when you put it that way—" He turned to the bed and eyed it in silence. "Well—" he said again.

"So that's it," I said, jumping up. I started down with the box. At the second floor, remembering, I stopped. "Another thing," I said.

"What?"

I entered my bedroom and took a book from the shelf.

"This is what. After you arrive in Springfield, you may have to wait, so I want you to start reading this novel. Later, whenever you have time, finish it. Then we'll talk about it. It's going to help you more than you realize with Juliet Lawrence."

Gingerly he took it.

"Believe me, Bunny, this is an essential part of my plan. I want you to read it at every opportunity."

"All right," he said resignedly.

He followed me down and out to his car.

"Drive straight home," I instructed. "Pack some things for overnight, and head for Springfield. See your father, then phone me by twelve. Afterwards, we'll stay over at a motel in Hillcrest."

"You think we'll really have the date?"

"Yes, Bunny. Just look at it like this. While you're selling my bed to your father, I'll be on the phone selling you to Juliet Lawrence."

I watched him out of sight, elated by my feat of salesmanship. I had properly motivated this son of a manufacturer to barge bravely in with my bed and sell it to his father. Keyed up as Bunny was, he could not fail. I wrote a note to my aunt, explaining my absence. I then threw a few necessaries into the overnight bag and drove to the office, so that if Bunny reported that his father was interested and wanted to see me, I could take off for Springfield in a hurry.

I did not, as Bunny was assuming I would, phone Kittery. For one thing, my best chance of catching Juliet at Gamma Delta House would be at lunch, just after twelve. And I did not intend to call, anyway, until Bunny reported as to his success with his father. It was just twelve when he called.

"My father isn't here, Gully. He drove down to New York yesterday, but he's expected back in half an hour."

Chagrined, I considered. Unwittingly, Bunny had out-maneuvered me. No longer could I wait to hear from him before calling Juliet. And once assured of the date, he would be even less enthusiastic about tackling his father. Still, he had done all he could.

"Where is the box?" I asked.

"I haven't taken it out of the car."

"Put it on his desk, Bunny, and wait there, so he doesn't get tied up with anything else."

"I will. I started to read your book."

"Good. Keep at it."

"Any news on Juliet Lawrence?"

"I'm working on that, and it looks good." This was, of course, an exaggeration. "Can you phone me again at twelve forty-five?"

"All right."

CHAPTER TWENTY EIGHT
A PRINCESS OF MARS

In the lobby, I station to stationed Gamma House. A bird-brained girl answered, I identified myself and asked for Juliet, and then sat back for the audible period of confusion at the other end.

"Hello, Gulliver!" at last came Juliet's pleasant and exciting voice. "What a surprise! Don't tell me you've changed your mind about my birthday dinner?"

I launched into the subject of the Tilton and Bunny, and it became clear at once that my original assumption was correct: he had made no impression whatever.

"You don't remember a tall, slim—"

"Gully, I was rushing around, so—were we introduced?"

"No. It never got that far. He isn't exactly the speedy type. In fact, he's as shy as they come. He only looked at you, and, according to his statement, you looked at him. Your eyes met."

"Our eyes met?"

"So he claims. But that was enough. He saw me talking to you afterwards, and by the time I got home, there he was waiting, begging to meet you."

"How exciting!"

My ears pricked up at the subtle change in her tone. She might very well be agreeable to my first thought—dropping in at her dinner with Bunny in tow. But then in a flash, I saw the decisive objection: of all the situations in which this pal would appear at his ultimate worst, surrounded by a gaggle of girls at a sorority dinner would be tops.

"As it happens," I said, I have to drive to Hillcrest on company business. I was hoping to bring Bunny along, and stop by. The trouble is, we couldn't make it before eight."

"Tonight?"

"Yes."

"Oh,Gully! I have a date."

"With Jim Williams?"

"No, my nosey friend. With Pete McGlue."

With an odd thrill, it struck me that this was just like old times! For thus, on many an occasion during undergraduate days, had I gone to bat over the phone for a pal. And so thinking, the old power and the old patter returned.

"Still on the spite kick?" I asked.

"Oh, *Gully!* I told you about that. But...what did you say your friend looked like?"

"Tall, for one thing."

"—and dark and handsome?"

"Well dressed, anyway," I said loyally. "Thin. A little floppy, and—let's face it—considerably on the shy side."

"You'll never be *my* agent!"

"There is, however, a lot on the plus side. I'm leading up to that, if you'll only—"

"How old?"

"Around twenty-six. As I say, we went through Hackamore together, except that he switched from engineering to business administration."

I then sat back. My throwing in this last had been a happy inspiration, for I have found that girls in general, and the Juliet Lawrence type in particular, incline toward men who switch from engineering to business administration. Or to anything else, for that matter. That my instincts had been sound was now indicated by a second subtle change in her tone.

"What is he like?"

"A jerk," I replied flatly, still carefully playing my cards from the bottom.

"Oh, *Gully*—!"

"But somehow I think you would like him, just the same. And since you've taught Jim Williams his lesson, breaking your date with Pete McGlue for an out-of-state neutral might be an easy ease-out."

She gave a short laugh.

"You don't know Pete McGlue."

This was not entirely true. We had met. Also, I had Jo's description of him on the football field, pressing the ball to his bosom in a there-there, don't-you-worry manner and heading in bulldozerish fashion for his opponents' zero-yard line, leaving dismay and destruction along the way. But this was no time for second thoughts. It was time to play my high cards.

"Juliet," I asked slowly and distinctly, "does Pete McGlue drive a new white Thunderbird?"

"No...you mean your friend does?"

"Yes. In fact, I was looking forward to pulling up there in his car, rather than mine."

"He sounds rather well-to-do," said a thoughtful Juliet.

"He *is*—and getting more so by the minute."

There was a spell of deliberating at the other end.

"Gully, why couldn't we arrange something for later?"

"We *could* arrange something for later," I replied, "—for any time you say. The only thing I'm afraid of is that in the meantime some other girl will latch onto him. It isn't every day in the year, Juliet, that you find the only son of a millionaire walking around loose and falling for you like a ton of bricks."

Two gasps and one gurgle, in that order, came from the Kittery end, and I realized with some satisfaction that I had timed my revelation well.

"Did I hear you correctly, Gulliver? Did I hear you say 'only son of a millionaire'?"

"My very words. Tell me, are you quite sure you don't even faintly remember the look he gave you at the Tilton, and the look you gave him in return?"

"I'm beginning to remember."

"When you see him again, it will all come back."

"Our eyes met—?"

"That's the stuff, Juliet!"

"What time will you be here?" she asked, in the tone of a sorority president who, accustomed to making decisions, had just made one.

"Well, not before eight. Is that all right?"

"Yes, Gully."

"We could drive down to Zaza's. Would you like that?"

"Of course."

I now mentioned that I had not yet asked Jo.

"I'll ask her to come over. We'll be ready."

It was twelve forty-five on the dot when Bunny phoned. With a chilly premonition of trouble, I again noted the lack of enthusiasm in his voice.

"My father didn't come in, after all. He phoned. He won't be back until tomorrow morning."

My heart sank. Just what I had feared. Now, Bunny would have his date before he saw his father, and so, when he did, would be less motivated in my behalf.

"Gully, I was thinking. How would it be if I took this in to the R and D boys, after all?"

"Wait." I asked for and jotted down his number. "Stay there, Bunny. I have good news. I'll call you right back."

In the lobby, I called station to station; he answered at once.

"Listen, Bunny. We'll stick to our plan. Is the box on his desk?"

"Yes," he said fearfully.

"Then leave it there. Tomorrow morning, early, you can drive back from Hillcrest and see him. Will you do that?"

"From Hillcrest? You mean—?"

"I mean," I said warmly, "that you and I have a double date with Juliet Lawrence and Jo for tonight. It's all set."

"Gosh! You did it! Did she remember me?"

"Of course!" I said, stretching the truth a bit in the interest of building up his self confidence. "And she wants to meet you."

"Gosh!"

It was time to get down to basics.

"How far are you on *A Princess of Mars?*" I asked.

"About fifty pages, I guess. But Gully—all those green men, fifteen feet tall, and those thoats and zitadars—!"

"Take them in your stride. Concentrate on the part where John Carter meets Dejah Thoris. Have you come to her, yet?"

"The captive?"

"The captive, yes! Good Lord, Bunny!" I exploded. "She's the Princess of Helium, the daughter of Mors Kajak of Helium, the granddaughter of the Jeddak of Helium!"

"Oh."

"Just concentrate on John Carter and Dejah Thoris. I'll explain how it all ties in."

"All right."

"And now, listen carefully, Bunny. To get off, I drummed up a little business for tomorrow morning in Hillcrest, so we'll have to take both cars to there." I gave him the motel name. "Go on and wait for me there. You should be able to finish *A Princess of Mars* by the time I arrive, which should be by seven."

"O. K. I'll try...Gosh! She remembered me!"

Upstairs, I loaded the Hillcrest documents into my briefcase and officially checked out. A minute later, I sprang into the cockpit and headed west.

The afternoon was sunny and clear, the foliage a blaze of yellow and orange and red. There was an invigorating nip in the air, and my mount, its tank newly brimming with economy grade, was giving out its usual eager small roar. As we topped a rise, I was afforded a tremendous view of the valley and mountains beyond, and my own spirits rose in response, filling me with the conviction that, bucked up by the magic of John Carter, old Bunny not only would become a new Bunny tonight, but on the morrow could not fail with his father.

In my mind's eye, I placed Bunny Wood and Juliet Lawrence together. Their dress and tastes were compatible. And Bunny was shy, while Juliet was warm, competent and decisive: the case of opposite poles which, if properly brought into proximity, should spark. But against this was Bunny's consistent record of one date, then a "no." What was needed was a different bringing together than in the past, and, pondering ways and means, I found myself eyeing the supersecret device I had employed in the case of Hackamore pal Chester Dunne and a rather independent sorority date of mine named Wilma Norton. With old Bunny's desperate record, the device, though dangerous, warranted serious consideration.

The silent asphalt of Massachusetts had long been replaced by the monotonous bump of New York's concrete, when, summing it all up, I thought I had my plans for Bunny as well in hand as they ever would be. The only unsolved problem was how to keep up his enthusiasm—if enthusiasm was the word—for tackling his father in the morning. Somewhere, an unexpected situation might provide the answer. In the dusk, I at last turned off the throughway and headed north. I turned in at the motel and parked beside the white Thunderbird. My engine's loud sound being as good as a knock at the door, I was not surprised when a wild haired and rumpled Bunny Wood strode out.

"The atmosphere plant!" he cried. "Did they get the pumps going in time?"

"It's in the next volume, Bunny." Inside, I opened my bag. "Tell me, do you remember all that happened in the throne room of Zodanga?"

"The fighting? Sure!"

"—how Sab Than was killed by the Tharks, freeing Dejah Thoris from her promise?"

"Yes, yes!"

"And now, John Carter and Dejah Thoris are alone in the throne room. Who places whose arms on whose shoulders?"

He eyed me, puzzled.

"How was that, again?"

"Bunny," I said earnestly, "I am getting around to the subject of passes, where you, in the past, have not excelled. So get this. It was Dejah Thoris who placed her arms upon John Carter's shoulders. Do you remember that?"

"Yes," he said thoughtfully. "That's right."

"What I want to emphasize," I went on, "is that Dejah Thoris made the first move. The girl makes the decision—not you. You are the hero; you love her, you fight for her. But you don't make any flowery speeches. You have driven two hundred and thirty-five miles to see her; that speaks for itself."

Meanwhile, in asides, I had ordered him to comb his hair, then to stand at attention; and making here a practiced pull and there a twist or pat, I finally pronounced him presentable.

I opened the door. We got in the Thunderbird.

"Head for the center of Kittery," I directed. " We'll have to stop there, first."

"What for?"

"Today is Juliet Lawrence's birthday."

"Her *birthday*? Gosh!"

"So we should arrive bearing gifts."

"But what should I get her?" he asked in panic.

I gave out a reassuring chuckle.

"Bunny, I wonder if you realize how lucky you are."

"Lucky? How?"

"Why, to have me at your side, rather than someone else—someone considerably less experienced, if at all, in such matters."

"Oh," he said, with less enthusiasm than he might have expressed. "I suppose so...How about candy?"

I looked at him in disbelief and shook my head.

"Candy! For you? Certainly not!"

"No?"

"No. You want to give her something that will both please her now and continue to remind her of you long afterwards."

"Why not a box of candy?"

"Bunny, you just don't know! Have you ever presented a box of candy to a girl in a sorority house?"

"No," he said promptly.

"It is obvious that you have not. Now, follow me closely. You enter the lounge. In your hands is a fancy box with a blue ribbon."

"Why blue?"

"Pink, then," I conceded. "Anyway, you hand it to her. She takes it, utters appropriate sounds, and asks permission, which you at once grant, to open it. She offers it to you." I paused. "Do you follow me?"

Jaw down, he nodded. "I think so."

"All right. Now, get this. You are in the lounge of a sorority house—no privacy. Other girls are looking on, relaying secret signals to still others as far away as two floors above."

"Two floors?"

"Yes. The nearest ones edge closer. With a generous gesture, your girl holds out the box to the nearest." I raised my hands in horror. "And suddenly, Bunny, there is a rushing as of a mighty wind—"

"A mighty wind?"

"Figuratively speaking."

"Oh."

"There is a rushing as of a mighty wind. Suddenly there are a thousand clutching, grasping hands—and then there is only an empty box, rustling with crinkled papers."

"I see," said Bunny thoughtfully. "Flowers, then?"

I smiled tolerantly and shook my head.

"Later, Bunny. After you have properly met and are far apart again, then you send her flowers on any appropriate occasion. For example, roses, with a note attached: 'It has been a week since I saw you, and by now—' You probably will be able to fill in the rest. If not, phone me."

"But not now?" he asked.

"Not at this time, no."

"How about a bracelet?"

I shook my head hard.

"A wristwatch?"

"No, Bunny. Jewelry would be a bit presumptuous. After you are engaged, yes. But not now."

"What, then?"

I did not answer. We were driving down the main street of Kittery. I saw the store I was looking for and directed him to park in front of it.

CHAPTER TWENTY NINE
BUNNY BUYS A PRESENT

"Bunny," I said, when we were safely berthed at the curb, "I want to tell you a story."

"A story?" he asked petulantly. "How about the gift?"

I sat back.

"I am laying the groundwork for the gift. Do you remember Chet Dunne?"

"Oh, yes. A mechanical, wasn't he?"

"Yes. I introduced him to Wilma Norton, but he didn't go over. So he took counsel with me. Her birthday was coming up, and I advised him what to get her. And when he did, the battle was won."

"It *was?*" he said, sitting up and displaying interest. "What did he get her?"

We were parked in front of an exclusive women's shop. I pointed to the window. "A pair of those, Bunny. Black silk."

He turned in the direction of my finger, then quickly shied away. "What—!" His jaw dropped to a new low. "I won't do it!" he cried desperately, turning as if to jump out of the car.

I laid a reassuring hand on his shoulder. "Consider this, Bunny, and consider it well. Three and a half months later, I was best man at their wedding."

Bunny's Adam's apple shot up and down. "I *could*n't!"

I considered. I did not know how much, if any, of *A Princess of Mars* by now remained in his overstressed mind, but it was worth a try.

"Bunny, think of John Carter. Would he have hesitated to give such a present to Dejah Thoris?"

"Well—"

"Bunny," I said quietly, "after they announced their engagement, I talked to Wilma privately. She confessed that, up to his birthday present, Chester to her had been just another jerk. But when she opened it, something shot through her, some new feeling. That gift broke the ice. It was the personal touch. And it will work for you, too." I opened my door. "So come along."

"Wait!" he cried. "We can't. It just came to me."

"Why not?"

"Because," he said triumphantly, "we don't know what size."

Snookered, I thought fast. "I'll phone Jo," I said.

"And have her tell Juliet Lawrence I want to know the size of—! Oh, no!"

"Jo won't have to ask."

"Why not?"

"Look." I pointed toward a girl half a block away. "See that girl? I've never seen her before, but I still can tell you this. Half the clothes she is wearing were borrowed from a pal."

"How can you tell?"

"Because, Bunny, the first thing girls do, they size each other up to see what they can borrow."

He eyed me in surprise, and then, as this universal truth sank in, shook his head in wonder. I got out. Fearfully he followed.

The adjacent drugstore, brightly lighted, was laid out in modern department store style. Halfway to the phone booths, he grabbed my arm and pointed excitedly to the counter we were passing.

"Look! Perfume! Something to remind her for a long time, you said."

"No, Bunny. A girl like that has very good taste, and you have no idea just what kind of perfume appeals to her. You might get her something which, every time she used it, would cause her to think badly of you. We can't risk that."

He pondered this, then nodded his head hopelessly. "I suppose you're right."

Both booths were occupied. Accordingly, I returned to the candy counter, where I selected a two-pound box containing many small pieces. The girl had turned to wrap and tie it with a red bow, per my instructions, when Bunny descended upon me.

"Gully!" he cried in a passionate whisper. "Why can't I buy her candy? Five pounds! Ten pounds! Anything but—"

"Bunny," I said firmly, "my present merely sets the scene, and then—pouf! Yours is a different matter entirely."

And accepting the attractive box and my change, I led him back to the booths, where, one now being empty, I soon was speaking with Jo.

"Remember Chet and Wilma?" I asked. "How you came up with the clincher? With a 'W'?"

A short silence followed. Glancing out, I saw Bunny eyeing the toothpaste and cosmetic displays in a desperate manner.

"A bit sudden," said Jo. "By then, they already knew each other fairly well."

"But the principle is the same, and old Bunny needs all the help he can get."

"Maybe so. Give it a try. But with a 'J,' not a 'W.'"

Rejoining Bunny, I held out the notebook sheet on which the vital figure was written. He shied away from it. Outside, as we neared the ladies' shop, he came to a mulish halt.

"Gully," he quavered, "I just can't. I've never been in such a place." He fumbled for his wallet and extracted a bill, which he thrust into my hand as if it were on fire. "You get them, will you? I'll wait in the car."

I considered. The main thing was to get them.

"O. K., Bunny." I handed him my box. "Hang onto this."

There is a party game of childhood in which one player orders another player to perform the most horrendous feat which that first player can think of. It then often happens, though I have forgotten just how, that the others cry *"Do it yourself!"* Which, incidentally, is the name of the game. At any rate, the hapless first player is then obliged to perform what he had ordered the other to do.

In the entrance, as my ears began to buzz in an overpowering manner, it occurred to me that this was precisely what had happened to me. I never was much on the Bard, but inside, the old lines came rushing back: that one about there being more things in heaven and earth than are dreamt of, and the part about secrets that would harrow up the soul, freeze the young blood, make the eyes start from their spheres and each particular hair stand on end. Sometime later, I became dimly aware of my own rigidly outstretched arm and of someone at the other end of it, who, with gentle words of encouragement, was attempting to extract my notebook sheet from between my hard-clamped fingers.

"Oh, yes," said this party.

She now gradually came into focus, and I made her out to be a kindly and psychic saleslady of middle years. Paper in hand, she chose a number of boxes from a shelf, and began to open them on the counter.

"Black," I croaked. "Silk. Very best. Present."

"Of course," she said soothingly.

"Do you have one with a 'J'?" I managed.

"No...I'm afraid we haven't, not here in stock. But we could get them for you."

"They have to be for tonight."

"Oh, I see. Well, we have one with a heart which is very distinctive."

She brought it out, and it was. I nodded hard. A period of gift-wrapping ensued, following which I reeled out into the reviving air with a thin, twelve-inch-square box with ribbon and bow, which I exhibited to Bunny while returning his change. He gave the box a petrified look, gulped and started the car.

That word petrified well enough keynotes what followed. Uttering no sound, and following my directions like a mechanical man, Bunny piloted the Thunderbird onto Sorority Row, a softly but gayly floodlighted avenue at this time of the evening. At the most impressive house of all—though this, I am sure, was lost upon Bunny—we at my direction came to a halt. I then, from long experience, sat back. I noted the steering wheel. Sure enough, he was gripping it hard. With appropriate gestures, I went into my routine.

"Now, Bunny, this is—?"

His jaw dropped and he leaned forward, concentrating.

"Miss Juliet Lawrence," he said, with a slight nod.

"Good. And your name?"

Mouth open, he eyed me blankly.

"Think of the phone ringing," I encouraged. "You pick up the receiver—"

"Oh. Mr. Wood speaking."

"Fine. And now, your first name."

"Bunny."

"Not right away."

"Bunnington. Bunnington Berkeley Wood."

"Yes, but save the middle name for later," I counseled. "Sometime when you can't think of anything else to say, ask Juliet what her middle name is. There's always a story behind that. Then, probably, she'll ask what your middle name is. You can kill half an hour, just with that."

Glassy-eyed, he nodded. Again I noted the steering wheel. Only one hand was gripping it—we were coming along.

"All right. Now, Georgette is ready to get into the back seat. What do you do?"

As if hypnotized, he got out and opened the rear door on his side. I got out, too, elated.

"Fine," I said. "but she probably will be on *this* side."

He came around and started to open the door, then straightened up with a stubborn air.

"Oh, *damn* it, Gully!"

I thrust his box into his hand and, ordering him to attention, gave him a final check. Then I locked my arm in his and we started up the walk.

Jo opened the door. She was wearing a tan sweater and skirt affair, quite chic but quite simple, and doubtless with the design of not competing with Juliet Lawrence in any way. No one was in the lounge, but as Jo led us to a divan near the fireplace, I noted that a group of girls was gathered in the smaller room across the entrance hall. Jo called to one of these to ask Juliet to come down, and the girl bolted up the stair.

"Is this your first time in Kittery?" asked Jo, promptly going to work on Bunny, who sat down in a frozen manner, holding his parcel on his lap with both hands.

"Kittery?" he stammered. "Yes. First time. Yes."

"Do you live in Boston?"

"Boston? Yes," he answered, after some slow motion pondering, and doubtless wishing he were there now.

I eyed Jo gratefully as, with a series of simple but well chosen questions she got Bunny to say "Yes" twice, then a "No," and "I guess so," and at length the admission—accompanied by his first arm-wave of the evening—that his Aunt Hattie harboured a Pekingese. At this point, I tardily thought to case the vicinity for table lamps and the like, and, quickly doing so, silently pronounced the area safe. My keen ear now detected the falling of a hush upon the group in the adjacent room, and, turning my head, I saw that the big event was at hand.

Juliet Lawrence was approaching. She wore a dark velvet gown, touched off by some stage jewelry at the neck and ears, and was, in short, devastating.

Alacritously I arose.

"Hello, Gulliver!" she greeted me.

Behind, meanwhile, Bunny struggled to his feet. Quickly I performed the introductions. As Bunny's hand grasped hers, his face turned the color of the heart inside the gift box—which he appeared to be trying to conceal by holding it edgewise behind his forearm. Which would have been a neat trick if he could have done it, which he could not. Instead, he dropped it, retrieved it and straightened up, redder then before.

"So we meet again," Juliet said warmly, calmly ignoring all the slapstick.

"Yes. Again. Yes!" said Bunny, rising to new heights of oratory.

Juliet, indicating that we should be seated, began smoothly to touch upon the salient points of the Tilton dinner. But the supreme effort of his three words had left Bunny pale and spent, and after a few glassy-eyed nods he began to sink back with the seizure of rigor mortis and multiple lockjaw which I had learned to expect at this point. Accordingly, I arose and held out my box.

"Happy birthday, Juliet!"

"Oh, Gulliver! Thank you so much."

At my invitation, she opened it, she and Jo emitting standard girlish squeals of delight over its contents. We all had one. A moment later, she called to a passing girl and extended the box. A few seconds after that, as I so accurately had predicted, the air was filled with reaching hands and soon the gutted box lay forgotten on the table.

All of this, of course, was accompanied by a necessarily swift series of introductions which at least got Bunny onto his feet again, but which also left him dazed. The other girls, gnawing away, promptly vanished again, and I turned to Bunny with a *You see?* in my eyes, but he only stared back glassily, until, misinterpreting my look, he with a supreme effort picked up his own box and lunged forward holding it out.

"For you," he managed.

"Oh, you dear!" said Juliet, taking it. "Thank you so much. Shall I open it?"

"Gah!" said a terrified Bunny.

"I'll tell you what," I broke in, suddenly also on the terrified side. "How about bringing it along? We were thinking of taking a breeze down to Zaza's, if you'd like to, and you could open it there."

"I'd *love* it," breathed Juliet, turning in question to Jo, who nodded eagerly.

CHAPTER THIRTY
ALL BLURRY-LIKE AND PERFUME

Zaza's, strategically located near a throughway exit, was not a college hangout, being both too expensive and too far away. It was "class," so far as Kittery dates were concerned, which was why I had suggested it in the first place. Its trade being split more or less equally between youngsters and oldsters, the smartly uniformed two-guitar, piano and drum combo would start out with a slow standard number and wind up with a fast one. Having established ourselves in a booth, it developed that, while both Juliet and Jo had suppered recently and well, neither Bunny nor myself had eaten a serious meal since noon. Juliet's quiet suggestion solved this discrepancy: one great Pizza royale, involving mushrooms, mozzarella cheese and a lot more.

When Bunny returned with Juliet from their first dance, I guessed that it had not gone too badly, for he, though still glassy eyed, was able from time to time to add a non-sparkling but at least coherent response to the conversation. The big question, of course, was how he was going over with Juliet, and dancing the next number with her, I went to work.

"What do you think of Bunny?" I asked.

"The question," she smoothly parried, "is what do I think of *you*—calling me up and calmly changing my plans!"

"Fellows like Pete McGlue and Jim Williams are not for you," I retorted. "In mental maturity, the male runs five years behind the female."

"What is the number of this course?"

"The course is one based upon considerable first-hand observation and experience. To cite a recent example, last summer at this very spot I happened to bring together a pal of Jo's, aged seventeen, and one of mine, aged twenty-six. They now are happily married and living in Brazil, where he pulls in the *cruzeiros* at an amazing rate."

"I see. And you thought it time to produce the right man for me?"

"Juliet!" I protested. "I had nothing whatever to do with Bunny's seeing you at the Tilton dinner—I wasn't even there. And I didn't know *he* was there. This date is his idea. So I repeat: what do you think of Bunny?"

"Why do you call him Bunny?" she countered.

"Don't you like it?"

"No, I'm afraid I don't. There's too much of the rabbit in it, and he isn't, really."

By now, my ear had detected a definitely protective tone in her remarks, and I was heartened. For any girl evidencing the protective instinct toward a male has at least not rejected him.

"So let's try his middle name," I said.

"Berkeley?"

"He told you?"

"Yes. You see, he had asked me mine."

"What is it?"

"I haven't any."

I reflected upon how old Bunny, at that point, must have felt like the novice mountaineer who, trustingly reaching up for the piton placed there by his instructor, feels it come off in his hand. Still, he somehow had survived.

She sighed.

"He is a lamb, though."

"You mean, you like him?"

"Gully, while we were dancing, I let drop about the Drama Club dance, tomorrow night, and he simply let it lie."

"What dance is that?" I asked quickly, intuitively sensing that the answer to a problem was just around the corner.

"A scheduled dance. Not big. No dress. I was going to suggest inviting Jo and yourself, to make it a foursome, if you could stay over. But—" She shrugged. "—he simply ignored it."

"What you don't realize is that he was too paralyzed to answer you." I thought fast. "Look, Juliet. Tomorrow morning, Bunny has business in Springfield and I have business in Hillcrest. I don't know if I can manage to stay over, but I think I can; anyway, I should know by tomorrow noon. Would you be willing to have Bunny ask you for a tentative date for the dance, to be confirmed tomorrow noon?"

"All right," she said. Then, to my surprise, she gave a start, gripped my shoulder hard and almost missed a step. "Pete McGlue and Babs!" she exclaimed.

Casually I glanced around and made them out. Barbara Stuyvesant was small but chunky, and had a flattened and spread nose which made her appear pugnacious. Her hair was a Cleopatra type, jet black, and she was heavily rouged and lipsticked. Although she no doubt was consciously concealing from her escort her reputation for being utterly spoiled and accustomed to having her own way, it showed. She was gazing up devotedly at the gorilla, hanging upon his every word—although this was not much to hang onto, his conversation as usual appearing to consist of an occasional grunt.

Puzzled, I turned back to Juliet.

"I thought your Jim Williams was dating Babs."

"So he was."

"Well, when you broke your date with Pete, Pete must have cut out Jim Williams for Babs."

"Probably. But I don't like the look Pete gave me. He's a vengeful sort, and he seems to think the honor of Zeta House is at stake. And he's not as stupid as he looks, either. He's quite the schemer."

I wondered if there was any significance to Pete's bringing Babs here. If a man wanted to make a hit with a girl, he would, of course, bring her here. But on the other hand, Pete obviously did not have to take Babs anywhere at all to make a hit with her. If he had revenge in mind, he might have followed us here merely to get a good look at the man who had usurped him, or simply with the hope that, by tailing us, an appropriate idea might occur to him. Or his presence could be pure coincidence.

During the girls' nose powdering absence, I told Bunny how Juliet was hoping he would ask to take her to the Drama Club dance, tomorrow night. "—Jo and I might go, too."

"Gosh!"

I repressed a look of annoyance.

"Didn't you even hear her mention it?"

He sighed.

"I don't know. While we were dancing, everything seemed all blurry-like and perfume." He stared into space. "Gosh!" he said again.

"This date, tomorrow night," I said. "Juliet has made the first move, just like in the book. Now, it's your move. Would you like to take her?"

"Yes—" He stopped, terrified. "You mean, alone?"

I relaxed. My plan was certain of success.

"You'd want to, if it was the four of us?"

He nodded hard.

"Look, Bunny. Tomorrow morning, while I attend to my business in Hillcrest, you'll be showing my bed to your father—selling him the idea, right?"

"...Right."

"Then you'll phone me, and if he wants to talk business, I'll drive to Springfield. Then we'll breeze back and take Juliet and Jo to the dance."

Seeing Juliet and Jo returning, I quickly asked Bunny's permission to do the negotiating, and as soon as we had seated them, I started in. It went over big, Juliet nodding and smiling at Bunny while I spoke for both of us.

Jo now noted the approach of curfew time.

"Oh!" exclaimed Juliet. "I must open my present."

"Go ahead," said I.

"Gah!" said Bunny, slipping back into his terrified state.

As Juliet undid the wrappings, I must admit that I, too, fell apprehensively silent. She started to lift the cover. Then, seeing what was inside, she colored and quickly shut it again. Jo at once giggled, which, I suppose, set about the right note; for Juliet, though considerably warmed, shot a smile at Bunny.

"You darling!" she said. "Thank you very much."

Jo now suddenly looked up, and Juliet and I followed suit. Pete McGlue with Babs, had danced up unobserved, and was eyeing the box. Now, seeing our eyes upon him, he glided away.

On the way back, Juliet invited me to lunch at Gam House, tomorrow, where Jo would join us, and where Bunny would phone me from Springfield. On the outskirts of Kittery, the time growing critical, Bunny was instructed to drop off Jo and myself at her Trevithick Hall, rush Juliet on to Gam House, and then return for me.

The lights in front of Trevithick were dim as Jo and I alighted, and just after Bunny and Juliet took off, they gave a significant flicker. An odd phenomenon now occurred, a number of cars screeched up, almost at a dead heat, and couples tumbled out and raced for the dimly lit doorway. Other couples on foot were legging it toward the same objective. The lights now shone out brightly, and at this signal the girls poured in, while a few fellows who had been sitting inside in the lounge pushed out. From inside came the strains of *Goodnight, Sweetheart.* Jo and & having concluded the personal part of our parting in Bunny's back seat, I gave her hand a final clasp and she ran in.

It was not long before Bunny returned. I got in.

"There's no curfew for the boys," I explained, indicating the groups we were passing. "Jo tells me the theory is that if you can get the girls in, there's nothing left for the boys, so they go in, too. And it works."

"What works?"

"Why...Never mind. What did Juliet say?"

"Juliet?...Gosh!"

"What did she say?"

He sighed.

"Just things. She thanked me for the present again."

"So you see, Bunny—"

"And the lights came on and she had to run in."

"That's the way it is, here. The theory—"

"She's wonderful, isn't she?"

"Yes, Bunny."

There was no use talking to him. In the motel, when I snapped off the light, he was lying staring at the ceiling. I suppose all blurry-like and perfume about summed it up.

"Everything is in the box," I coached, Friday morning, as, after a hearty breakfast, I saw Bunny to his Thunderbird. "The doll, the mattress—just plug in the cord."

"I know."

"First the red light goes on. Don't forget what that means."

"Coffee. I know."

"And the special, catchy name—?"

"What name?"

"For the bed."

"Oh...'The Bachelor's Friend.'"

"That's it, Bunny! Good luck."

I stood watching until the white car carrying my hope for a better life passed out of sight. Then I went inside to prepare for my encounter with the Dean.

"She's a pusher," Jo had said. "—the punctual, get-to-the-point, no-nonsense type. Her next step will be college president, somewhere, and then on to Washington, D. C. Some day you'll see her signature on the southwest corner of the dollar bill." And considering her ruthless classroom exploitation of Professor Rowbottom, I did not doubt Jo's estimate in the least. As to her alleged punctuality, however, Jo proved to be wrong.

"I'm Mr. Gates," I announced to the keen old buzzard at the desk, having arrived at the Hillcrest Town Hall, a large old wooden structure topped by a bell tower, at a few minutes of ten. "I was to meet the chairwoman of the Town Committee."

"Oh, yes. She hasn't arrived." And so saying, he arose and ushered me into a musty conference room, where I proceeded to lay out the contents of my briefcase in an orderly manner. I then sat back to eye the large clock on the wall for fifteen uneventful minutes.

"She didn't phone?" I asked, at twenty-five after.

"No...Ah!"

And he pointed toward the street, where a smartly tweeded woman was alighting from a taxi.

CHAPTER THIRTY ONE
GULLY BETRAYS HIS OWN

As she approached at a brisk and businesslike gait, I took hard and calculating note of this town committee chairwoman who, unknown to herself, represented the end to my association with B, R & W. Her forehead was high, her blonde hair severely drawn back. Her nose was straight, long and thin, and her chin firm. Two nights past, I had seen from behind the Tilton column that she could be quite pretty when she chose, but right now I was looking at the tough chief of police for a thousand girls.

"Dean Van Eyck?" I queried.

She gave me a businesslike smile and nod.

"I suppose you are from Bell, et cetera?"

With a sinking sensation, I realized the significance of that light "et cetera": she had avoided saying "Rowbottom."

"Mr. Gates," I said.

Coolly she extended a hand.

"What time is it?" she asked, more to herself than to me, with a glance at the clock over the desk. "Oh, dear! I must apologize for my lateness."

"Not at all."

"My car was damaged, early this morning. I left it at Kittery Garage, but when I stopped by, it was not quite ready. You have brought the reports?"

"All laid out," I said, extending my arm toward the conference room, where, seating her, I invited her to choose at random one of the seven copies—this copy, upon her approval and initialling, to become B, R & W's copy of record.

She did so, and rapidly paged through it. "It seems thoroughgoing."

"Yes. But there are certain points, which, if you will permit me—"

"I am perfectly willing to accept your firm's competence in the working out of technical details," she said—the statement of an executive if ever I heard one. She now, to my surprise, yawned openly; then, catching herself, made out to stifle it. "Oh, dear! You must excuse me. I'm afraid I didn't get much of a night's sleep."

"Quite all right," I said, and asked if she had any questions. She did not. I accordingly reached for my ballpoint and asked her to initial the copy. When she had done so, I promptly shoved it into the manila envelope addressed to Rowbottom—over the safe return of which, you will recall, he had been so much more concerned than of myself. I then laid in front of her the receipt form.

"Here?" she asked, stifling another yawn.

"Yes, if you will, please."

When she had signed, I slid the form into the envelope.

"These are for me?" she asked, reaching for the six copies and starting to rise.

"Yes, but first I wanted to talk to you about the next step."

She looked at me in surprise.

"What next step?" she asked sharply.

"The next step, of course," I said, quickly launching into my sales pitch, "is the preparation of final plans and specifications. Naturally, my firm is anxious to do this work for Hillcrest, and there are several reasons why a considerable saving to the town will result if—"

By now, she had risen, a hard glint in her eyes and a hard set to her chin. "Thank you," she said evenly, "but since the Board is about evenly divided on the matter, I shall advise an indefinite wait. I appreciate your coming," she said, turning away.

No dice, about summed it up. She was halfway to the door when an inspiration hit me.

"Dean Van Eyck," I said amiably, "I was hoping that you would allow me to drive you back to your car."

She hesitated, doubtless swayed by the thought of her taxi wait.

"Thank you, but I don't feel—"

"No trouble at all."

She turned over her copies to the clerk for safekeeping, then accompanied me to my car.

As I started off with a silent and aloof Jewel Van Eyck beside me, I wracked my brain for a new approach. I had failed to sell the job because, I was sure, it would force Jewel into further association with Sampson Rowbottom. The logical thing, then, was to try to sell her on Rowbottom! I straightened my shoulders and shot her a glance.

"I have always felt fortunate," I remarked, in the largest lie of my career to date, "in being given the opportunity to work under such a remarkable man as Mr. Rowbottom. You may not be aware that he, in addition to being a partner in the firm of Bell, Rowbottom and Witherspoon, is also an associate professor of sanitary engineering at one of the highest rated universities in the United States. While an undergraduate, because of his outstanding scholarship, he was admitted to Tau Beta Pi. You may have noticed his gold key." With my right hand, I tapped significantly at a spot some inches north of my navel.

Whereupon Jewel made a choking sound, and I, guessing the cause, paused, for it set my own teeth on edge to recall the repellent way in which, by the device of persisting in wearing a vest even in the warmest weather, old Rowbottom always managed a prominent display of this emblem of superiority. He was a "key swinger." With an effort, I buckled down to my disagreeable task.

"While he was studying for his master's degree—which he received *cum laude*—he did valuable research on septic tanks and anaerobic decomposition, and for this he was honored by admission to Sigma Xi. Also—" Glancing to the right, I saw Jewel stifling still another yawn. "—also, he has written many technical and scientific papers on sewerage and has received a number of national honors and awards. You may not be aware that he is the author of two textbooks on the subject, *The Sewer* and *Some Aspects of Sewage*."

"I am aware of that," she said in a frigid manner. "I am quite aware that Mr. Rowbottom is a recognized authority on the subject of sewers."

"Oh," I said, and rang off, for the tone of her voice clearly indicated that, while conceding his professional excellence in that field, she personally regarded Sampson Denhardt Rowbottom as something that had crawled out of one.

Visitors' score still zero, we entered the outskirts of Kittery. She having already mentioned the name of her garage, I, without waiting for her directions, turned down the street that led to it.

"You appear familiar with Kittery," she observed.

"Why, yes—" Up to now, mindful of the part which Jo had played at the Tilton, I sedulously had avoided revealing that any relative of mine was enrolled at Kittery. But could this be my opening, after all? Could my admission lead to a hair-down, parent-to-teacher type discussion, and thence to a warmer relationship between Jewel and myself? "—my cousin, Georgette Gates, is a sophomore at Kittery."

To my amazement, her manner promptly underwent a change which sent my spirits soaring. Solicitously she turned toward me.

"Then you haven't heard?"

"Haven't heard what?" I asked, wondering what, in the few hours since I had deposited her at Trevithick Hall, could possibly have happened to Jo.

"I am sorry to inform you, Mr. Gates, that your cousin has been hospitalized with an attack of appendicitis."

"What!"

I was dumfounded. At the time of our recent parting, and, in fact, throughout the entire evening, Jo had appeared particularly sound and fit.

Jewel nodded sympathetically. "I'm sorry," she said.

"When did it happen?"

"Early this morning."

"Oh," I said. My ears, meanwhile, dwelt curiously upon this recurrent use by Jewel of the expression "early this morning." Her car, you may recall, had been damaged "early this morning." Then, remembering, I laughed unbelievingly, for only yesterday morning I had been explaining to Bunny Wood how the little experiences of one's past could suddenly interlock to form some great new idea—in this case, my automatic bed—and one of those experiences had been Jo's appendectomy. "That's impossible! Why, Jo had her appendix out when she was fourteen."

"Are you sure?"

"Of course. I brought her flowers. She even—" I stopped. At the time, Jo had wanted to show me the scar, but I firmly had restrained her and had followed up with a short lecture on the proprieties. "—I brought her flowers," I amended.

"I see."

By now, Jewel's manner had undergone still another change, and one entirely in the opposite direction: her tone was metallic and ominous. A chill shot up my spine. There was, without a doubt, some monkey business afoot. Jo was in the middle of it, and I unwittingly had given her away!

"It probably is something else," I said hastily, "like that time back in Cambridge when my cousin Marjorie Miller had her tonsils out, and they grew back in."

"I hardly think—"

"Or Asian flu. That's been going around a lot, I understand. Hits you just like that."

"Dr. Washburn definitely diagnosed an attack of appendicitis and recommended a period of observation—" Abruptly, with a clicking of teeth and a faint hissing sound, she cut off. "Mr. Gates," she said stiffly, "I wonder if you would be so kind as to drive me to the infirmary, rather than to the garage."

"Glad to," I said hollowly, and wheeled about.

Somehow, I had betrayed my own.

With Jewel apparently as immersed in her own somber private thoughts as was I in mine, we drove to the infirmary, where, with short thanks, she got out and strode purposefully inside, leaving me to sit behind in the car at the curb with visions of her imminent reappearance leading young Jo by the ear.

Apprehensively I eyed the glass entrance doors and unrevealing windows of the new two story brick structure—the result of a former drive such as the one now winding up. Somewhere inside was Jo, doubtless being given what-for by Dean Van Eyck. Why she had wanted to be there, I could not fathom, but how she successfully had faked appendicitis, I could: Juliet had prevailed upon admirer Washburn to aid in the deception. If so, the affair also involved Juliet.

With a start, I looked hard at a figure up the street. It was Pete McGlue, standing in conversation with another fellow—who now took off, leaving Pete alone. I saw him take a long look at the infirmary. Then another fellow came up to him, and their conversation appeared more than casual. Was there some connection between Pete's presence outside and Jo's inside? This second fellow took off, and Pete McGlue again stood there alone and purposeful. I saw him eye the infirmary entrance again, and I did not like it a bit. Ten minutes later, Jo emerged—not, as I had expected, with Dean Van Eyck, but alone.

Perceiving the VW with myself inside, she stalked toward it with arms akimbo and the usual love-light lacking in her eyes. She flounced in and slammed the door.

"You," she hissed, "have queered everything!"

She was steaming, and there is no telling what havoc might have followed, had not, at the very instant of her slamming the door, a familiar black limousine pulled up to the curb ahead. Meanwhile, I automatically had started the engine, but as I came down on the clutch, Jo flung up her hand.

"Wait! Let's see what happens."

"All right," I said, anxious to please.

She sat back.

"The Dean—" I started.

"Quiet!" she hissed.

The uniformed chauffeur was getting out. Jo leaned forward, tensely watching. The man walked around and opened the rear door, from where tall old Austen Stuyvesant emerged and strode toward the infirmary entrance. The chauffeur followed, darting ahead to pull open the door. The two disappeared inside.

"Babs' father," said Jo, in awe.

"Would you mind telling me—"

"Pete McGlue!" she exclaimed, now making him out.

"He's been standing there," I informed, "for the last ten minutes."

"He has?"

"Yes."

From Jo came a descending whistle.

"The question now is whether Pete will get a chance to talk to Babs. If he does, we're sunk."

"Barbara Stuyvesant is in there?"

"Yes."

"Would you mind—"

"So what we do is wait and see. Oh, Gully!" she cried. "Why did you have to tell the Dean I'd had my appendix out?"

"I'm sorry. At our meeting, she told me her car had been damaged, so to try to make a hit, I offered to drive her to the garage, and on the way, I happened to mention that I had a cousin enrolled here. Then she told me how you were in the infirmary with appendicitis. So naturally, I said that it was impossible because you'd had it out at fourteen. I could hardly forget that! I'll always remember how you wanted—"

"Ha! Well, just now somebody else had a look at the scar, and guess who?"

"Who?"

"The Dean. She called in the doctor and insisted."

"Dr. Washburn?"

"Yes. He'd do anything for Juliet, so she asked him to diagnose appendicitis for me. Now, he's due to lose his job and his license, and I'm to report to the Dean after lunch, likely for suspension."

I shook my head, puzzled.

"I'm sorry, Jo, but I still do not grasp the scheme of things entire."

She sighed.

"Gully, last night we had a panty raid."

"What!"

CHAPTER THIRTY TWO
PETE McGLUE'S REVENGE

Jo nodded, then yawned.

I stared at this yawn, one much like those of the Dean's, which, at the time, had surprised me.

"A, er—, raid, did you say?"

"Yes, if you prefer it—a raid."

I sat back. This explained Dean Van Eyck's out-of-character yawns at our conference; also, probably, the way her car had come to be damaged "early this morning." For the coeducational institution's first reaction to such uprisings is a riot call to its campus security police and to the faculty. But I still found it hard to believe, for at the late hour when Bunny and myself, motel-bound, had last cruised through the campus streets, all had been peaceful and quiet.

"When did it start?"

"Around two o'clock."

"Was it big?"

"Big, it was! Eventually, the whole school turned out."

I shook my head incredulously. Five miles away in Hillcrest, Bunny and myself had slept soundly through the whole thing. Suddenly, a horrible thought struck me and I shot straight up.

"Jo!"

"What?"

"What about Bunny's present? Is it—are they—all right? I mean, during the excitement, she didn't, by any chance—?"

Jo sighed.

"You are warm, very warm," she said, maddeningly adopting the jargon of another of those childhood games.

"Jo! What do you mean?"

"I mean, they're not all right."

"*Not* all right?"

"No. Pete McGlue stole them."

I gave her the most incredulous look of my career to date.

"*Jo*—! Did you say that Pete McGlue—?"

She yawned.

"—stole them. Yes."

It was to an open mouthed, all ears audience of one that Jo, meanwhile keeping an eye upon purposefully loitering Pete McGlue, related an incredible tale.

"Last night at Zaza's, do you remember how Pete danced up with Babs just as Juliet opened the box?"

"Yes. But I doubt that he really saw what—"

"He danced away with a mighty good idea of what was in that box."

"How do you know?"

"Because Zeta Nu House got the raid going. When the Alphas heard and started out, they found the whole Zeta gang already making the rounds of the dormitories. There's no doubt that Pete McGlue had it started for a cover-up."

"A cover-up?"

"Yes. While Juliet was downstairs, a Zeta climbed the porch, got into her room, found the box and tossed it down to Pete."

"What!"

"Yes. But by then, the Alphas had begun to arrive. You see, they're supposed to stand guard when anything is up. They spotted Pete, and about ten of them took after him. I guess it was quite a chase, although all I saw was the end of it. Babs' dormitory, Proxmire Hall, is right across from mine. A crowd of boys was all around below, cheering and singing and shouting 'We want silk!' and all that, and the girls were at the windows, all excited and tossing the stuff out mighty enthusiastically, by then. So Pete came running past and looked up and saw Babs Stuyvesant at her window—she, of course," Jo noted snippishly, "has a room to herself."

"I suppose so. But go on."

Jo shrugged.

"As you probably saw for yourself at Zaza's, Babs has it bad for Pete and would do anything at all for him. So he called to her to guard the box with her life, and she said she would. Then he threw it up, and Babs caught it."

I shot her a keen look.

"So Babs has it?"

"That's the question."

I was at the point of asking just what she meant by this, when my attention was diverted by the sight of egg-shaped Chancellor Fogwell trotting diagonally across the grass toward the doors of the infirmary.

"Just what—" I started, as he purposefully disappeared inside.

When Babs, leaning out her window, caught the box—Jo continued—she caught a corner of it in the eye. So later, hysterical with excitement and with a slightly black eye, she was taken to the infirmary.

"Rather special handling," I observed.

"Not when the college is looking for a large donation from her doting father."

"He didn't come across at the Tilton dinner?"

"I don't think so. He, too, gets special handling."

"Oh."

Following Babs' exit—Jo went on—the quick thinking Alphas had by secret means obtained a key and ransacked her room for the box, but had come out empty handed. Then Jo had had her idea of faking appendicitis, and with the help of Juliet and loyal Dr. Washburn had done so, the latter seeing to it that she was bedded down next to Babs, where Jo, by keeping her eyes and ears open, had hoped to glean some hint of the box's whereabouts.

And this desperate and well executed scheme, I singlehandedly had spiked.

Jo, who probably had had no sleep at all, gave another yawn.

"Pete McGlue's gang had the idea of searching Babs' room, too. They got in right after the Alphas left."

"They didn't find the box, either?"

"No."

"How do you know?"

Jo started to answer, then froze.

A distinguished group was filing from the infirmary: Babs, her father, Fogwell, my late passenger Jewel, and the chauffeur. The five entered the limousine and drove off.

"They're probably lunching with the Chancellor," said Jo wearily. "And you, I believe, are lunching with us—look!" she broke off.

Pete McGlue had turned and was rapidly walking away.

"Now his chance at Babs is gone," I said.

"For the present, anyway."

I tried to think.

"Jo, how do you know for sure the Zetas don't already have the—the Items?"

She turned and pointed.

"See that flagpole?"

I turned. In a lawn down the street, I made out a tall but bare flagpole.

"Yes, I see it. But no flag."

"No. That's the Zeta flagpole. It's all ready. If the Zetas had them, they'd be flying."

"What?"

Jo nodded.

"That is Pete McGlue's whole idea." She said quietly. "—to fly Juliet's Items from that flagpole. That will be the Zeta's revenge."

It was a badly shaken Gulliver Gates—one much more so than Jo, lacking the vital facts which I so far had found no time to impart, could realize—who drove her toward Gam House and lunch. As is her practice in such moments of unresolved danger, she had drawn up her knees, and, hands tightly clasped around them, sat with her head bent forward in an attitude of intense concentration. To have ventured to intrude upon her thoughts would have elicited only an impatient exclamation, and so I silently strove to think of some way to redeem myself for my blunder—some way to cause Jo and also Washburn to escape punishment in the matter of her fake appendicitis. The time was short: her appointment with Dean Van Eyck, as she had said, was for right after lunch; but I could come up with nothing.

But that was not the half of it: I now had a problem of my own which, though stemming from the same source, put theirs in the minor leagues. For unknown to her, Jo's final information had revealed a danger to myself of a far greater magnitude: if Pete McGlue got his hands on those Items and flew them as planned, the attendant notoriety would mean not only dishonor to Gam House but disaster to the Gates Automatic Bed as well! For when Bunny Wood learned of it, as he doubtless would tonight, he would be so mortified that he probably never again could face Juliet. And except for the unlikely event of old Thomas Wood entering into a binding contract with me this very afternoon, before Bunny heard, he would have no further incentive to push the bed deal with his father. And failure there, with all hope of saving my job at B, R & W already dashed by Dean Van Eyck, would bring on the final disaster of disfranchisement.

As we pulled up at Gam House, several sleepy girls, spotting Jo and apparently knowing of her hospitalization, gathered around for questions. But she, firmly adhering to a policy of "no comment," pushed on inside, where she quickly briefed a non-smiling Juliet.

"I'm sorry I queered it," I said.

"You didn't know. Besides," Juliet noted wisely, "once Babs left,

Jo wouldn't have been able to learn anything."

"That's right," conceded Jo. "So it boils down to this: after the luncheon, Pete will make every effort to contact Babs, and when he does, we're sunk. We have to get those Items—"

"Those what?" asked Juliet.

"Gully calls them the Items."

"Oh."

"We have to get them," said Jo, "before that luncheon ends."

"Which still won't solve the problem of your suspension or of Dr. Washburn's job," I noted.

"We'll worry about that later," snapped Jo. "This won't wait."

Juliet gave me a worried look.

"Gully, Bunnington is so shy. What do you think he would do if he learned his present had been flown from a flagpole?"

"I don't think you'd ever see him again."

"That's what I think, too." Juliet shook her head. "Whatever possessed him to buy such a present?"

I looked at Jo. She eyed me noncommittally.

"I see," said Juliet. "Well, it's done."

"There is just one thing we have to do," I said, summing it up, as the gong sounded for lunch. "We have to find out where those Items are and get them back, quick."

"Yes," said Juliet. "But how?"

"And first," Jo added practically, "where?"

"Start thinking," I said.

And this, with a sober Juliet on one side and as sober a Jo on the other, and surrounded by some two dozen or so sleepy girls, I did all though that luncheon, but without result—until, over dessert, a stray vision of my Uncle Roscoe flitted across my mind.

"Tell me about Austen Stuyvesant," I said to Juliet, grasping at a straw.

"He started out as an engineer," she said, "and apparently did fairly well. Rather late in life, he married a rich woman. She bore him Babs and passed on. He dotes on Babs."

One of Uncle Roscoe's stories began to ring in my ears.

"He was an engineer?"

She nodded.

I calculated.

"He would have been an undergraduate during prohibition?"

Juliet and Jo considered.

"Probably," said Jo.

I sat back, almost sure I saw the answer.

I turned to Juliet.

"If," I said quietly, "you can produce the key to Babs' room, I am about ninety per cent certain that I can produce the Items."

"Gully!" cried she, grasping my arm.

"Gully!" cried Jo, grasping the other.

Poker faced, I turned to Jo. Her eyes registered first incredulity, then hope, then trust, and finally hero-worship; in her eyes the old love light again burned bright. There was an electric new feeling all around as we abruptly arose and excused ourselves. Juliet called a trusted girl from the table and sent her racing off to Alpha House. And I, after swift thought, directed Jo to telephone for a taxi for myself.

"A taxi? But Gully, it's only—"

"I am well aware of the distance. For reasons of my own, I want a taxi."

And under my firm gaze, Jo cut off and dashed to the phone. I went out to the car, opened the front hood and busied myself thereunder. I then took out my briefcase and donned my fedora. When Jo and Juliet came out, I noted that both were silently impressed, and I was encouraged, for it augured well for my plan. Soon, the breathless messenger dashed up with the key and handed it to me, together with the information of Babs' floor and room number.

"Gully," said Jo, "don't you know they won't let you above the first floor?"

"I am well aware of that, too," I said, as the taxi pulled up. I handed my VW key to her. "Drive to the Administration Building," I instructed, for it was there that she was due to report to Dean Van Eyck for trial & punishment. "I'll meet you there shortly."

"All right," she said, mystified.

I entered the taxi, and, to Jo and Juliet's fervent calls of good luck, drove off.

"Where to?"

"Proxmire Hall."

At this, the driver, a seedy little man of middle years, muttered under his breath, for it meant, as I well knew, a minimum fare. In a sulky manner, he drove the short distance to the imaginative brick & glass affair—for as might be expected, Babs Stuyvesant had drawn the choicest dorm. Following my well-laid plan, I had taken no notice of the man's obvious displeasure, and when he pulled up in front, I made no move to get out.

"Why," I asked innocently, "are we stopping here?"

"Because this is it," he said irritably.

"This is Proxmire Hall?"

"Yes, sir," he snapped.

"What!" I raised my hands in surprise. "Why, I was given to understand it was much farther. Had I known, I could just as well have walked."

He nodded in a highly aggrieved manner.

Suddenly I laughed.

"I see it now! My young cousin back there was having her little joke."

"Some joke," he said sourly.

"But to call you all the way out from town!" Soberly I shook my head. "Well, although the joke is on me, it certainly is not going to be on *you*. Here—perhaps this will make it right."

And so saying, I took from my wallet a large bill and held it out.

His face lit up.

"Why, thank you, sir!"

And with a half-somersault-with-twist, he was out of the cab, around to my door and opening it with a flourish. As I alighted, he raced up the steps to the entrance, wrenched open the door and stood beside it at attention. Fedora on head and briefcase in hand, I ascended the short flight in a deliberate and purposeful manner. At the doorway, to the cabbie's repeated thanks, I, with the air of one with weightier matters on his mind, returned a brief "Not at all," and he, with a final touch at his cap, carefully let the door close after me.

CHAPTER THIRTY THREE
OFFICER PINZIO

That my expenditure had been well advised was at once evident, for at the desk ahead, one girl, apparently in charge, and another to whom she had been talking, both stared open-mouthed at my approach. And I should note that, during the short taxi ride, I had not been idle: when the building hove into view, I had taken hard note of its machinery penthouse and in my mind's eye had projected lines vertically down to the main floor, where I had plotted their relation to the entrance. Accordingly, with a nod and preoccupied glance at the pair, I turned sharply toward where the elevators should be—and they were. One was open and waiting, and—as I had been almost certain it would be—automatic. I strode in, pressed the third floor button and was off.

At the third floor, I stepped out into the floor lounge where several bevies of girls, sprawled over the smart divans, looked around in mild surprise. Acting my role to the hilt, I gave the room a preoccupied stare and turned toward the swinging doors behind which, ordinarily, positively and absolutely, no male may pass. With no hesitation, however, I pushed through and started down the long hall, keenly eyeing the door numbers en route. At a scream from far down, I merely waved a tolerant elder's tush-tush toward a scattering covey of half-clads.

At the door in question, I rapped importantly.

"Miss Stuyvesant?"

There was, of course, no reply.

The key was ready in my hand. Looking neither left nor right, I inserted it, opened the door, removed the key and dropped it into my pocket. Making sure the catch was set to lock, I entered and closed the door. Not pausing to survey the utter shambles of the twice-ransacked room, I picked my way across the debris to the lavatory bowl and swung open the mirrored door of the medicine cabinet. From my briefcase I extracted the screwdriver from the faithful VW's kit—a part of my careful preparations outside Gam House. Quickly I loosened the three screws, lifted the cabinet out and set it against the wall. And from down within the thus exposed pipe chase I reeled up the dangling box that contained Bunny Wood's present to Juliet Lawrence—a secret handed down from father to son at matriculation time, or, in my case, from Uncle Roscoe to nephew in a tale of his undergraduate days during Prohibition; and one which I had counted on old Austen Stuyvesant in like manner to have revealed to his only child.

But even as I gloated over the much-sought box which now was in my hands, there came a rapping even more authoritative than my own, and my heart leaped upward in my throat.

"Open up!" called an authoritative voice.

The thing we learn early in life—my Uncle Roscoe once said, pointing to a new puppy of his which, though at all other times exceeding friendly, at this particular time had a bone and was giving out small growls at our approach—is to hold on to what we have. This advice, along with a number of other thoughts, flashed through my mind as, following the authoritative knock and authoritative voice, I re-swallowed my fast-beating heart.

I did not panic. The old brain continued to hit on all four, and one of its thoughts was that the box which I now held was a lot more rightfully mine than Babs', for I was acting as agent for the true owner, Juliet Lawrence, from whom it had been stolen. And so, whether or not I ended up in the local hoosegow for the crime of breaking and entering in the daytime, or whatever—I would hang onto this box. And with a sudden inspiration, it occurred to me that I might very well bluff my way out of the whole thing.

"It's unlocked," I called cheerily. "Come in!"

Meanwhile, I swiftly plunged the box into the briefcase. As I did so, I saw my notebook and pencil, and was inspired to snatch them out. Meanwhile, a futile tugging and twisting appeared to be in progress at the opposite knob.

"It is not," concluded the voice. "Open up, I say!"

"Oh, sorry," I called. "My mistake. One moment, please."

Briefcase and notebook in hand, I made my precarious way to the door, opened it and beamed affably at the scowling figure in blue.

"You," he announced, "are under arrest!"

He was not the tall-in-the-saddle policeman you sometimes see astride a horse in downtown Boston, or even the type that briskly marches down the street chalking tires. He was the soft, bulgy campus type that strolls about the grounds jollying the kids or at night noisily approaches parked couples to advise that they had better move along. He was a short, dark-complexioned campus cop in a rumpled uniform, and his eyes were bloodshot, as if from lack of sleep.

Preoccupiedly I paused, took a look behind, and then, as an important afterthought, paused again to jot down an additional word in my notebook.

"Indeed?" I said, pencil poised. "And may I have your name, please?"

"My name," he said, drawing himself up, though still to no great height, "is Officer Pinzio, and—"

"S or Z?"

"P-i-n-z-i-o. What are you doing here?" he demanded, determinedly regaining the initiative.

I shrugged and pointed.

"Merely attempting a preliminary assessment of the probable damage, which, as you can see, is likely to run high in the three-figure range, and possibly beyond."

He looked beyond me with obvious surprise, then eyed me in silent thought. At length—apparently having concluded that, having been called to investigate an intruder, not a wrecked room, he would stick to his original purpose—he spoke.

"Well, you'll have to come along."

"Certainly. As you say. Although I'm afraid I don't quite understand. As a friend of the family—an 'advisor,' let us say—"

"You're not allowed in."

"I see."

I accompanied him back along the hallway, conscious of doors opening after we passed, and of informations being hissed from the openers to those behind. We reached the lounge. At the elevators, Officer Pinzio pressed the button.

"Perhaps," I suggested casually, "you might care to phone my good friend Dean Van Eyck, to check."

He turned.

"You know Dean Van Eyck?"

"Yes, indeed. As it happens, we spent most of the morning together in Hillcrest, although on an entirely different matter. I dropped her at the infirmary, but by now she should have returned to her office. The name is Gates—Gulliver Inchmore Gates—of Bell, Rowbottom and Witherspoon."

Red eyed and sleepy, he gave me a baffled look. Having arrived with a gentle, unseen bump, the elevator opened its doors invitingly. Silently he debated, then yawned. It was, I reflected, a great day for yawning. He was still standing there when, called by some unseen finger, the elevator closed its doors and departed again.

"All right," he said decisively. "I will. You wait here."

"Certainly."

He crossed to a counter on the far wall, where, with one distrustful eye on me, he began to dial. Our audience of girls gaped and whispered. Uncomfortable under their scrutiny, but affecting boredom, I moved to an adjacent window and looked out.

And it was well I did!

On the grounds below, calculatingly dispersed, stood Pete McGlue himself and about a dozen others, who, from their alert demeanor, I was sure were Zeta Nus. This put a different aspect on the matter, and suddenly a trip to the campus pokey in the protective custody of Officer Pinzio appeared much more desirable than before, I thought fast. Pete McGlue must have put two and two together, and, when he saw Jo leave the infirmary and join me in the VW, must have assigned an agent to tail me. Learning that I had entered Babs' dormitory, he had correctly guessed my mission and now suspected that, when I emerged, I might have in my possession the object of his futile search. My thoughts, however, were interrupted by a respectful tap on the shoulder.

I turned.

"Mr. Gates," said my recent companion. "Dean Van Eyck happens to be in conference with the Chancellor. What you ought to do is go down to the resident's office and ask her to come back up with you."

"I see," I said, not too enthusiastically. "I will, then. Thank you."

Had it not been for my recent look out the window, I would have been glad to be so luckily dismissed, but as it was, I found myself reluctant to take leave of this new-found friend. At this point, however, the busy elevator disgorged a bevy of co-eds, and one of them saluted him and asked:

"What's up, Pinzie?"

And he, with a dismissing "Do that," to me, happily turned to her.

I entered the elevator, pressed the 'M' button for the main floor and again thought fast. And with, I might add, instant results. Opening my briefcase, I quickly removed the unnerving Items from their box and slipped them into the envelope which, in spite of old Rowbottom's careful instructions, I so far had not dispatched. As I sealed it, the doors opened. Stepping out into the main lobby, I spotted the adjacent wall-mailbox, strode to it, and through its slot thrust the envelope.

And at the sound of the soft 'plop' within, I paused for a well earned sigh of relief. Juliet Lawrence's Items, the honor of Gamma Delta House, the future of the Wood-Lawrence romance, and the future of the Gates Automatic Bed as well, were saved!

My own safety, however, was in considerable doubt. Casually I strolled past the desk and to the glass doors. Outside, Pete's men stood at their distances. Thoughtfully I turned and paced the lobby. While Pete McGlue could not know, so far, that I actually had found the Items, I had not the slightest doubt that his presence indicated that he had guessed my mission. If I now ventured outside, he would demand a look into my briefcase, and there would be rough stuff. I stopped. I debated phoning for a taxi and making a dash for it. But I never would reach that taxi with my briefcase. As I started to pace again, the elevator's doors parted and Officer Pinzio stepped out.

I rushed up to greet him as a long-lost friend.

"The resident wasn't in?"

"Resident? What—" I had forgotten all about the resident. "—oh, no. I didn't even go to her, because I believe I have seen enough, after all. Also," I said in a rush, "I realize that inadvertently I have overstepped my authority and so would consider it a great favor if you would accompany me to Dean Van Eyck's office and simply state the circumstances—just for the record."

He eyed me, puzzled. He yawned. He tipped back his cap, scratched his head and ruminated. He yawned again.

"All right," he said. "I might as well."

As we set out together from the entrance, I saw a flurry of intelligences fly between the posted Zetas. Glancing back, I saw three of the gang dash for the doorway and enter; the others, in casual groups, started to follow us at a distance. Hardly two minutes later, hearing a distant pounding of feet, I looked back again. The three who had dashed inside were dashing out again to rejoin the mob, and now, with no further attempt to conceal their unity, all went into a close huddle. The three, I surmised, had entered Babs' room and had noted the newly removed medicine cabinet, and so were convinced not only that I had succeeded where they had failed, but that I now carried the Items in my briefcase. And when they broke from their huddle and with a tense new air resumed their stalking, I was sure.

I almost laughed aloud. It was a case of the experienced professional winning out after the bumbling amateurs had failed, and they would not soon forget it. And in the second place, I had adhered to a fundamental rule of the trade: never get caught with the goods. I stifled a second laugh: the goods they thought they were following actually were behind them!

Meanwhile, I made an effort at conversation with Officer Pinzio. To my questions as to the outbreak of the night before, he observed that, while it was the first for the year, there had been reports of similar raids at nearby colleges, and so it was "in the air," and had come as not too much of a surprise. For his part, he had gone off his regular duty at midnight, only to be aroused and recalled again, and so had gotten little sleep.

"Dam' kids," he concluded, lapsing into thought.

Now, taking another glance behind, I saw a most beautiful sight: white above and blue below, the two colors separated by a horizontal band of red, a squared-off truck was pulling away from Proxmire Hall. I restrained a cheer. The most sought Items in Kittery were riding in that truck, which was bearing them irretrievably away.

"They're beautiful, don't you think?" I enthused.

"What?"

"The new mail trucks."

Officer Pinzio gave me another puzzled look.

"I suppose so," he said, and plunged again into silent thought.

As we approached the Administration Building, I saw both Austen Stuyvesant's limousine and my VW parked in front. It thus was likely that the conference which Officer Pinzio had reported included Stuyvesant, and that Jo was waiting somewhere above. But as we entered the old structure and took the stair to the second floor, I began to fear that he, having unwittingly provided me with safe conduct across the campus, might now turn into a liability.

CHAPTER THIRTY FOUR
IN THE DEAN'S OFFICE

Across the large anteroom, from which doors opened to the Chancellor's and deans' private offices and to a conference room as well, Jo sat like an Indian. Two chairs away, Babs Stuyvesant slumped back, pouting. To Jo, I made no sign of recognition, and she, wide eyed, noted the policeman at my side and stared back in rapt silence. My fears, however, as to Pinzio's questioning my lack of greeting to Babs Stuyvesant disappeared as he crossed to Dean Van Eyck's office and knocked, for it was apparent that he did not recognize her.

To the knock, to my relief, there was no response, and I began to hope that with a well framed phrase I might send him on his way.

"The Dean is in the conference room," Babs informed.

"Thank you," said Pinzio, and, assuming an at-ease stance, lapsed into another of his periods of silent thought.

A few seconds later, from the open doorway through which we had entered, there issued a sharp hiss. Turning, in the middle distance I saw Pete McGlue standing and beckoning to Babs. Beaming, she arose and floated out to her Dream Man, from where his urging gutterals and her acquiescing squeaks reached my ears. I had hardly taken a chair when Babs marched back in, and straight for me. From her eyes—one slightly black, and both hard with purpose—it was clear that she had been briefed as to my having unearthed and made off with the loot. With Jo and Officer Pinzio looking on, I arose and bowed in a courtly manner.

"Miss Stuyvesant!" I said cordially. "I see that you remember me. Mr. Gates, of Bell, Rowbottom and—"

"Never mind that jazz!" she said fiercely, "I want exactly one thing from you, and I want it quick!" She thrust out her hand and snapped her fingers in a peremptory manner. "Give!"

The situation, I must admit, was sticky. Nevertheless, and with the tentative plan of simply taking out and handing Babs the empty box and informing her that its recent contents were now in the hands of the United States Postal Service, I uttered an amused, disarming chuckle.

"Miss Stuyvesant—" I began, and then I stopped, for to my surprise, I heard my words echoed.

I turned. So did Babs, Jo and Officer Pinzio.

The double doors labelled *Conference Room* had parted, and

between them stood Dean Jewel Van Eyck, beckoning toward Babs in her official charming manner.

"Miss Stuyvesant," she repeated. "Your father would like to speak with you, inside."

With a baleful glance at myself, Babs flounced about, strode toward the doors and entered. Jewel, remaining outside, closed the doors after Babs. Officer Pinzio, who since my no doubt puzzling interchange with Babs, appeared to be having second thoughts, stepped forward, hat in hand.

"Dean Van Eyck?"

"Yes, Officer?"

"Dean Van Eyck, this gentleman here—" He turned and waved a fat hand to indicate myself; and Jewel, with a start, recognized me. "—is this gentleman really Mr. Gates, of Bell, Rowbottom and—" He flapped the hand helplessly. "—and all that?"

"Yes," said Jewel, with a curt nod which clearly added an unspoken but derogatory *so what?*

"Oh," said Officer Pinzio, working at his hat. "Well anyway, he hadn't ought to go up in the girls' rooms alone."

"What?"

"Yes, mam."

Jewel's eyes widened and her mouth opened. Snapping the latter shut, she glared from myself to Jo, then from Jo to Officer Pinzio.

"I will handle it," she snapped.

"Thank you, mam," said Pinzio.

And obviously relieved to be out of it all, he took off.

I looked after him, then at Jewel.

"Well!" she gasped.

She extended her arm, and Jo and I, following the direction of her rigid finger and in the order named, filed into her office.

Although I had been through it enough times in undergraduate days, I had, with the passing years, about forgotten the experience of a dean's office. But the old room was about the same, high ceilinged but with dark-paneled walls, so that the total effect was somber and brooding. And now, as a formidable Jewel took her place behind her formidable desk and as broodingly eyed an offending paper thereon, the years rolled away and it all came back in a rush.

I dared glance at Jo, who sat beside me not moving a muscle. It was too bad that I could not at least have conveyed to her the good news of my success at Proxmire Hall, even though this left unsolved the problem of her faked appendicitis. Meanwhile, behind her desk, Jewel picked up a pencil, eyed it disapprovingly, and let it drop. The crash caused both Jo and myself to start.

"Mr. Gates—"

My case, it appeared, was first on the docket. I snapped to seated attention.

"Yes, mam?" I said faintly.

"Mr. Gates—"

She paused.

I squirmed.

"—I do not wish to appear too inquisitive, and I appreciate, of course, that it was your own kind offer to drive me back to my car in Kittery that brought you here."

"It was nothing," I breathed, having another squirm.

"But I would like to ask," she went on, in that disarming manner of which the experienced undergraduate has learned to beware. "Are you in the habit of calmly walking into Trevithick—it is Trevithick Hall, is it not?"

This last was addressed to Jo.

"Yes, Dean Van Eyck," she said quickly.

Jewel returned her attention to me.

"Are you in the habit of calmly walking into Trevithick Hall and up to your cousin's room, unannounced?"

I smiled and shook my head.

She had assumed that I had been in Jo's dormitory, and Jo had assumed that the dean was asking the name of her dormitory. The whole confusion stemmed from Officer Pinzio's failure to state to Jewel the name of Babs' dormitory where he had found me.

"Why, no," I said.

"But you did."

"Well, no."

"You did not?"

"No, mam."

"I am afraid I do not follow you. I was given to understand by the officer who arrested and brought you here—"

Again I smiled and shook my head. I would have to straighten her out on this, too.

"Officer Pinzio did not arrest me. I brought him here."

She took a long breath.

And as she did so, something hit my brain with a sickening thud: tardily I realized how my razor-sharp cousin had set up an easy out for me—which, by my thickheadedness, I now had destroyed. For Jo had seen her chance and by her deft reply had led Jewel to assume that I had been found in Jo's room in Trevithick—a thing perhaps excusable for a visiting out-of-state cousin. I should have seen and gone along with that, but now it was too late.

I drew myself up.

"As a matter of fact, Dean Van Eyck, I was not in Trevithick Hall at all. I was in Proxmire Hall. I had gone there hoping to see a certain party in regard to an important matter, but this party, as it turned out, was not there at the time. I explained all this to Officer Pinzio when he happened to come upon me there, and asked him to accompany me here, in case there should be any question as to the propriety of my act."

At this, she eyed the ceiling in the familiar manner of a dean who places no credence in an offender's tale.

"And who was this person?"

"I prefer not to say."

With a sharp click of the teeth, she began to repeat her silent initial routine, brooding and toying with the pencil, while I for my part reverted to the uneasy squirm. She clearly was an expert at the slow windup. But what would have been, I am sure, a blistering for the book, never left the mound, for at this point there sounded a frantic buzzing, and on the wall, over the caption, *Chancellor's Office*, a red light blazed—and Jewel, in an amazing metamorphosis from master to slave, sprang to her feet and with a briefest by-your-leave hurried to the door.

As it closed behind her, Jo whipped around.

"Talk!" she said. "And fast!"

I looked toward the door. There was no telling how long it would be before Jewel would re-open it again, but I wanted to enjoy the telling of as much as I could of my inspired and successful adventure.

"In a word, the Items have been rescued. The honor of Gamma Delta House is secure."

"You did it?"

"Yes."

"Oh, Gully!"

"And in another word, thanks for your try on Trevithick. Good thinking, and I'm sorry I muffed it."

"That you did," she said wryly. "But how did you—"

Quickly I sketched out the taxi bit, my effecting the grand entrance, my unchallenged boarding of the elevator, my passage down the hall and into Babs' room, taking out the medicine cabinet—

"The pipe chase!" exclaimed Jo. "Nobody thought of that!"

Rapidly I sketched the subsequent events: Officer Pinzio's knock, my passing myself off as a junior member of the family's law firm, my making out to be palsy-walsy with the Dean, his phoning her and dismissing me—then the threat of Pete's gang, and my solution.

"You *mailed* them?"

"Yes."

"Oh, Gully!" she cried admiringly.

I was in the middle of telling a spellbound Jo how, fearing for my personal safety, I had reattached myself to Officer Pinzio, and, followed by the Zetas, had achieved safe passage here—when the door opened and Jewel re-entered.

We promptly arose.

I had heard of her as the charming heartbreaker, I had seen her this morning as the businesslike chairwoman—and just now as the stern judge & jury sitting on the various matters of Kittery College versus Gates. But the Jewel Van Eyck who now rejoined our little group was, to my amazement, still a different Jewel: a white-faced and wild-eyed Jewel, and one from whose mind all thoughts of infirmaries and girls' dormitories had been expunged.

"Mr. Gates!" she exclaimed, striding toward me.

"Yes, mam?"

"Listen carefully," she said in a desperate rush. "The trustees have Mr. Stuyvesant in the Conference Room. You could hardly be expected to know that he is a man of great wealth and that he has considered donating the million dollars we so urgently need for a hall of science..."

To sum up the story which she proceeded to pour into my ears, old Stuy, on news of his daughter's injury, had rushed to the infirmary, as Jo and I had observed. Now, much impressed by the college's solicitous care, he was ready to sign. But pen in hand, he had summoned Babs in—as we had witnessed in the anteroom—and had asked his "little girl" for a final assurance from her that she was completely happy here. Whereupon smart operator Babs had called Chancellor Fogwell aside and had privately advised him that no such assurance would be forthcoming until "that guy out there with the cop" turned over to her "a certain something."

The Chancellor, accordingly, with a million dollars at stake, had set off the above described buzzing and had ordered his lieutenant, Dean Van Eyck, to produce the "whatever-it-is" for Barbara Stuyvesant, instanter.

"I see," I said thoughtfully, as Jewel, quite out of breath, concluded her tale.

"So where is this something?" she demanded.

I did not at once answer.

CHAPTER THIRTY FIVE
VICTORY AND DEFEAT

During the whole of her account—which, for the most part, though she did not realize it, came hardly as news to me—the Gates brain had been turning over fast. And by the time of her final question, that brain had produced a fine, juicy idea. And so, with the realization that for a change I was in the driver's seat, I drew myself up.

"Dean Van Eyck," I began, in a calm and assured manner, "this 'something' of which you speak does not belong, and never did belong, to Barbara Stuyvesant. It was stolen from its rightful owner and entrusted to Barbara to hide. It was in order to right this great wrong that I just now personally undertook to enter Proxmire Hall and Barbara Stuyvesant's room—" The widening of Jewel's eyes at this point indicated that at least one mystery, though by now one of much less importance to her, had been cleared up. "—and remove this something. Or, more properly," I added in a scholarly manner, "'these somethings'."

"But where—" Jewel cried, and was within an ace of screaming, "—where are these 'somethings'?"

Calmly I took a breath, then gave her a grave smile.

"I have caused them to be removed to a safe place—a place so safe, in fact, that for the time being I could not, if I so wished, regain possession of them myself."

Jewel clenched her fists and opened her mouth, but nothing came out. She stood quite stiff, then trembled.

"*Oh!*" she cried.

Jo eyed her with concern, but remained silent.

"A thought, however," I went on calmly, "has just occurred to me. A plan, that is—one whereby Barbara's demand may easily be satisfied."

"What is it?" demanded Jewel hoarsely.

I held up my hand. "But first," I said gravely, "there is another matter to be taken up."

"There is no other matter to be taken up!" cried Jewel. "Any other matter can wait."

I took a breath and slowly shook my head.

"Not this one."

"Then what is it?"

"I understand, Dean Van Eyck, that for all their well-intentioned efforts, though failing wherein I finally succeeded—" Here I could not refrain from a smug glance toward Jo, who, except for her alert eyes, was standing like a stuffed Indian. "—my cousin Georgette, here, faces suspension, and the infirmary head, Dr. Washburn, is due to lose his position."

From Jewel's eyes, it was apparent that still another mystery had, at least to some extent, been dispelled.

"I see," she said faintly.

"And so, Dean Van Eyck," I continued in a firm tone, "I therefore will not offer this saving plan unless and until I am assured by you that all charges against both parties will be dropped."

"Yes!" cried Jewel. "Yes!"

"You will drop the charges?"

"Yes! If you will only—!"

"Very well, then."

I stooped to my briefcase, opened it, took out Bunny's box and placed it on the table. Jewel lunged for it and opened it. It was, of course, empty. Blankly she eyed the lid.

"But this is only an empty box!"

"And yet," I said, "it is going to provide our solution, as you will see." And so saying, I turned to Jo, who during the whole of my new role as master of the situation had looked on in silent wonder. "Last night, Jo, everything happened in a hurry and in the dark. Probably no one except Juliet and yourself knows exactly what the Items in question look like."

"True," said she.

I pointed to the box. "So the thing to do, Jo, is donate *yours*, while I," I added gallantly, "step out into the waiting room." And suiting action to word, I started for the door.

Halfway there, I stopped at her cry of dismay.

"But Gully—!"

"What?"

"The idea is wonderful," she said with a look of anguish, "except for one thing."

"What?"

"Last night I threw them to the Cause."

I clutched my brow.

"You threw—! What—!"

She nodded.

"Yes, Gully."

"But—"

She shrugged, "And then, while I was out of the room, my excited roommate tossed out all my others."

"What?"

Shocked to the core, I backed a step from Jo, and probably would have backed another, had not Jewel, who during the above interchange had maintained a mystified silence, now frantically demanded to know what this was all about. Jo at once shot back an explanation that was brief, to the point, and left me red around the ears. Toward the end, she stopped in midsentence to stare speculatively at Jewel.

Jewel stared back.

Jo raised a finger to her chin, then from the elbow unbent her arm toward Jewel. "You—" said Jo.

"Me? "

"Yes."

Jewel stiffened, backed and turned a light green.

"No," she whispered hoarsely.

"It's the only way!" urged Jo.

Jewel backed again and clutched at her throat.

"No!" she said faintly, the green deepening.

Suddenly we all gave a start: to the beat of a slow waltz, the buzzing had begun again.

Jewel looked wildly around, then decisively at me.

"Out!" she cried.

"Yes, Gully!" cried Jo.

In keeping with my recent character, I started off at a moderate pace, whereupon Jewel and Jo, newly united in common cause, pushed me to the door and slammed it after me. Inside, I heard the bolt turn.

"Hey, you," said a deep voice.

I turned. Across the waiting room a huge Pete McGlue, lackadaisically leaning against the door jamb, beckoned.

"Hey, you," repeated this larger-than-life apparition.

I whipped around, wrenched at the knob and pounded on the door. In a moment, it was opened a crack. I fought my way back in past an exasperated Jo and Jewel.

"Pete McGlue!" I explained, re-slamming the door and turning the bolt.

"The closet, then!" cried Jo.

"Yes!" cried Jewel.

And once again, with what any referee would have blown the whistle on for unnecessary roughness, I was propelled toward a door destined to be slammed behind me.

In the closet's dark interior, between bouts with ingeniously located hard edges, including one low shelf against which my head fetched up at once, I finally probed through a slippery layer of ladies' galoshes and came to firm footing. Thus in equilibrium, though forced to maintain an unnatural stoop, I removed a coathanger from my left ear. As to closets, Dean Van Eyck apparently opened the door, tossed in whatever she did not need, and shut it again. It was not a closet that I would have chosen for any extended stay. And I was thinking with disapproval of Jo's enthusiasm in the matter of the late panty raid, an enthusiasm which had almost jinxed my plan to deceive Babs Stuyvesant, and had made mental note to speak of this in the role of *loco parentis* at some appropriate time, when the door was opened.

"You can come out, now," said Jo.

At once I glanced at the table. The box was gone. So was Jewel, and I deemed it indelicate to inquire further as to the details on that score.

Jo, with the undone air of a young mother who has just dispatched the last of her brood for school, sat down with her head in her hands. It is not every day of the year that a sophomore coed causes her dean to part with what Jo had just now caused Dean Van Eyck to part with, and I did not begrudge her a period of silent meditation.

And I was preparing to indulge in a bit of the same when from outside came a great cheer. Jo, reviving at once, rushed to the window, and I was right behind her. Below, Pete McGlue and his exultant crew were bearing Babs away on their shoulders.

"Zeta Nu! We can do!" they chanted.

Babs, thrown about, laughing, and probably feeling at the climax of her young life, was waving the box up and down like a baton.

"She fell for it!" I said.

They hardly had rounded the building when through the woodwork behind us filtered the sound of subdued clapping. Jo crossed to the door and cautiously opened it a crack. We peered out. A distinguished group was filing from the conference room, and out of their happy babble my ear several times picked the words "Stuyvesant Hall of Science." Beaming Chancellor Fogwell held his arm tightly around the waist of Jewel Van Eyck, who walked as in a dream.

When all had gone, Jo closed the door and rushed to the telephone on Jewel's desk. She dialed, asked for Juliet Lawrence, and soon a great deal of classified information was pouring into the mouthpiece, its gist being the happy fact that Juliet's Items were safe and that those soon to fly were spurious. As to whose, however, Jo wisely remained silent. The important thing, she urged, was for Juliet to instruct the loyal Alphas to allow the duped Zetas to proceed without opposition in their ceremony; and Juliet appeared agreeable to going along with the hoax. Jo then reported that Dean Van Eyck, for reasons which she—Jo—had best not divulge, had agreed to withdraw all charges against Dr. Washburn and herself, and this appeared to go over big at the other end. The names of Bunny Wood and myself were then mentioned, and Jo, after jotting a number on a pad, hung up.

"Bunny was trying to get you at the Gams'. You're to call this operator."

I eyed her in surprise. Caught up in the local maelstrom of events, I had forgotten all about Bunny. Now, remembering, and sure that soon he would be telling me what I wanted to hear, I indulged myself to the extent of a preliminary piece of bragging.

"Jo, there's something I haven't told you."

"Oh?"

"Yesterday morning, I evolved a plan to end up on easy street. The final chapter is about to be enacted. I will explain as soon as I talk to Bunny."

"I can wait," she said, unimpressed, for she always had been strong on the principle of not counting chickens before they were hatched—and, as I now recalled with sudden misgivings, she usually had been right.

I replaced her at the phone, and, after some delay, the voice of Bunnington Wood came on. There was a certain lack of enthusiasm to his salutation, and I did not like it.

"Did you see your father?" I queried.

"Well, Gully, old man—"

"Did you? "

"Yes, and I showed him your bed. I worked it, and I told him the story about Pug Pendlebury and the hotel rooms, and all that."

"Great! So what did he say?"

"He—well, he said no."

My heart dropped with a dull thud.

"No?"

"He said no. In fact, he said that if I ever...well, anyway, he said no. I'm sorry."

"That's all right. Thanks for trying. Well, that's that."

"Yes, but about tonight. I guess that's off, too."

"Off?" I asked in surprise. "Says who?"

"Juliet," he answered in his voice of doom.

"Why—!" I was flabbergasted. "When did she say that?"

"When I tried to get you. She said something had come up, and she didn't know. She's going to call me back."

I sat back, limp. Had all my efforts been for naught? Last night, everything had seemed to be going strong. What had happened?

"She said she'd call you?"

"Yes. She asked me to wait right here."

"Then wait, Bunny. All is not lost. You'll see."

But as I hung up, I didn't think so. It sounded just like the way all of Bunny's other romances had ended: one date, then a no.

I sat with my head in my hands, realizing to the full how all of my recent exertions had not one whit altered my own circumstances.

"What's wrong?" asked Jo.

"Everything."

"Not everything! Why, you saved the day! You saved the honor of Gamma Delta House! You cinched the million dollars for the Hall of Science! You saved Washburn's job, and you saved me from suspension! Why, everything's mighty all right, I would say!"

I shook my head, and with a sigh, filled her in.

"Oh, Gully!" she said sorrowfully, when I had finished. "When you were being so masterful with Dean Van Eyck—"

"I was, wasn't I?" I said, recalling the scene with pleasure.

Jo shook her head.

"—you could have made her sign that order, as well. She'd have done anything, then." Jo paused. "Why! With all that's riding on that Hillcrest order, you could have held out for a partnership with B, R & W, too!"

My mouth dropped open. I had muffed it, but good! I hung my head. And I was just gathering myself to tell her of my final failure, the conk-out of Bunny with Juliet, when the door opened and Jewel entered.

CHAPTER THIRTY SIX
SHUFFLE OFF TO BUFFALO

After a rough voyage from Nantucket, I often have continued for a spell to walk as if I were still on the ship. The present Jewel appeared to be in the grip of that same sensation, and dazed as well, so that it was some time before she became aware of the presence of Jo and myself.

"Oh, yes," she said, in a dreamy manner. "Miss Gates, you are excused."

"Thank you."

"And Mr. Gates. In the future, you will kindly stay out of—" Helplessly she waved a hand. "wherever it was."

"Thank you. I will," I said, and turned to follow Jo.

But at the door, Jo slowed, stopped, turned back and shot me a secret look which started the old pulse beating faster.

"Gully, weren't you going to drive Dean Van Eyck to her car?"

It was not a question, I sensed, but a command.

"Oh, yes," I said. I turned. "Dean Van Eyck," I said, "we had better drive you to your car."

She gave me a vacant look. "My car," she said mechanically. "Yes." Like a sleepwalker, she turned and followed us.

Out at the old VW, Jo quickly climbed into the back, and I ushered Jewel into the same seat which she had occupied, not many hours before, on the fateful journey which had ended at the infirmary. We drove a block in silence; then something caught Jewel's eye and she let out a wild cry.

"Oh, *no!*" she ended weakly.

I turned my head. We had just passed the Zeta house, and I saw that the counterfeit act of vengeance had been performed. Resolutely I faced forward. After a decent interval, I cleared my throat.

"Dean Van Eyck," I said in a reassuring manner, "you must look at it philosophically." Here I paused and debated throwing in a pat on the shoulder, but decided against it. Instead, I raised my hand in an effective gesture. "Think of them—think of it—as a small personal loss in exchange for a large gain to society: the new Stuyvesant Hall of Science."

Jewel, in reply, said nothing, but sat like a statue, so I could not tell whether this had bucked her up or if she still was unreconciled to her recent loss. Now, however, I became aware of an odd, prickly sensation, like that of ozone from a sparking motor. And from long association I realized what it was: behind, Jo's brain had revved up to top speed. I therefore, though not at first perceiving her design, was not surprised when she, in a loud and clear voice, began to upbraid me.

"Gully, you shouldn't have mailed Juliet Lawrence's panties—Items, rather; excuse me—to Mr. Rowbottom in the same envelope with those documents that Dean Van Eyck signed. What will Mr. Rowbottom think?"

"What will Mr. Rowbottom think?" I parroted, puzzled.

"Yes. What will—"

With a start, Jewel returned to life.

"Mr. Rowbottom?" she asked.

"Yes, Mr. Rowbottom!" replied Jo, emphatically. And slowly she repeated her opening remarks. "—those Items," she went on, "had a big 'J' embroidered on them."

I blinked. This was a flat misstatement of fact, I having settled, you will recall, for a heart. But prudently I remained silent and wondered what was coming next.

"Mr. Rowbottom doesn't know Juliet," continued Jo. "But he would know that Dean Van Eyck's first name is Jewel. So—"she concluded with merciless logic, "—what will Mr. Rowbottom think?"

The ensuing short silence was broken by Jewel's loud squawk. She sat erect, wide eyed, staring at me.

"Mr. Gates! Am I to understand that you mailed these—these Items—with a 'J' on them to Mr. Rowbottom with the papers I signed?"

I nodded. "I had to," I explained earnestly. "Pete McGlue's gang was after me. They—"

"Never mind that...Mr. Gates," she said decisively, "I want you, right now, to call Mr. Rowbottom long distance and explain about that envelope, before he receives it. Tell him—tell him—"

She stopped, stumped.

"Tell him," there came from the rear, "that you bought them for your cousin Georgette and that you put them in the wrong envelope by mistake."

I nodded appreciatively. "That should do it," I said.

"But who," objected Jewel, "would buy a 'J' for Georgette?"

"Gully would."

Jewel looked at me. "Yes," she conceded, "he would."

I resented this slur, but said nothing.

"I mean," said Jo, "—for Jo."

"Oh," said Jewel.

But now, with the scheme apparently approved all around, I began to experience laser pains in the back of the head, and, glancing into the rearview mirror, caught Jo's electric beam right in the eye. In a moment, the whole inside of my head was glowing with her message! She had set it up for me!

I took a long breath. Good old Jo, still in there fighting! Feeling my way along, I announced in a tone of some concern: "The only trouble is, Dean Van Eyck, before I left Boston, I happened to have a considerable disagreement with Mr. Rowbottom. And losing out on the Hillcrest order this morning has rather soured me on the sewerage and drainage business as a career."

Jewel shot me a sidelong look.

"So—?" she asked guardedly.

"I had intended," I continued, "to let the success or failure of this morning decide for me." I glanced into the mirror. Jo, lips pursed and slightly rocking to and fro, and in a manner which somehow oddly reminded me of my Aunt Orpha, was faintly but rhythmically nodding her approval. "And the fact is," I said roundly, "it has. I have decided to sever relations with Bell, Rowbottom and Witherspoon. And having completed the assignment, I do not wish to communicate further with them at this time."

Jewel eyed me in dismay.

"You—you won't call Mr. Rowbottom?"

"Not at this time."

"You refuse?"

"Yes."

And so saying, I faced straight ahead and gripped the wheel in a determined manner. We drove a block in tense silence before Jewel spoke.

"Mr. Gates. If I were to reconsider and give your firm the work at this time, would that change your mind?"

I gave this half a block. "If you did," I then admitted, "it would."

"Then I will, if you will telephone at once."

We were in downtown Kittery, approaching the same drugstore from where Bunny and I had phoned the night before. I pulled to the curb. From my briefcase I extracted the order. Jewel signed it. I thanked her.

"And now," she said, "if you will just go in there and—"

"Certainly."

The same young lady who, the evening before, had wrapped and tied my two pound box of candy with a red bow, while, behind, Bunny Wood hoarsely demanded to be allowed to buy the same, was at the candy counter, and I called out a friendly greeting as I passed. Threading my way toward the telephone booths, I pictured the ensuing course of that evening—and I just could not believe that Juliet was giving him the brush-off.

As I sat down in the booth, there flashed before my eyes the summer's unbroken series of deeds well done: Chris Beanfield soon would wed his Ellen Hill, Randy Bohr his Marj Miller; the threat to Ted Prentice and my Aunt Flo's future had been removed; and Lucy Kerensky was back with her Boris in Cincinnati. Also, Fizzo Fitzwilliam was wed to his Winnie Stubbs, and—though I could not claim full credit, I had only caused him to be fired—Homer Hart to his Ethel Montgomery. And after all this, was my final score for Bunny Wood to be a flat zero?

With a sudden resolve, I dialed Gam House, where Juliet Lawrence, to my surprise, greeted me effusively. "About the Items," I said. "I'll have to mail them to you."

"Do that. I'm going to frame them."

"Frame them—?"

"Yes, and I'm sorry about the dance. You see—" Her tone turned conspiratorial. "—I was so afraid that, if we went, Bunnington might hear talk about the flagpole and all. So I told him—"

"You phoned him?"

"Just now. I told him that something had come up, and I had to make a quick trip home. I asked him if he would consider driving me there, instead, tonight—and he is."

"He's driving you to Buffalo?"

"Yes," she said dreamily.

I sat back. She had said it dreamily! I had done it, after all! Except for the finishing touches.

"Juliet—"

"What?"

"Listen carefully," I said, and in a few words I sketched out how, to buck up Bunny, I had had him read *A Princess of Mars*.

"What's it about?"

"It's about John Carter and a certain princess of Mars named Dejah Thoris. In brief, John Carter goes to Mars and wins the hand of

Dejah Thoris."

"Just how does this affect me?"

"Well, John Carter was a brave fighting man, but with the woman he loved, he couldn't speak."

"Like Bunnington?"

"Yes. So in the end, it was Dejah Thoris who placed her hands upon his shoulders, and then he came to life. He took her in his arms."

"I see," said Juliet thoughtfully.

"She made the first move, is the point."

"I'll bear that in mind..." She gave a dreamy little sigh. "Yes, I'll certainly bear that in mind."

And with a thrill, I realized that at last I could cross the one flat failure from my record.

I took out another dime and then, heady with success, paused. Why not climb the highest mountain, why not solve the hardest problem of the heart—Rowbottom's? Confidently, matching Rx to ailment, I mentally reviewed my files: Chris, Randy, Ted, Lucy, Fizzo, Bunny—Ah! The Homer Hart-Ethel Montgomery mechanism! Yes. Like Ethel, Jewel objected to her suitor's occupation. So change it, was the prescription. But to what? At once I saw the answer: to engineering's glamour specialty of the future, pollution and ecology control. And while Rowbottom learned and brought in assignments in that field, new partner Gates would take over the firm's prosaic sewerage and drainage activities.

I negotiated the call. Quite as in the case of my call from the Stubbs' on Nantucket, I did not mince words with Rowbottom. I was prepared, I stated, to deliver the Hillcrest award in return for a partnership in the firm. This time, however, no period of gargling set in at the other end, but only a stupified silence.

"By the way," I asked, "does the Dean address you as 'Sam?'"

An outraged cry came over the wire.

"I fail to see how that concerns you!"

"You can be frank with me, Mr. Rowbottom," I said calmly. "I have handled many problems such as yours, and always with a happy ending. In fact, only today—"

"I have no problem!" he roared, quite unconvincingly.

I now sought for some different matter to throw in, to give him time to calm down—and found it.

"The electric," I said. "I could take it apart in your garage and dispose of it piece by piece."

"Why—!" he stammered. "Well," he said gruffly, "I certainly would appreciate that."

"Glad to," I said, for those parts would be invaluable in my attic lab for developing the Gates Electric Automobile. "—but as to your problem. The solution has occurred to me."

He did not answer for half a minute. Then:

"...what?" he asked cautiously.

"We can discuss it later," I said. "What about the partnership?"

It took him another half minute to say yes.

"Fine," I said. Then something hit me: no longer was I a wage slave! And though I was not yet exactly a capitalist, and though this was not the way I had planned it, I was a big step on the way. I thought of the order, already signed and, literally, in the bag. It was not dated: I could insert whatever date I chose. And suddenly the old refrain, *Shuffle Off to Buffalo*, flashed across my mind. If Jo wanted to, we could do just that, confer with the registrar there, and perhaps Juliet and Bunny would consider remaining there long enough to stand up for us. "This may take a few days," I said.

"Take whatever time you need," he growled.

"—and a certain amount of expense."

"All right," he grudged, "within reason."

Happily I strode out of the drugstore. As I approached the car, an anxious Jewel called, "Did you get him?"

"Yes." I waved reassuringly. "Everything is all right."

But as I stepped off the curb and went around to my door, it struck me that not quite everything was all right. Something vital was missing. And dead ahead over the top of the old VW, in the window display of the adjacent women's shop, I saw what it was.

I opened my door and tilted my seat forward.

"Jo," I said firmly, "please get out."

She looked at me in surprise, then eeled out. At the curb, I pressed into her hand a large bill and circumspectly pointed.

"I thought you might like to buy something in there, as a present from me."

"Oh, Gully!" she gushed.

"For Dean Van Eyck, too, also as a present from me."

"Oh, *Gully!*" she dittoed.

I opened Jewel's door. She gave me one of those inscrutable looks that girls sometimes do, then got out. I watched happily as they entered the shop.